WITHIN
THE
PINES

Thank you to my heavenly father for EVERYTHING!
A heartfelt thank you to my Beta readers and support team:
Sandi Tutolo, Heather Payne, Heather Garent, Kathy Tripp,
Sandra Harvey, Anna Fernandez, Brooke Wolfe, Dawn Dugle,
Otto Schafer, Kamy Lavin, Martha Kate Shiels, and April Berry.

*

A grateful thank you to my readers (aka, Rockfishers),
social media followers, and fellow authors:
Your support keeps me going! All of the reviews, videos, tags,
recommendations, likes, and shares mean the world to me, and
though we may be physically miles, states, or even countries
apart, your support is felt daily and greatly appreciated!
Thank you for loving my Rockfish Island Mystery series!

*

And, of course,
To my wonderful family and friends:
Your love, encouragement, and support means the world.
I can't thank you enough for telling everyone
and their dog about my series!
Don't stop!

*

Cheryl Corbin
Your input was greatly missed, as you are every day.

*

Research Acknowledgements:
Sheriff Robert Udell, Deputy Robert Tripp, Robert (Papa Bob)
Hutchison, and Tanya Hagel.
Thank you for your time and guidance!

*

Editing and Cover Art: Payne Design
Author Photo: ELF Photograph

CAMP HOSTS

Tanya Bennett – Island Resident, Assistant Horse Guide, Cook, and Cousin of Angie Bennett

Angie Bennett – Island Resident, Owner and Horse Guide of the Campgrounds

Witt Reyerson – Mainlander, Co-Owner of Vita Mineralium, Spouse of Nancy Reyerson

Nancy Reyerson – Mainlander, Founder Of Vita Mineralium, Spouse of Witt Reyerson

CAMP GUESTS

Clint Carson – Mainlander, Witt's Best Friend, Stay-At-Home Father, Spouse of Cami Carson

Cami Carson – Mainlander, Nancy Reyerson's Assistant/Accountant, Spouse of Clint Carson

Aaron Coletta – Island Resident, Bank Manager, Spouse of Sandi Coletta

Sandi Coletta – Island Resident, Stay-At-Home Mother, Vita Mineralium Reseller, Spouse of Aaron Coletta

Nick Mason – Mainlander, Vita Mineralium Reseller, Spouse of Maddie Mason

Maddie Mason – Mainlander, Vita Mineralium Reseller, Holds Top Sales Spot

WITHIN THE PINES

A ROCKFISH ISLAND MYSTERY BOOK IV

BY J.C. FULLER

CHAPTER 1

The dwindling campfire, neglected as much as she, struggled to fend off the encroaching darkness, the glow barely touching the surrounding pines, their spindly tops moving with the midnight breeze, towering in judgment, unpleased with the group of city slickers daring to venture among their midst.

"I'm cold. Can someone..."

A log was tossed onto the starving fire, and sparks cascaded, flirting upon the air with the laughter and conversation of the camp. Bits of flame mingled with the spiraling smoke, narrowly missing the swaying branches before extinguishing from a violent red to a fluttering ashen grey... much like her marriage.

She watched her spouse and their fellow campers, the group moving further away from the fire, laughing and cajoling, migrating to the mess tent, a shout for more whiskey and s'mores, the warrior cry.

Her gaze lingered on her husband's back as his hand slipped down and cupped the butt cheek of their young guide, who moved away from his touch a tad slower than expected. A heavy sigh of disappointment escaped her lips, and Nancy Reyerson, instead of joining the festivities or admonishing her husband, focused on the flames, her thoughts drawn to the charcoaled splinters fueling the small inferno, very much mimicking her internal turmoil.

"So much for your promises, Witt."

An unexpected crunch of needles and pine cones underfoot, a heavy step beyond the tree line, caught her ear, and her head jerked up, eyes darting past the fire pit and out into the trees.

What was that?

The group, successful in their campaign, flowed from the mess tent, shouting their triumph, and made their way back to the fire pit. She ignored their antics, her eyes searching the condensed darkness and the tall, crowded pines stark against the starlight bleak.

A scarlet glow, an ember at the end of a cigarette, suddenly inflamed and exposed an outline, a blotting black matching the denseness of the evergreens, standing still, reverent, like the trees, a silent observer.

Who is that?

She leaned forward, curiosity piqued. Her plastic red solo cup crackled under the pressure, and her grip tightening as she strained, fearful of taking her eyes from the silhouette, unsure she'd be able to find it again, the outline barely noticeable.

A head, shoulders... definitely a person. What were they doing?

"Cami?" she called and then, realizing the shadow was more masculine in stature than her petite friend, tried, "Aaron? Or is that you, Nick?"

There was no given response, and she leaned forward, head cocked, eyes slit, wondering if she was seeing things. Perhaps it was the day's fatigue, conjuring a figure, smoke and darkness tricking her eyes. She tried again. "Clint?... Witt? What are you doing? Watering the tree? We have a perfectly fine outhouse!"

The shadow shifted, sliding behind a vast pine and out of sight, her call unanswered.

"Nance..." A whispered hush against her ear caused her to start, the source stepping back and announcing loudly, "Looks to me like you need more "toddy" in your hot toddy, ya hottie!"

A glass bottleneck suddenly weighed heavy upon the rim of her plastic cup, the sharp smell of whiskey reaching her nose. She peered down, her solo cup dipping under the pressure, the pourer sloppily cascading Crown Royal all over. She quickly transferred the drink to her other hand and shook out her fingers, dispelling overcast droplets from her skin.

"Clint! Watch it!"

"Cheers!" Clint threw her a wink, along with one of his best disarming and charming smiles, before moving on to their fellow campers and heavily tipping his bottle into each of their cups, a double pour into Witt's. As if her husband needed more liquid courage.

She continued to follow his drunken path, all the while taking count. One... three... five... seven. She leaned forward and peered into the mess tent, counting two more. Nine... nine people. Everyone accounted for... and drunk. Well, almost everyone.

Her frustration rose as the group arranged chairs and log stumps around the rock-bordered pit, tossing an additional log onto the fire and pulling out their pilfered goods: marshmallows, chocolate, and graham crackers.

"What is that smell?" Nancy's nose crinkled at the overwhelming aroma of weed, which suddenly outweighed the stench of campfire smoke, and muttered, "You've got to be kidding me." She gave a pointed glare in Clint's direction, knowing full well who supplied the additional merriment, and it suddenly occurred to her that it might be the explanation for the figure in the woods. She sat up, her voice dripping with disappointment. "You're all acting like this is a frat party. We have a ride in the morning!"

"Hey, now! Get that woman a s'more!" Aaron Coletta bellowed loudly, his wife Sandi hanging on his plaid flannelled arm, an infectious laugh following his declaration, the outburst very unlike his usual uptight bank manager demeanor. The small group cheered the edict, and Nancy flopped back into her canvas chair, defeated.

This was supposed to be a corporate getaway, a reward for their top sellers, with she and Witt as the gracious hosts.

Vita Mineralium, their small garage-headquartered business, within a year, was on the brink of becoming an empire, practically an overnight success! Between her enthusiasm and Witt's business savvy, they had enlisted an army of friends and family, who engaged and created a litany of internet resellers via various and numerous social media outlets, the enthusiastic militia, selling and promoting their vitamin products, the initial small group growing and reaching astronomical numbers.

The new members, all of whom continuously bragged about the benefits of their product, gave them free advertising and spread the word like wildfire across the nation, boosting their sales and expansion. Their foothold in the Pacific Northwest, home base, was just the beginning. Witt had set his eyes on the East Coast, hiring a publicist who arranged several small interview slots with the top morning news affiliates and minor talk shows, landing her husband a coveted five-minute stint on a financial segment of CNN.

That's when their progress with the business exploded. Though head twirling to Nancy, it wasn't fast enough for Witt. He was hungry for more, pushing for additional airtime and larger crowds, their P.R. agent insisting they needed to have patience, hinting that self-help books and seminars were the next step... that this was the beginning of a windfall of success, and that they simply needed to trust him. Frustrated with impatience, Witt was tempted to take things into his own hands... Much like he did in other aspects of their life. This trip, for instance.

Initially, Nancy had hoped for a few days away without the kids, an intimate adventure all their own. He saw it differently and turned the horseback riding-camping excursion into a tax-deduction opportunity, pushing her to arrange the gathering, transforming her romantic suggestion into a corporate gift trip. A formal celebration for their top sellers. As Witt put it, a jumping point of encouragement, a time and place for a serious discussion on how people could reinvest and expand on their platform of followers. A declaration that if Vita Mineralium was going to make it to the top of the health industry, it had to be a joint venture. Everyone had to carry their share of the load, everyone needed to be invested and... INVEST.

"Nancy? Can I get you anything?" Cami plopped down her camp chair and inched closer, their knees touching, her puppy-dog eagerness instantly annoying. "Are you still cold? Should I grab a blanket from your tent? Here, I'll get one—"

"I'm fine, Cami." She looked at her self proclaimed assistant, in truth, her right arm, and smiled, the expression failing to reach her tired eyes. "I was trying to enjoy the fire and a bit of quiet." The hint went unnoticed.

"Oh, I don't blame you!" The spiky-haired blonde lowered her voice to just above a whisper, leaning further into Nancy's space, her hand lightly landing on her forearm. "Things are starting to get a bit rowdy. Don't you think?" Cami failed to acknowledge that it was her husband, Clint, who was hyping the party atmosphere. "Have you noticed how much Sandi has had to drink tonight?" She tilted her head toward the pretty brunette clinging to Aaron's arm, a thirty-something like them, and added, "Like she's upset about something? I don't know if you noticed, but Aaron and Maddie disappeared for a bit... TOGETHER. Wonder what they were up to?" She raised an eyebrow, giving a knowing nod with a lopsided smile, and flicked her eyes sideways in the direction of Maddie and Nick Mason, the superstar sales couple of Vita Mineralium.

Nancy followed her gaze, her own attention instantly drawn to Nick, a smoldering cigarette in hand. She forgot he smoked when drinking. Possibly it was him she had seen, and he hadn't heard her call his name...

"How long ago was this, Cami?"

"Oh, forty minutes or so." Cami inched even closer, her voice rising in volume instead of lowering. "Both were gone for QUITE a while." She twisted toward the fire and caught Sandi's eye, giving her nemesis a mock cheer with her solo cup before turning back to Nancy with a wicked smile. "Look at the way Sandi is clinging to Aaron. She can barely stand!"

Nancy frowned at the observation and noted, despite Cami's claims, that Sandi was having no problem standing under her own power. However, the woman's eyes and ears were pinned on Witt, devouring his every move and syllable.

Did she need to worry about Sandi?

Cami's face bobbed into Nancy's line of sight, breaking her train of thought, Cami's eyes wide with curiosity, her voice dropping to a whisper, "Will you say something to Nick? I... I know you don't approve."

"Of course, I don't approve!" Nancy huffed and then smirked in triumph. "But it's no longer an issue. I had a little chat with Maddie this afternoon and told her to end the affair with Aaron. If not, I'd be forced to tell Nick. I also strongly suggested she keep the Vita Mineralium family in mind before jeopardizing her standing over a man... especially THAT man." Nancy smugly sat back in her chair, a pleased smile on her lips. "I would imagine Maddie and Aaron disappearing for a bit was so that she could end things."

"Or squeeze in a quickie."

"Cami!" Nancy's eyes slit, and she twisted in her chair. "I really don't think you are in a position to throw rocks at a glass house."

At the rebuke, Cami leaned away, stung, and, feigning ignorance, gave a confused shake of her head with a weak smile.

"Ohhhh!" Nancy suddenly gave out a long sigh, her scowl morphing into shame. "I'm sorry, that was rude of me, Cami." She lightly patted the other woman's hand. "I'm on edge, but that's no excuse. You know the new accountants will be looking at our books come Tuesday?" She shifted in her chair. "You'll have everything in order, correct?"

"Oh, yes." Cami's head joggled up and down. "On your desk, Monday morning."

"And there won't be any discrepancies, like last time?" Nancy arched an eyebrow. "Because if there were, I think you know how disappointed I would be."

"There won't be, Nancy. Everything will be in order. I promise."

Worried she'd displeased her employer, Cami quickly added in a chipper, change the subject tone, "Everyone seems to be having a good time! We really should make this a yearly thing." She glanced toward the mess tent where Angie and Tanya, their guides, were putting away the chaos caused by the raid for midnight snacks. "Especially if you can get the same deal. How hard did you twist Angie's arm?"

"Twist her arm? I did nothing of the sort! If anything, I am helping her!" Nancy gave Cami a severe look and then leaned in herself, her tone lifting. "With my circle of friends and a raving review, Angie's business should quadruple. Besides, the poor girl has no business sense." She waved toward the rest of the camp. "If it hadn't been for me already... Seriously, nylon tents? Who would pay the kind of money she wants to sleep in a nylon tent? I helped her elevate things. The price decrease in her quote was in gratitude."

Cami furiously nodded, as if she would dare to disagree, and turned in the direction of Nancy's wave, indicating the rest of the campsite, a "glamping" campsite, to be precise. Large yurt-like tents were erected behind them, Italian solar-powered lights strung from one pole steeple to the other, enhancing the cream canvas flaps, pulled back, exposing sheer mosquito fabric allowing one to look in, revealing a full-size queen mattress piled high with blankets and fluffy pillows, accompanied by leather chairs and matching ottomans, trunks full of books and other merriment stationed in the corners – a far cry from camping if ever there was.

As if her ears were burning, Angie Bennett stepped within the circle, a tin bucket in hand, and cleared her throat, garnering the group's attention.

Huddled in a conspirator's whisper directly in front of her, Nancy and Cami looked up, curious, while Maddie, drunkenly hovering marshmallows on a stick, did the same.

Witt ignored her entrance and continued speaking. Nick was seated to his right and Aaron, with Sandi still clinging to his arm, was seated on his left. Clint stood behind them, refilling their drinks after every sip.

Witt's brow was furrowed, his tone serious, the conversation ongoing, "Invest their college fund in Vita Mineralium now, instead of waiting, and in two years' time, rather than sending them to some community college, you'll be shipping them to one of the big four, the tuition fully paid. I'm telling you. Commitment is the driving force for a successful..." His words faded as Angie stepped closer, his blood-shot eyes following the lines of her leg, stopping on her Levi's back pockets.

Angie plastered on a patient smile and raised her voice, "Okay, folks! Time to call it a night. We've got the sunrise mimosa ride in the morning."

As if on cue, a loud whinny from the corral went up into the night, and everyone turned as Angie's assistant, Tanya, locked the pen's makeshift gate, giving a final pat to the rear of a lingering dapple grey, encouraging the horse to move along, it pining for another apple.

"We'll need to leave by five-thirty a.m.," Angie continued, "And you'll want to dress warmly. The October mornings can be pretty chilly here on the island." She turned toward Tanya, the young girl making her way to the group. "We'll have muffins for breakfast at the sunrise point and then a full brunch waiting for you when we arrive back at camp."

"Ang? I don't know if I'll feel up to a ride," Maddie confessed, stumbling to the side, Sandi's arm jetting out, stopping her from taking a tumble. "I have a funny feeling I'm going to have one hell of a hangover tomorrow."

"And you're very welcome, Maddie!" Clint cheered, taking the final swig from the Crown Royal bottle, and tossing the empty over his shoulder with a self-congratulatory smile. Tanya quietly circled behind him and retrieved the discarded item.

"Maddie, you'll be fine." Nancy's voice shot out, her tone authoritative, "All of you will. I suggest everyone drink a good amount of water before hitting the pillow, which is NOW."

"That's not a bad idea," Angie agreed lightly, "I'll have Tanya bring some water bottles to everyone's tent." She hurried, a chorus of grumbles igniting, "Besides, the view really is to die for. Not only do you have the gorgeous sunrise, but the ocean view is spectacular, and you can see a miniature Seattle in the background." She stepped forward and tilted the bucket in hand, sending water sloshing down upon the campfire, a hiss of hot steam rising with a large plume of white smoke"You might even see some whales!"

The enthusiasm Angie had hoped for did not come as everyone rose from their spots and began heading for their designated tents.

Sandi quickly released Aaron's arm and made a straight beeline for their hostess.

"Um, Nance, one second." Sandi put a polite hand on Nancy's back, her other still gripping Maddie's arm, the latter teetering from side to side. "Sorry, hold on." She gave a pleading nod to Nick, who was taking the last drag from his cigarette before tossing it into the doused fire, and silently asked for him to take his drunken wife's arm. Releasing Maddie to her husband's care, she turned to Nancy with a concerned look.

"I don't know if you overheard, but Witt was pushing pretty hard on Aaron and Nick tonight."

"Pushing? About what?" Nancy gave a friendly wave and mouthed, "Sleep tight!" to Nick and

Maddie, her eyes watching Witt over Sandi's shoulder, her husband still speaking to Clint and Aaron, his hooded stare focused on Angie's backside.

"Investing our savings. ALL of our savings, Nance. Listen, we don't have the kind of money that you and—"

"Oh, that's not pushing!" Nancy gave a light laugh, her full attention now resting on the anxious woman. "That's sound advice, Sandi! He's a financial adviser. I mean, that's what he did before we started our business and... Well, Sandi...You and Aaron, you're in the inner circle. You're practically family, and if you ask me, you'd be wise to heed any advice he gives."

"But he's advising we invest our kid's college funds! We're already sinking several thousand dollars in product monthly and—"

"And I've signed your commission checks!" Nancy's face suddenly blossomed into a proud smile. "Sandi, if you continue to do as well as you have, in six months, YOU will be the breadwinner of your home, NOT Aaron. That's an incredible accomplishment for a stay-at-home mom! And if Witt is recommending you invest more than just your time into Vita Mineralium, which..." She lowered her voice to a whisper. "Is on the verge of becoming a multi-million-dollar company..."

Sandi's eyebrows raised in surprise as Nancy gave

her a subtle nod, assuring her it was true.

"Well, it's because we love you guys!" She suddenly leaned in and squeezed Sandi's shoulders in a half-hug. "Don't believe me? Ask Maddie and Nick. Each month they put eighty percent of their commission check BACK into the company, and EACH MONTH, they earn its return, plus twenty-five percent." Nancy patted Sandi's arms and stepped back, adding, "Aren't you tired of being in second place? You know, Sandi, if Aaron applied himself a bit more, you two could knock Maddie and Nick from the top."

Sandi shook her head, apparently still mystified by the figures.

"Eighty percent? Even with commission chargebacks? Our last check was far below—"

"Maddie does an excellent job of up-selling. She moves more Titan packages than anyone, and because of that, chargebacks on the lower items have no effect on her commission. They basically wash each other out, and she knows that investing in the product is investing in her and Nick's future. She has faith in the process, and you should too."

"I understand the concept, but Aaron doesn't make the money that—"

"You wait and see. The growth within this last year will be nothing compared to what is coming, and knowing Witt as I do, the few measly thousand you have sunk away for the kid's college will come back a thousandfold, if not more! Think hundreds of thousands. Now..." She patted Sandi's arm, her tone motherly. "Get some sleep. We've got an early ride in the morning!"

CHAPTER 2

An hour before sunrise, Angie unbridled the antsy dapple-grey mare and spoke softly as she gently removed the bit from its mouth and tossed the leather bridle over a corner post. "You get to stay put today, Grailee." She ran her hand up and down the long forehead and stopped at the velvet nose, giving it a gentle cup. "Here."

Whiskered lips eagerly brushed her palm in search of a sugar cube, the token happily accepted as Angie lovingly tousled its dark mane. "You like that, huh?" The horse threw its head back and moved forward, nuzzling her hand greedily, looking for another sweet. "No, there's no more. Go on, join the rest of the gang."

She gave a coaxing push and encouraged the disappointed speckled grey to unite with the other horses, all freshly untacked, the restless string anxious for a ride that would not be.

With a sigh, Angie tiredly leaned against the corral and rested her chin on the rough wood, her attention wandering to the separated horses, three of them, left saddled and tied to a post at the end, waiting...

"Twenty-four hours." She closed her eyes and inhaled deeply, the crisp morning air mingled with the scent of horses and evergreens. "Twenty-four hours, and then you're free."

These exact words had become a mantra, first whispered to the dark an hour earlier when she awoke at four a.m. They had been repeated, unconsciously spoken, when sending Tanya with the sunrise necessities, all packed on a pony to arrange the ride's destination, leaving her the chore of saddling the remaining horses and waking the sleeping campers, the exception being Nancy and Witt, an already lit lantern inside their tent, accompanied by raised and angered whispers.

She had tipped-toed past their tent, choosing not to linger, the hisses of conversation abundantly clear.

"You're sleeping with her, aren't you? You can't keep your eyes off her!"

"You're crazy!"

"Don't do that! Don't try to make me feel like I'm seeing things! Admit it!"

"I won't! Because I'm not sleeping with her!"

"Not yet!"

Cringing, Angie had moved past to the Carson's tent, giving a gentle rap upon the wooden plank hanging by the entrance.

"Rise and shine! We'll be riding out in forty minutes."

There was movement from inside, and Cami's chubby face had poked through the canvas flaps, her short blonde hair smashed to one side of her head.

"Oh, Angie... I think we're going to pass." She squinted against the lantern's light and peered back inside, the flap moving askew, her husband Clint splayed on the mattress, half on, half off, looking dead to the world. "Clint is not feeling up to it."

The horse guide had given her a knowing smile with a nod and moved to the next tent, suspecting she would hear roughly the same excuse, the whole group having drunk themselves silly the night before.

She'd been correct, experiencing an irritated "Go away!" from the Mason's tent and a dual chainsaw sonata from the Coletta's. It was clear the two couples, along with Cami and Clint, would not be joining the sunrise mimosa horse ride.

Anxious but slightly relieved, Angie had headed straight to the corral to unsaddle the horses.

"Twenty-four hours."

This long weekend was her last-ditch hope to stay afloat.

Running into Nancy earlier in the spring had, at first, seemed like a God send. She'd been struggling financially for various reasons, wondering where or how she would come up with the money to pay her land tax and mounting vet bills, Jerry Holmes hinting he wouldn't be able to extend any more credit for his services on his last vet call.

Sinking further into debt and behind on her utilities, she was also dealing with a broken heart. Kevin Givens, the man she thought she would marry, had left her for one of her best friends, Amy. It was bad enough to be stuck on the same tiny island, constantly bumping into the lovey-dovey couple, but Amy's father, her vet, didn't seem to realize things had not ended amicably, giving her constant updates on the budding relationship, chatting away happily when visiting her horses.

Life looked bleak, but then she'd run into Nancy. Reacquainted after six years, the pretty bottle-blonde had done well for herself since they'd last seen each other, having gone their separate ways. Nancy had mentioned to Angie that she was looking for someone to give her daughter riding lessons, and Angie had jumped at the chance. It ended up not only being Nancy's daughter but a group of four girls, all family friends, and before Angie knew it, Nancy, or some other parent, was carpooling a large SUV of excited five-year-olds to her farm twice a week for lessons.

One afternoon, while the girls were helping her clean out stalls, the two women had a moment to visit, and Angie confided a desire to someday open an outdoor adventure business. The budding supplement entrepreneur, delighted with the vision, began to encourage Angie to take the plunge, advising her on how to bring glamping and horse riding to the wealthy Seattle tourists of Rockfish Island at a profit.

Desperate for success, Angie proceeded to sell a portion of her inheritance, a section of land she'd been unable to maintain, and used the proceeds to buy the necessities to make the dream a reality, hiring her cousin, Tanya, to help assist.

The business plan was solid... She already had the horses and a great working relationship with the national park, Ranger Russell, having created a new campsite section not far from the horse trails and charging her a decent rent for the camping season.

Unfortunately, the dream, now a reality, had begun to sour due to unforeseen and unexpected expenses, such as insurance costs to cover every eventuality and advertising to get the word out to the mainland, all adding to the already established pile of debt. Along with special requests from customers, some remarkably outlandish and lavish, and mounting vet bills, her clients unfamiliar with horses and less careful than she'd prefer.

As her business mentor, Nancy reassured, it was

all the cost of doing business, and soon, the profits would begin to roll in, and since the season was coming to an end with Angie drowning in red ink, Nancy suggested she could help bring business in, guaranteeing reservations for the next year by offering to hold her own corporate getaway through Angie's company. Of course, at a discounted rate. Claiming her review and word of mouth from her guests would be well worth the discount, and the circle of friends she rubbed elbows with, the ideal customers, would be new prospects for Angie to meet and impress.

With the beginning of October and bills past due, Angie readily agreed and purchased additional tents and furnishings to accommodate the guest list of ten couples, arranging another month's rent for the campsite and practically cleaning out Hattie's General Store for food supplies to feed the coming masses. But when the time came, there were cancellations, leaving only four couples, all of them already known to Angie in one capacity or another.

So much for the new business connections... and so much for the supposed life raft in the sea of debt.

"Where is everyone?" Tanya called, having arrived back at camp atop Tamarack, Angie's appaloosa, a long rope tied to the horn of her saddle, a round and pregnant pony at the end. "They're gonna miss the sunrise if they don't—"

"Aren't they up yet?" Flinging a tent flap aside, Nancy stepped out into the crisp morning air dressed in a white knit sweater and jeans, her words, wisps of vapor, illuminated by the lantern in her hand as Witt emerged from behind her, dressed in all black, looking grouchy and hungover. "Didn't you wake them?" Her inquisitive glare swiveled from Tanya to Angie before grazing the entirety of the campsite, it deserted like a ghost town. "I don't see anyone up!"

"I tried, Nance. But I'm afraid last night's frivolity impacted today's participation." Angie motioned to Tanya for the pony's lead, the corded rope untied and tossed in her direction. "Looks as if it'll only be the three of us." She peered up at her cousin, the girl's red hair platted, damp with the morning dew. "You'll need to start brunch early for the group staying behind. I suggest your famous bacon omelet and lots of coffee."

"Greasy bacon? No, no." Nancy firmly shook her head. "What they need is a Vita Mineralium morning shake! It's the perfect cure for a hangover and a great way to start each morning. It's full of antioxidants to clean out the system and—"

"Nance..." Witt croaked, both hands at his temples, fingertips white as he rubbed in circular motions, his stare set on Tanya's chest. "Let everybody be. In fact, why don't we—"

"No, wait!" Nancy followed his gaze, her words

tumbling out in a rush, "I mean, you're right, Witt. We could, uh, we could use some alone time. A romantic sunrise, just the two of us? Good idea, Honey." She gave her husband a bright smile and tugged on his arm, tearing his eyes reluctantly from the young redhead and leading him in the direction of the pine-logged corral. "Uh, hold on!" She stopped mid-step, and Witt bumped into her as she abruptly turned, giving Angie a questioning look. "Why is Grailee not saddled, Ang?"

"She threw a shoe this morning. But I have a filly I picked out—"

"I'll take Tamarack then." Nancy decided, lightly shoving Witt aside as she reversed course and extended her hand toward Tanya for the reins. In return, Tanya unconsciously pulled the leather ties protectively to her chest and shook her head, darting a nervous look at Angie, her eyes wide.

"Ahhh... I don't think that'd be a good idea." Tanya tightened her grip on the reins. "I'm afraid Tamarack got a little rambunctious on our ride. He stepped on a rock, and now his back leg is acting up. The same one as before." She winced and then hurried on, "Sorry, Angie. Better to let him rest."

"Another stone bruise? Dang it, Tanya! My vet bill is already sky-high!" Angie marched over and put a comforting hand on the appaloosa's back side before gently pulling the left foot up, the horse shuffling to the right at her touch. She gently put the foot down and sighed, "Okay, then. Corral him with the rest. I don't want the bruise to abscess like last time." She shook her head as her hand ran the length of Tamarack's body up to his neck, giving his mane a loving tousle. "And give him some extra hay."

Tanya gave a bashful nod of an apology as she dismounted, accepting the pony's rope returned from Angie's hand and walked both animals to the corral as Nancy, her lantern held low, observed the stride of the appaloosa with interest.

"His step looks fine to me." The statement was a combination of a pout and disbelief. "Maybe I should look at it?"

Witt suddenly gave an annoyed grunt, his fingers running through his hair, spiking it in every which direction.

"For crying out loud, Nancy! If she says the horse is lame, it's lame! You're not a damn vet." He nodded towards the horse corral. "Now, pick a nag already, and let's go!"

"Witt, please!" Nancy practically hissed as she grabbed his arm, jetting a panicked glance at the unlit tents. "Don't raise your voice. Remember, we're the face of the company and need to set a proper example." Her eyes suddenly scrunched in wariness. "You took your pill pack this morning, right?"

"Like a good boy," Witt grumbled and jerked his

arm out of her grip. "You're not my mother. I wish you'd—"

Angie quickly intervened and stepped between the couple, pointing to the three saddled horses, singling out the painted mare. "Here, Witt." She led him toward the corral as Nancy narrowed a suspicious glare on their backs and followed slowly behind. "I saddled this one just for you. He's a bit of a slow poke."

"So, nothing like me." Witt conjured a smile and leaned in, his voice low, "As you already know."

CHAPTER 3

With the sky above a twilight blue, the three horses progressed single file through the dark woods, their path bordered by leafy maples and skinny pines, the ground beneath their hooves obscured by discarded leaves and encroaching ferns. Lanterns swung from their saddles, doing little to light the way, the darkness failing to deter their confident stride, the path well memorized, spurred forward by the promise of an apple.

Despite leaving camp at the desired time, Angie knew by the skyline that there was no way the trio would catch the sunrise in its full glory. Not with the two riders ahead of her stopping every few feet to holler a sniping word or toss a rebuke in the other's direction.

Out of politeness, Angie hung back, attempting to give the unhappy duo some resemblance of privacy and, at the same time, avoid their bickering. It did little to no good, their voices raising higher, all pretense of a happy couple collapsing.

"...And you need to get off my back, Nance. I'm trying to build a business!"

"More like a self-proclaimed dynasty! ...Witt, your ego is out of control!"

"If it weren't for me, honey, you'd still be selling your cheap vitamins out of the garage! Try showing some gratitude!"

"By gratitude, do you mean turning a blind eye to your affairs? We had a deal."

There was no follow-up retort, and silence descended, the only sound being the clippity-clop of the horse's hooves.

Taking advantage of the silent pause, Angie inched her mount forward and cleared her throat, her leather gloves gripping the reins in nervous tension. "Um, over this small rise, you'll see Crescent Meadow." Both Witt and Nancy twisted in their saddles and peered back at their guide. "It's a beautiful, long grass pasture shaped like a crescent moon."

Neither responded but faced forward again, their horses plodding on, the tree line breaking and the path widening, the lush meadow a few feet ahead revealing a pink horizon, the sun starting to ascend.

"Oh, we've missed the sunrise!" Nancy huffed, her shoulders sagging. "If we hadn't stopped to adjust your saddle..." She gave a pointed look back at Witt, who frowned in return and awkwardly spurred his horse forward. The speed of the cadence startled him, and he pulled hard on the reins, the path now wide enough to walk side by side.

"You know, not everything is my fault, Nancy," he sniped, his horse falling into step. "I wish you'd give me some credit."

"Credit?" Nancy's eyes grew wide, her voice awed. "Six years I have stood by you through thick and thin! With no money, mounting debts, unemployed, practically homeless, and STILL, I stayed with you, telling people you were going through a rough patch. Trying to find a way to scrape enough money together to keep food on our table, and when I did just that, with my CHEAP vitamins, you took over and pushed me aside. Proclaiming your strategies of success to anyone who would listen while I stood behind you, smiling and nodding, and never publicly questioning your decisions. Credit?" She pointed to her chest, her voice rising, tearful. "This was my business idea, my dream, Witt! And you take ALL the credit!"

"Oh, you'd love to make yourself out to be a

saint, wouldn't you?" He leaned in, spit flying from his lips. "You're lucky we're not embroiled in a lawsuit!"

"Luck had nothing to do with it, Witt. Money talks."

"Ha!" Witt's head fell back, his voice dripping with disdain, "You talk as if I don't already know exactly what you're willing to do for cold hard cash."

"Then you'd be wise to keep it in your pants. Divorce is expensive." Nancy smirked, and Witt's eyes went wide before willowing into a glare of contempt.

"So, money WILL buy me happiness..."

"Witt, please. Let's not—"

"Let's not fight?" His voice suddenly softened, "Oh, Nance, I remember when we used to enjoy each other. When everything was a laugh. You used to be fun..." Witt's eyes suddenly raked down his wife, his mouth contorting into a sneer. "Now you're just a chubby prude."

"Is that any way to speak to the mother of your children?" Nancy bit back in mock surprise. "What a grand example you are for our kids!"

"Our children have nothing to worry about. I'll never stop loving THEM!" Witt suddenly spurred his horse, this time prepared for the leap, the mare taking off and running the entire course of the bend with a cloud of trailing dust behind, disappearing into the crescent's tail and out of sight.

Exhaling a heavy sigh, Nancy pulled on the reins as her chin fell to her chest, a sob catching in her throat. The filly obediently stopped, its hooves pawing the ground, anxious to keep going.

This wasn't what she had wanted. What she'd wanted was a romantic getaway where time would stand still, and the world waited at their doorstep while they salvaged their marriage. Not this finger-pointing and bickering, constantly looking over her shoulder, suspicious of every look, whispered comment, or stolen touch. If they could reconnect, put everything to the side, and find some common ground. It could all be saved. His softened tone gave her hope, even if for a moment. If only they could... She turned her head to the side, Angie's voice calling from behind.

"What?" Nancy called, twisting at the waist, her right hand resting on the back of the saddle. The horse beneath her twitched, dancing a few steps forward as she tried to peer back at Angie, still stationed at the entrance of the meadow. "I can't hear yo—"

Without warning, her body jerked, the crack of a gun following seconds later as she tumbled from the saddle, the startled filly rearing up and crashing down, free of its rider.

CHAPTER 4

Angie jerked as Nancy fell from the saddle, a deafening thunder echoing in her ears, reverberating across the meadow as the filly startled and bolted, dust billowing behind. Shocked, her eyes darted to the surrounding woods, peering through the long grass, frantic, searching back and forth as birds exploded from the surrounding timber, their cries jarring her wide eyes back to Nancy, unmoving, lying on the ground.

"Nance?"

There was no movement or response, and Angie's breath hitched. Without thought, she clicked her tongue and nudged her horse into a full gallop, racing forward, her head swiveling side to side, scanning the dark woods, fearful.

Reaching Nancy, the horse's hooves dug into

the trail as Angie pulled hard on the reins and dropped from the saddle, scrabbling to remove her gloves. She paused, gulping in air, her chest heaving with each breath, and once again, risked a glance into the thicket of Shore Pines before bringing her eyes down and connecting with Nancy's unblinking stare. She let out a shuttering breath with a shake of her head and squeezed her eyes shut, her bare hands settling on the holstered pistol on her hip.

Nancy lay unmoving, blood blossoming like a weeping flower across her white sweater, a black centered dot the source.

Seconds ticked by...

There was nothing more to be done and nothing she could do to change it.

"Hey! Did you hear a gunshot?" A disembodied voice rang out, Witt coming into view at a slow canter from the crescent's tail, the runaway filly trotting close behind, its reins clasped tightly in his hand. "It sounded close! ...I didn't think hunting... was allowed... on the island—" Witt sputtered to a stop as he grew closer, Angie standing over a sprawled body, her hand lying on top of her pistol grip.

"Get off the horse," she hissed and quickly squatted down, her head bobbing low, signaling for him to hurry. "We were shot at."

Witt, stunned, scrambled from the saddle and

practically fell to the ground, both horses forgotten as he half crawled, half ran to Angie's side, his eyes wide and confused as her trembling finger pointed across the meadow towards the tall grove of pines.

"Look over there," she commanded, her voice shaking as badly as her finger, Witt's wild eyes not following the indicated direction but drawn to the slumped body. "Witt, please!" Angie frantically groped for his hand and squeezed tight, yanking his attention to the tree line. "I thought I saw someone. Can you see them?"

Witt squinted, mystified, turning his bewildered stare from the empty meadow to Angie.

"In the trees. Look!" She tore her eyes from his and peered back into the dense evergreens, her pistol now outside its holster.

"No... I... don't see anybody!" He leaned forward, his body ridged with fear, his head turning on a swivel as he scanned every direction, unsure. "No. I... I don't see anyone."

"Straight ahead! At the base of the tall pine. There is a bit of orange! Look hard."

He straightened and peered directly ahead, suddenly tensing, his mouth dropping open, his eyes narrowing. "Wait..."

"You see them?" Angie inched closer, excited, her grip tightening, her finger resting on the trigger. "You see the hunter's orange?"

"No, I don't see any orange." He abruptly shook his head. "I can't! I'm color-blind!" His tense shoulders slumped, frustrated. "Orange looks green to me. I don't—" His released gaze landed on his wife. "Oh, dear God! Nancy! She looks..."

Angie's attention remained on the giant pine as birds descended back into the looming branches, returning to their roosts, the danger deemed gone. "I'm so sorry, Witt. I think..." His hand still trembled in hers, and she quickly let go. "I think whoever was there is now gone." She half stood as if testing the motion and then straightened completely. "We need to get—"

Free from Angie's grip, Witt crawled on all fours to his wife, his hand grasping her shoulder, giving it a timid shake. "Nance? You, okay?" He nudged her again. "Nance? ...Nancy? Can you hear me?"

Deaf to his plea, his wife continued to stare at the open sky lit in bright pinks and purples.

"Witt, she's gone." Angie grabbed his arm and yanked impatiently. "Listen, my radio is dead. We're going to have to leave her here and ride back to camp. We need to let them know—"

"I can't... I can't leave her behind! What would people think? I mean, the girls..." Witt tightened his grip on Nancy, her head lolling to the side. "What would they think? ...They'd think I abandoned their mother."

"The girls will get over it!" Angie snapped, irritation tingeing her tone. "They need their father too! Now, come on, Witt!" She gritted her teeth and pulled harder, forcing him to sit back on his haunches. "I need to get you back to camp." She clucked for her horse, the big bay nudging her shoulder. "And contact the authorities—"

"This is a nightmare. I shouldn't have said the things—You won't tell anyone... I mean, you couldn't hear us, so..."

"We don't have time for regrets." Angie edged around her horse, her eyes darting across its back and into the woods, her brow creased with worry. "Witt, we don't know if they or whoever, is still out there."

"One of us should stay behind." He shot up, twisting to face her, edging away from the stomping bay. "And you're the better rider."

"I can't leave you behind!"

"Yes, you can!" He stepped forward and grabbed the horse's bridle, jerking its head out of his line of sight, his stare determined. "I abandoned her in life, Ang. I won't abandon her in death!"

Angie bit off her retort and instead pressed her lips together in indecision, her boot already in the stirrup.

"Damn it." She hauled herself up and onto the

horse. "Stay low and... and don't touch her, Witt. This... is a crime scene. Do you understand?" Angie waited for his response, but he simply nodded, his eyes nervously scanning the tree line. "I'll be as fast as I can."

With a grunt, she twisted the reins and turned the bay sharply, pointing it back the way they came and spurred forward, her heart in her throat.

Flying down trail, branches slapped Angie's cheeks and shoulders as she raced, urging the bay onward, anxious when forced to trot or come to a walk, spurring to a full gallop once on open ground, determined to reach the camp and the two-way radio.

Thoughts pounded her as rapidly as the thundering hooves below her... Who was in the woods? A poacher? A stranger? Someone from camp? She had seen someone... hadn't she?

Tearing into the clearing, she leaned into the muscled stride, minutes later, falling upon the camp, her mind occupied with curious possibilities. She yanked on the reins, and the horse gave a nicker of protest as it bounced on its front hooves.

At her unexpected entrance, upturned faces and cautious cries of surprise greeted her as Tanya flew from the mess tent, a look of confused concern on her freckled face.

One by one, Angie took them all in... Cami taking a seat by the fire, Sandi standing by the horse corral, Nick coming from the direction of the creek, Aaron coming out of the trees, an axe in hand, and Maddie, tying her yoga pants, coming from the direction of the outhouse, and Clint, hungover, his head sticking out of the entrance of his tent.

All accounted for...

CHAPTER 5

Carrying an oversized pumpkin in her arms, Sheriff Lane shouldered the lobby door to the Sheriff's office open and stuttered to a stop, her eyes widening in surprise.

"Oh, for the love of... Martha! What is all of this?"

Descending from the corner window sat a massive fake spider with spindly legs dangling, its multiple beady eyes pointed straight towards Lane and the front door. Stationed below the eight-legged hairy beast stood her dispatcher and the town gossip, Martha Barnes, tugging and yanking on a large wad of cotton, doing her best to create a cobweb from the white fluff.

"Morning, Sheriff!" Martha cheerfully trilled, continuing to pry and pull. "It's looking pretty good in here." She happily nodded toward various locations within the room. "Don't ya think?"

Lane stood stunned and surveyed the office, mouth slightly agape.

Scores of miniature pumpkins were placed around the lobby, along with colorful swaths of autumn leaves over the archways, the station's posted signs and artwork slightly obscured by fake cobwebs housing tiny, black plastic spiders with cutouts of Frankenstein, Dracula, and other various monsters taped to the office windows. Down the hall leading to the back rooms hung white-sheeted ghosts descending from ceiling tiles and crime scene tape plastered across the walls. A life-size scarecrow, pitchfork in hand, was even propped by the coffee station, an actual bale of hay sitting by its feet.

"Martha..."

"Now, I know you said only a few decorations..." The older woman quickly crossed the room with pleading eyes, hoping to head off the sheriff's complaints, the cotton now clutched to her chest. "But I got so excited, and it's not like I can decorate at my house for Halloween... or any holiday, really. Being the mortician's wife, I mean, that would be considered in bad taste, *wouldn't you say?"*

With a sigh, Lane placed the huge pumpkin on the corner of Martha's desk.

Decorating the funeral home with ghoulish glee would be in very bad taste, almost as improper and unprofessional as decorating the Sheriff's office with crime scene tape. Then again, Martha was married to the island's funeral director, and their house was attached to the mortuary, with people traversing between the two locations for burial services and bereavement receptions afterward. Lane could understand Martha's desire to "celebrate," even if it was still wildly inappropriate.

"I guess it's fine, Martha. Only..." Lane shook her head bemused, the smell of burning dust from the furnace tickling her nose. "Only, no spider decorations in my office, okay?" She gave a playful squirm as she shrugged off her coat, eyeing the scarecrow guarding the coffee station.

"Oh, not a problem!" Martha waved a dismissive hand at the thought of spiders and returned to her task of cobweb making. "Besides, I have other plans for your office, Sheriff." She suddenly smiled deviously and added, in a whisper, "Spooky plans."

Lane opened her mouth to protest but, seeing Martha so happy, asked instead, "Where's Deputy Pickens?"

"Oh, we got a call about an hour ago. Sue Carter hit a deer on her way to work." Martha held up the strewn cotton fibers to the window and the oversized, dangling spider. "She's fine, but her BMW had to be towed." She peeked over her shoulder, her voice dropping in pitch. "Edgar Rowles told me when he arrived, MISTER Allister was already on the scene. *Looks as if Sue has him on speed dial.*"

"Hmm... You're not jealous, are you?" Lane hung her jacket on the coat rack, her eyes on the older woman, curious.

It had been six months since Martha had called off the affair between her and the semi-retired lawyer, Mike Allister, due in part to a miscommunication. Or rather, Lane letting it slip that the lawyer had another woman on the side with whom he'd jetted off to Florida. The "other woman," however, had turned out to be his sister.

Though Lane couldn't feel bad about unintentionally breaking up the affair, she hadn't done herself any favors with the crotchety lawyer, the two clashing since her first day on the island, his life mission, to have her removed from office.

"Of course not!" Martha brought the cotton down in a huff, stretching and pulling the material with gusto. "Cougar Carter is welcome to him!"

Lane raised an eyebrow, noticing the reference to Sue's nickname, dubbed by the town folks for being an insatiable flirt, and made for the coffee station, taking a wide berth around the scarecrow, wisely changing the subject, "I heard it was all elbows and knees at the city council last night." She picked up the coffee pot. "Is it true they nixed the idea for the soccer complex but approved the

Starbucks drive-thru at the end of the street?"

"It is!" Martha's eyes lit up as she crossed the room, Sue Carter and Mike Allister forgotten. "And you should have seen the commotion Coach Rick made! Threw an absolute fit! Got so red in the face I thought for sure he was going to keel over in his chair! Scared me to death!" Martha dropped her cobweb-holding hand, it having been placed over her heart, and waved it in Lane's direction. "Instead, he popped up, rigid as a nail, pointed his finger straight at the board, and said..." She paused, lowering her voice, "Well, I won't repeat what he said, but... He told the council EXACTLY where they could stuff..."

The phone on Martha's desk rang, cutting off the gossip intel.

"Shoot! I was just getting to the good part," Martha tsked in annoyance, adding, "Excuse me, Sheriff," as she started for her desk, Lane barring the way.

"Hold on, I'll get it." Lane placed her coffee cup on the desk. "You finish putting up your decorations." She shooed Martha back to the unfinished window and picked up the handset. "Rockfish Island Sheriff's Department."

"Sheriff? It's Kody at the ranger's station. We've got a gunshot fatality..."

CHAPTER 6

"I don't like this." Lane looked up from the blood-stained trail, her fingers plucking at the long grass bordering the worn path, her gaze meeting the park ranger's before being drawn to the bright orange chopper, now a dot in the sky, carrying Nancy Reyerson's body to the mainland.

"There's not much to like." Philip's eyes were pinned on the grey horizon as well.

"No, there's not." Lane's attention swung to their lone witness, Angie Bennett, the young woman standing beside a big bay, her fingers buried within its thick mane, her stare glued to the ground, face blank and pale. "Poor Angie is pretty rattled."

"It's understandable. I'd imagine everything has started to set in. Now that the adrenaline has worn off." Philip crossed his arms and nodded in the horse guide's direction. "Not only did she witness a shooting, but she kept guard over the grieving husband."

"Grieving, indeed." Lane gave a huff and shuffled to the side, Witt visible over her shoulder, standing a few paces from Angie, scrutinizing the heavens, the orange helicopter disappearing into the mid-day horizon. "Do you see how he's dressed? All in black. If you ask me, seems rather prophetic."

An hour earlier, their small group had arrived to find, as reported, the victim beyond help, a single gunshot wound to the chest, dead center of the heart, with additional abrasions and cuts about her head and torso, likely inflicted by the fall and the hooves of the bolting horse. With the death confirmed, Lane had radioed the Coast Guard for extraction, her focus quickly switching from the fatality to the survivors while Philip searched the area for the shooter, scouting all the way to the sunrise point destination and back.

Lane was left to question the witnesses on her own, having directed Deputy Pickens to remain behind at the campsite and take statements from the guests. She had immediately separated Angie and Witt, trading off with Ethan Richardson, the local EMT, who checked their vital signs for shock and other injuries.

Angie, upon request, relinquished her pistol, even though unfired, for exclusion testing, and willingly submitted to a gunshot residue test. She had then shakily recited the whole morning from the moment she woke, to Lane's arrival on the scene, insisting she had seen someone in the woods dressed in hunter's orange, her trembling finger pointing to the arched tree line and the tallest pine. Lane, trying to remain impartial, gave a curt nod with a warm smile and squeezed Angie's shoulder before moving aside, letting the EMT step between them with his stethoscope.

Witt, who had only heard the shot, admitted he hadn't seen anyone within the tree line, and though he didn't outright discount Angie's claim, he was unable to lend authenticity to it. Rather, he was more concerned and curious whether the news media outlets had gotten word of the shooting and his wife's passing.

That did not sit well with Lane.

"Maybe black is his favorite color?" Philip nudged her arm with a smile. "It's not against the law, and you're not the fashion police."

The comment earned him an eye roll as Lane pulled her notepad from her back pocket and stepped off the trail, asking, "Ranger, how fast do you think someone could get from the end of the meadow to that tall tree in the center there? Back, through the woods, I mean?"

Philip gauged the distance, his head swiveling

from the end of the crescent and back, following the forest line to the indicated pine.

"Oh, I'd say... a good fifteen minutes, maybe less if they were running full force." He followed behind her, Lane crossing the meadow, heading for the trees. "Why? You think the husband, once he was out of sight, hoofed it behind forest cover and shot her from there?"

"Might be why he was dressed in all black, for camouflage, and he did have trace amounts of gun residue on his person." Lane shrugged. "Then again, so did Angie."

"From handling the victim?"

Lane nodded. "Most likely... yet, if Witt is our shooter, it might also explain why Angie said she saw someone in the trees, yet he claims he didn't."

"Orrrrr..." Philip picked up his pace, Lane still leading. "It could be that the shooter was long gone by the time Witt showed back up. At least, that's my vote. The guy claimed to be off his horse, taking a pis...um, using the outdoor facilities at the time of the shot. It's not too hard to believe he had trouble getting back in the saddle." Philip met Lane's eyes and shrugged, his eyebrows rising with the motion of his shoulders. "I mean, his wife's runaway filly comes rearing around the corner, so he tries to calm the startled horse down and grab the reins. That probably took a while, and once he managed to climb on, he then started back, having heard the gunshot."

"Pretty good excuse to be out of firing range, if you ask me."

"I don't know..." Philip frowned. "It has a ring of truth."

Lane shook her head, a small smile playing on her lips.

He would say that, and it was no surprise, as the two of them had developed this back and forth over the last couple of years. Philip, always taking the side of virtue and human decency, and Lane, exposed to the worse of human nature, suspecting anyone and everyone of devious plots and schemes. In all fairness, both had been right and wrong in equal amounts, but Philip never seemed jaded, whereas Lane felt vindicated in suspecting such evil intents.

The two were polar opposites... yet, maybe that was why their relationship worked?

It was no secret that the pretty blonde sheriff, who was still considered new by the locals though she'd held the position for almost two years, had caught the eye and heart of the friendly and hand-some park ranger. They'd done their best to keep the budding relationship under wraps, but with the is-land being the size it was and having the town gos-sip as a dispatcher, well, word got out, and there was no point in pretending otherwise.

Though they were no longer a secret, Lane still insisted on keeping things professional when on the job, maintaining a strict policy of no public displays of affection... Philip, however, struggled with this rule from time to time, forgetting himself and planting a kiss on Lane whenever the whim hit him. She found this both infuriating and endearing in equal measure.

"Well, until the coroner digs out the bullet or we find some casings in there..." Lane motioned toward the forest and then stopped short. Philip's attention was pulled back to the trail, the big bay giving a loud knicker of protest, the painted mare nipping at its neck.

"Lane..." Philip twisted his focus between the tree line and the bickering horses. "If our poacher was hunting deer and shooting from about here..."

"Alleged poacher."

"Unless they had terrible eyesight, I'd say it would be hard to mistake a horse and its rider for a buck or doe. This is open ground."

"True, but open ground with long grass."

"Still... Might want to talk to Ol' Mark Jamison." He gave a shrug. "The poor guy is in his late seventies with lousy eyesight."

"I think I've seen his son around. Big guy, tall and broad shouldered. Around thirty-something?"

"That'd be Jay. Helps take care of his dad's place."

Philip nodded toward the woods, his feet turning in the same direction. "The two live on the edge of the park, right over that rise." He gave his head a subtle shake, a smile budding. "This time of year, the old man's memory gets a little fuzzy on where the border lies between the park and his property."

"Then not an alleged poacher but an accidental poacher?"

"So, he claims."

"Mark Jamison." Lane wrote the name in her notepad. "Bad eyesight would explain an accidental shooting." She stepped into the trees, the small meadow disappearing behind the tall timbers. "Unless this is a 'lay in wait' scenario?"

"Lay in wait? As in... a sniper?" Philip made a face. "I think that's a little out there."

"Why?" Lane turned, surprised. "Angie made it very clear the victim and her husband weren't a happy couple, constantly bickering since their arrival on the island. What if this is actually a murder for hire?" She paused, tucking her notepad into her back pocket and trudging ahead. "Think about it, Ranger. The husband provides the details of their weekend. The time and place of opportunity." She swiveled and peered out toward the meadow, the view slightly obscured by low-hanging limbs. "From this location, the sniper would have a clear shot and plenty of cover."

"So, Witt removes himself from the equation by galloping off in a huff?" Philip entered a few paces behind, watching his step, eyes cast down upon the moss-covered twigs and mushrooms littering the needle-carpeted ground.

"Exactly. He starts a fight and leaves his wife as the lone target. Then the shooter picks her off and vacates the area. Job over." Lane paused a few feet ahead, standing in front of a swept section bordered by fingered ferns, and gave Philip a questioning look, her eyebrow arched, indicating the bare, oval-shaped spot.

"That's a deer bed. You can tell by the pellet scat," Philip answered in response and continued to march past, his eyes pinned to the base of the large pine. "Here is something, though."

Lane abandoned her find and followed, her steps deliberate, eyes trying to track along.

"We got footprints." Philip squatted at the base of the wide stump, his hand hovering above two set marks in the dirt. "Can't make out a sole print, but it looks as if they were standing here for a while. You can see where they shuffled their feet." He suddenly stood up, his brow creased, and examined the tree bark at eye level, running his hand against the rough surface.

"What are you looking for?" Lane inched closer and pulled out her cell phone, swiping through the menu for the camera. "I doubt they carved their initials in the tree."

"Ha. Funny." Philip stepped back, his mouth quirking into a half-smile as he pointed down at the prints. "Look how close they were standing to the trunk. If they were shooting from here..." He paused and peered upward, suddenly lifting his arms, miming a rifle hold, and squinted one eye closed, leaning forward, taking aim. "They would've had to press the rifle right up against the tree, standing here, in this spot." He suddenly shook his head, dropping his arms. "The recoil from the rifle would have scarred the bark, and I don't see that."

"And I don't spy any leftover casings. But if this was a crafty poacher or a professional hitman... that's not surprising." Lane bobbled her head, trying to see past Philip, looking the trunk over herself. "You don't think they climbed into the tree?" She suddenly glanced up, searching for snapped branches or broken limbs.

"Don't think so. There's no sign of where someone landed if they came down." Philip absently scratched the back of his head. "And no need for a rifle scope at this distance either." He moved aside so Lane could step closer. "Look. Those horses stick out like a sore thumb, and you can see everyone clearly." He suddenly shrugged. "A scope would be unnecessary unless their aim was incredibly off."

"It was a direct shot to the heart." Lane snapped a few photos and then put her phone away, pulling out her notepad and referring to the third page. "Angie stated our victim had been turning, twisting around in her saddle to face her." Lane shook her head and flipped the notepad closed. "I thought it was a lucky shot, but..."

"At this range, there was no luck about it," Philip finished for her, his tone gruff. "In fact, a handgun could have done the job." He circled the tree, then pivoted, stopping short to scrutinize the grassed meadow. "Hey, Lane? Check out the horses."

Inspecting the tree bark, she looked up, spotting the string clearly. "Yeah? What about them?"

"Their saddle bags are orange," Philip groused. "Hunters,... even poachers, know better than to take aim at anything in orange."

"Then this wasn't a hunting accident." Lane's mouth gave an involuntary quirk of satisfaction before setting into a proper frown.

"I'm seriously starting to doubt it." Philip turned away from the meadow and, once again, began examining the forest floor, moving further from the tree line into the dense woods. "I mean, if the shooter was in hunter's orange like Angie said... They should have known better."

"Okay, then..." Lane twirled in a slow circle, gauging her bearings. "Can you tell which direction they left or came in from?" She stopped and faced toward the end of the crescent. "Did they come from this end or the entrance of the meadow?"

"Neither." Philip jutted his chin towards the ground. "Looks as if the footprints peter out here, into obscurity." He pointed forward, away from the meadow, his face concerned. "In the direction of Ol' Jamison's place... and Angie's camp."

CHAPTER 7

In shades of grey and purple, peppered with twinkling points of brilliance, dusk fell upon the sky as the riders returned to camp, the weary bunch greeted by flying tent flaps and calls of welcome, followed by consoling sentiments and a barrage of curious questions.

Shoulders squared and a brave face on display, Witt greeted his fellow campers with assurances he was fine, allowing himself to be led to the roaring campfire, where one by one, guests broke away to bring him a token of comfort, be it a blanket, a plate of food, or a stiff drink.

With the focus on Witt, Tanya had taken the horses' reins and a firm hand on her cousin's elbow, steering them both to the pine corral, where now they sat upon the top rung, a comforting arm draped over Angie's trembling shoulders.

The camp was clearly divided.

Watching them all was Lane, standing by her patrol truck, having allowed Ethan to return to town. She stood with her back against the driver's door, her notepad and pen in hand, making small notations, the dynamics of the group noteworthy. She glanced up at the sound of footsteps and flipped the pad closed as Deputy Pickens slowly approached, a brimming tin cup in hand.

"So, there were footprints leading back to camp, huh?" Caleb turned slightly and peered back at the campfire, his voice kept low, "You think one of them was the shooter?"

"It is one of several working theories," Lane admitted, having radioed her deputy instructions before leaving the meadow. "Ranger Russell is looking into one of his own at the moment."

"Ahhh, I wondered why he hadn't returned with you." Caleb indicated the tin cup, extending his arm. "Here, Sheriff. This is for you." The corners of his mouth hitched into a lopsided smile. "Be warned. It's hotter than hell and doesn't taste much better."

Lane arched an eyebrow, the rich aroma seeping into her bones, and dared a tentative sip, a pleased and playful smile breaking her stern expression.

"Liar." She took another, gauging the risk of burning her tongue well worth it. "This is divine!"

"Yeah, top-notch. Much like the rest of this camp." Caleb nodded at the yurt-like tents, then gave a backward tilt towards the line of parked luxury cars. "Nothing but the best. Must have cost Angie a fortune to set this place up."

"Every penny, I'd say." Lane's gaze roamed to the horse pen, the two cousins still perched upon the corral, Angie's wide eyes occasionally darting towards the campfire and their guests. "Everyone, been cooperative?"

"All but one. Nick Mason. He's the tall, lanky guy standing on the edge of the firepit. The gal with the bobbed haircut... That's his wife Maddie. She was friendly enough, but all he wanted to know was when they could leave."

"Back to town?"

"No, off the island." Caleb shrugged, pushing his hands into his coat pocket, the evening chill setting in. "Struck me as odd because he was the only one out of the bunch that didn't ask how Witt was or if we knew anything more about Nancy. I mean, it's human nature to be curious. Everybody else was."

Lane nodded slowly, agreeing, and took another sip. "What about a timeline?"

"Well, from what I gathered, the weekend started with the mainland couples..." He paused, discretely pointing out each as he spoke with a nod of his head, "The Masons, from Bellevue, the Carsons and Reyersons from Seattle, all headed over the ferry, reaching the island around nine a.m. Thursday morning, uh... yesterday. Their first stop was the general store to pick up a few last-minute supplies and a couple of bottles of Crown Royal. Sounds like they were pretty enamored with the place and took the opportunity to pose for a few touristy shots around the picnic table with Miss Hattie."

Lane smiled at the image.

Miss Hattie Vickers, the owner of the general store, known as plain "Hattie's" to the locals, was an island favorite at the ripe ol' age of a hundred and three. Her grandson, Harry Vickers, ran the place for her, but she could be found in her rocking chair not far from the gossip circle's picnic table stationed in the front window, sales tag still attached, eager to share a tall tale over a hot cup of cocoa.

Caleb pulled out a notepad of his own, a birthday gift from Lane, and referred to the first page, his notes barely legible.

"Then, purchases in hand, the merry bunch ventured to the bank next door and stood outside the main window, jeering friendly waves and catcalls at Aaron Coletta, stuck at work until five p.m., who ignored their antics.

Denied their fun, the group spent an hour wandering the small shops before climbing into their cars and heading for the park and Angie's camp. There, they were greeted by the two-person staff and Sandi Coletta. They all quickly settled into their tents and enjoyed a light lunch while listening to Witt, who shared some upcoming news about the business and announced that the vitamin-distributing company was thinking of going public, apparently offering an invitation to become an actual board member to those that proved themselves faithful."

Lane stood a bit straighter, noticing Caleb had the last word in all caps and underlined.

"From my understanding, the news was received well. Though I have to say, even though they're a friendly bunch, there seems to be a sense of competitiveness and jealousy bubbling just under the surface."

"I can see that." Lane's attention returned to Witt, still surrounded by his fellow campers, the small crowd hanging on his every word, the couples practically elbowing each other to get an inch closer to his presence.

"Then, in celebration, the group went on a two-hour horse ride which was guided by Angie. The trip up the trail was uneventful, but on the way back, two men, one described as elderly, the other middle-aged, both holding rifles but seemingly on friendly terms with Angie, had stopped to chat. No one caught their names. The two men were out rabbit hunting and, apparently not realizing they'd crossed over onto parkland, were sent back the way they'd come with no complaints on their end. Just a farewell wave to everyone before disappearing back into the woods."

"Mark Jamison." Lane flipped open her own notepad again and circled the name Philip had given her earlier, the park ranger currently on his way to speak to the old man, having convinced Lane there was no need for her to tag along, assuring that if Mr. Jamison had indeed been their accidental shooter, the old man would turn himself in willingly. "That's the name Tanya said as well when I asked who she thought it might have been." Caleb shrugged. "She said he and his son, Jay, are harmless. Wouldn't hurt a fly."

"That's usually why it's called an accident."

Caleb didn't disagree and continued, "Upon returning to camp, Aaron Coletta had arrived, and together, they unsaddled the horses before the whole group was invited into the mess tent, where Tanya served dinner. With Aaron present, Witt rehashed the earlier business discussion, this time disclosing figures of profit." He stepped closer, his voice dropping even more, "Have you seen the prices they're charging for these vitamins?"

Lane nodded, having been subjected to one of Sandi's sales pitches. A box of free Vita Mineralium samples still sat in her office untouched.

"Anyway, in celebration of the positive report,

bottles of whiskey were brought out, and a party atmosphere developed, leaving Angie and Tanya to clean up the dishes and settle the horses for the night. It wasn't until a little past midnight that everyone was directed to their tents so they could get up bright and early for another ride.

However, come dawn, the majority of the camp was crippled by a hangover, leaving only Angie and the party hosts to venture out, tackling the morning horse ride on their own, leaving Tanya behind to make breakfast for the remaining three couples."

"Sounds like they were having a nice time." Lane pulled her eyes from Witt's direction and nodded towards the vacant tents. "What's with all the empties?"

"Cancellations." Caleb shook his head, his mouth set in a flat line. "Tanya said that seven other couples canceled at the last minute."

"Seven! She know why?"

"I didn't think to ask."

"Find out and get their names," Lane directed and tilted her mug in the direction of the group before taking another sip. "Any of them hear the gunshot?"

"They all did, except Clint Carson. Says he was passed out in the tent with his wife playing nursemaid. She, on the other hand, did hear the shot. Said she'd gotten tired of listening to his snoring and snuck out, deciding to sit by the fire and sketch for a bit." Caleb referred to his notepad. "Aaron Coletta said he was chopping wood when he heard the shot, whereas his wife Sandi was in their tent reading. Tanya was in the mess tent, cleaning up breakfast and washing dishes. Both Maddie and Nick Mason said they were down by the creek. Nick, fishing, and Maddie, doing her morning yoga."

"So, the Carsons and Masons, each, can vouch for their spouses?"

"Not exactly. Nick and Maddie both seemed surprised to find the other was down by the creek at the same time. Either they were in different areas or..."

"One of them is lying."

"And as for Cami Carson?" Caleb flipped his notepad closed with a wry smile. "Sandi Coletta stated that when she finished her book, she decided to check on the horses, and there was no sign of Cami, only a sketchbook in her chair."

"Cami snuck off somewhere?"

"Maybe to the little girl's outhouse?"

Lane nodded, acknowledging the possibility.

"But then, if Aaron was off chopping firewood and Cami wasn't sketching at the firepit, then there is no one to verify Sandi was in her tent reading... if we're going to be fair." Lane's eyes bounced from one couple to the next, finally landing on the corral, Tanya and Angie now feeding the horses. "What was Tanya doing?"

"She was in the mess tent."

Lane made a face. "Was she able to verify everyone's movements?"

"Nope. Said she was cleaning the breakfast dishes and getting lunch prepped." Caleb tucked his pen into his shirt pocket. "Which I guess means no one can say for sure she was in the mess tent the whole time either?"

"Yeah. That's what I was worried about. Seems as if no one can really vouch for anyone else." Lane gave a subtle shake of her head, her brow creasing as she turned to meet Caleb's eye, handing him back the empty coffee mug. "Did you have any trouble getting the warrant?"

CHAPTER 8

"Hello! Anybody home?" Philip called out as he slid from the dapple-grey's back, his boots landing hard on the ground. "Mr. Jamison? Jay?"

Clucking his tongue, he coaxed the mare forward as he tossed her tethers over the handrail of the steps leading to the cabin's front porch. He had learned with Ol' man Jamison, it was always best to announce your arrival at his homestead, indicated by the numerous hypocritical no trespassing signs littering his property, than risk a shotgun pointed in your direction. He tried again, "It's Phil! With the ranger station."

He strained for a response, but there was none. Noting the smoke rolling from the brick chimney and the front door left wide open, Philip took the wooden steps two at a time and strode across the porch, stopping short of the cabin's entrance and giving the door jamb a solid rap, not stepping inside. A sharp bark greeted him, along with a wagging tail, as Jamison's grey-muzzled chocolate lab came to the door, his tongue lulled in delight at a visitor.

"Hey ya, Jasper. Where is everybody?" The lab, without comment, bounded past him and briefly paused at the sight of the speckled mare, offering her an excited woof of welcome before heading in the direction of the backyard.

The dog disappeared around the corner, and Philip followed, spying a skinned black-tail deer hung by its hind legs, the pelt stretched on a rack a few feet away with ol' man Jamison sitting on a large stump, knife in hand and blood smeared across his front and forearms.

Jasper, tail still wagging, was giving a veracious report in staccato barks, all of which were ignored or unheard, depending on if Mark Jamison had his hearing aids in or not, the old man unconcerned, his head cocked back, looking up at his work, face set in exhausted wrinkles. "Jasper, will you hush up?" The old man dropped his knife in the grass and placed a large hand on the dog's head, giving the lab a loving tussle. "Is Jay back?" He looked up, slightly startled at the sight of Philip. "Oh, well! We've got company!" He turned back to the dog, his smile widening.

"Why didn't you say so, Jasper?" His next remark was for Philip, "That you, Phil? Come help an old man up." He extended his arm out and then, thinking better of it, pulled it back, instead running his palms down the front of his blue overalls, wiping them clean before taking Philip's offered grip, the ranger pulling the elderly man up to his feet with ease. "This is a surprise!"

"That's a nice doe. Get'er this morning?"

"The boy did." He suddenly elbowed Philip with a wink. "Lucky shot if you ask me."

"He shoot her up by Crescent Meadow?" Philip thought he'd take a stab in the dark.

The old man, in turn, frowned and shook his head. "Now, that's park land. He wouldn't be up there." His smile returned, but not as bright. "What brings you around, Phil?"

"Well, I need to ask you a question." Philip unconsciously rubbed the back of his neck, suddenly embarrassed. "Where...uh, where is Jay? Is he around?"

"Nah. He's checkin' the fence line. I noticed a section knocked over the other day." The old man pulled a dirty handkerchief from his back pocket and wiped his brow, squinting up at Philip, his faded blue eyes crinkled at the edges. "Should be back for dinner any minute. Got a stew on the stove. You're welcome to join us."

"I appreciate the offer, but..." The growl of an ATV drowned out the beginning of Philip's gracious decline, and a wide smile split Mr. Jamison's face, Jasper taking off at a full run to the front of the cabin.

"Sounds like he's already back. Come on inside, Phil."

Not prone to be impolite and thinking it best to tackle father and son at the same time, Philip followed as Mr. Jamison led the way up the back steps and into the house, Jasper returning, his baleful yelps announcing the new arrival.

"Now, shush, Jasper. You'll bark the walls down." Mr. Jamison pointed Philip to a round oak table and then bellowed, "We got company!" as the front door slammed shut.

Heavy footsteps marked the arrival of Jay Jamison as he marched into the small kitchen, his wide shoulders filling the door frame, dressed in a flannel shirt, and dirty jeans, a bright orange baseball cap atop his head. Spotting Philip sitting at the table, his curious expression softened in relief, and his shoulders relaxed, giving the ranger a polite nod, before making his way to the kitchen sink to wash his hands, tossing his baseball cap down onto the counter.

"I wondered whose horse that was out there. Thought it might be Angie coming for a visit."

"Sorry to disappoint, Jay." Philip leaned back, Mr. Jamison placing a bowl of piping hot stew down on the table. "That's her horse, though. A sweet little grey."

Mr. Jamison gave a slow nod of recognition.

"Ahh, that'd be Grailee. Had her since she was a colt, she has." He placed two more bowls on the table, jamming a spoon in each one. "Come on, Jay. Get it while it's hot." He settled himself into a chair and beamed at Philip. "We don't get visitors all that often, except for Angie." He paused, vigorously shaking salt into his stew. "Which usually is the way we like it, but it's nice every now and then."

"So, what brings you around, Phil?" Jay tucked into his bowl as well, choosing pepper over salt.

"Well, I'll be honest. This isn't a social call." Philip gave an apologetic smile, mindlessly stirring his stew. "One of Angie's group was shot and killed this morning, up at Crescent Meadow—"

"Is Angie all right?" Jay sat up straight, his spoon clattering against the side of the bowl.

"She's fine." Philip put up an arresting hand. "The assumption is a hunting accident or a misfire. So, I have to ask, and I hate to do it, but I know if it were so, you'd do the right thing... Were either one of you hunting this morning in or by the meadow before sun-up?"

There was an awkward silence as neither father

nor son spoke. Philip looked to one and then the other. "Fellas, if it were an accident..."

"No, of course not, Phil!" Ol' man Jamison groused, his hand slamming down onto the table. "You just took us by surprise, is all!" He pointed a gnarled finger at Jay, it slightly trembling. "I was sound in bed until seven this morning, and the boy, well, he roused around eight, and we went straight into our chores. The boy went off to feed the live-stock and happened to find our supper." He groped for his spoon, the utensil hitting the side of the bowl with a loud ting. "And I was busy restocking the wood pile."

"That's right." Jay held his father's stare, his head bobbing up and down. "I didn't come back around until ten? Maybe ten-thirty?"

"And I promise you, he found that doe on our property, fair and square."

Jay continued to nod. "I can even show you the spot, Phil. It was along our south fence, by the woodshed. Now, I'll be honest. I used bait, but it was on our land and..." Jay suddenly frowned. "You don't think a stray bullet..."

"How many shots did you take at it?"

"Two, but—"

"No, son. If you got the deer where you said you got 'em, you wouldn't have been shooting in the right direction. The meadow is east of us. Besides..." Mr.

Jamison's eyes whittled down to a squint, and he leaned in, peering hard at Philip. "You mentioned sun-up. Exactly what time did this shooting happen?"

"Around six-thirty this morning. Three of them were heading up to the point to catch the sunrise."

"Well, there's your answer! Both of us were still in bed, sound asleep!" Mr. Jamison leaned back with a smile, his good mood returning. "Understand why you needed to ask, so no harm done, us being the only ones this close."

"Thank you." Philip took a deep breath as Jay, sitting across from him, kept his eyes pinned on his father, his brow knitted. "You, uh, you notice anybody around wearing hunter's orange? Besides yourself?" Philip gave Jay a wry smile, nodding at the orange baseball cap sitting on the kitchen counter.

Jay, his eyes drawn back to Philip, gave a curt shake of his head. "Haven't seen anybody, well, except Angie and her group of riders—" Mr. Jamison unexpectedly coughed and dropped his spoon with a clatter, pounding his chest.

"Hey, you, okay?" Philip slapped the old man's back, jarring him forward, and handed him a glass of water from the table.

Mr. Jamison quickly nodded, eyes wide, and Jay hurried on, "That is, yesterday. We stumbled across them while we were out hunting rabbits. Right, Dad?"

Gulping down the water, his father held up a

hand, indicating he wanted to speak, then slammed the empty glass down, excited. "Yeah, that was a surprise, let me tell you!" The old man dived back into his stew, his head swaying side to side. "Never would have believed it if I hadn't seen it."

"Seen what?" Philip asked, turning in his seat, curious.

"Now, Dad. You're not sure it was her."

"Her, who?" Philip asked.

"I sure as hell know it was her!"

"Dad, it's been years!"

"Don't matter! I'd know that conniving woman anywhere. Even with that peroxide hair!"

"Know who?"

Ol' man Jamison turned to Philip, at the same time, waving a dismissing hand at his son and growled, "Buck Bennett's widow."

"Buck Bennett? Angie's dad?"

"May he rest in peace." Mr. Jamison made the sign of the cross and then rapped on the table. "Could have knocked me over with a feather when I spotted her yesterday. Never thought my ol' eyes would see Nancy Bennett in the flesh, step foot on this island ever again."

CHAPTER 9

"Widow!" Lane dropped the goose-down pillow and its corresponding pillow-case upon the Carson's queen-size bed, the inside of their tent torn asunder, clothing, bedding, and personal items laid out orderly on the ground, Lane's tedious efforts of searching for evidence interrupted by Philip's arrival back at camp. "You're telling me Nancy was Angie's mom?"

"Step-mom," Philip clarified. "And only for about a year. Buck Bennett met her on the rodeo circuit after losing his first wife, Suzanne, that was Angie's mom, to cancer six months prior, and then, of course, there was his own untimely demise that cut the relationship short."

"Was it a suspicious, untimely demise?" Lane asked, her voice curious in pitch as she paused her search and arched an eyebrow at Philip, standing just outside the canvas structure.

He shook his head. "Heart attack in his easy chair at home."

Lane, disappointed in the answer, snatched up the two remaining pillows lying at the end of the mattress and shook them out.

"Though there were rumors," Philip added with a sly smile, stopping Lane mid-shake. "I mean, there were bound to be, I guess, with Buck showing up with a new bride, much younger than himself, a pretty little redhead, full of piss and uh,…" Philip cleared his throat. "Vinegar."

"A redhead, huh?"

Philip nodded. "And a little rough around the edges, if you get my drift."

"Party girl?"

"And then some. Folks used to say that Buck had a hard time keeping her home at night." Philip wiggled his eyebrows. "She liked the bar…and the male patrons."

"A loose party girl. Got it. So, what did she and Buck have in common?"

"Couldn't say. He'd lost Angie's mom in a rather short period of time, and Angie, well… She was a handful, a typical teenager testing her boundaries, working through her grief." Philip crossed his arms. "I think he was taken in by good looks and the desire not to be alone."

"But what drew Nancy to him?"

"Oh, well... that's easy. Money and horses. Buck had been a rodeo rider turn announcer. Traveled all over the place. One night, on a whim, he bought a lottery ticket and managed to beat the odds, winning. A month later, he'd retired from the circuit and returned to the island with his new bride, spoiling her and Angie with his newfound money and using the bulk to buy all the land around his farm. Turned it into a horse ranch, stocking it full of the finest ponies he could find. Made his own little equestrian paradise." Philip shook his head, his face falling. "Too bad he didn't get to enjoy it for long."

"And let me guess, he left everything but the house and land to the new wife when he died?" Lane cocked a questioning brow, knowing Angie still lived on the horse ranch. Though, now, it was more of a farm, whittled down in acreage and livestock.

Philip shook his head. "Nancy was executor of his will, but he left the bulk of his fortune and property to Angie."

"How many years ago was this?"

"Um, six or seven?"

"That would have made Angie, what? Seventeen?"

"There about. If I remember right, Nancy only stuck around for about a month or so after Buck's passing before taking off for good, so Angie had to have been of age when she left."

Lane tossed the pillows aside and faced Philip, her expression miffed, "You sure his death wasn't suspicious?"

"Lane, the man never ate a salad in his life."

She tossed her head side to side with a roll of her eyes as if to say, "Okay, fine." And then placed her hands on her hips, surveying the disarrayed tent. "Well, it seems the woman of six years ago is a far cry from the Nancy Reyerson of today. A mother of two, head of a successful multi-level marketing vitamin company, business mentor, and, may I add, a short-haired blonde with designer clothes, who wears three-thousand dollar cowboy boots. I'd say she could have held her head up high, coming back to the island. Why would Mr. Jamison think otherwise?"

"It was the way she left. The consensus on the island was that as soon as she found out she wasn't getting any money in the will, well... she basically abandoned Angie. Though, I think Angie was happy to see her go at the time."

Lane sighed and dropped her arms, grabbing the edge of the comforter and stripping it from the bed, the pillows flopping to the canvas floor.

"Odd that Angie didn't mention the relation, though brief." Lane shook her head, bending over and yanking the sheets off before running her hand underneath the mattress. "Or Tanya, for that matter."

"Shock, maybe?" Philip shrugged, his mouth curving down at the edges. "As for Tanya, maybe she assumed you knew since you'd already talked with Angie up at the meadow?" Philip suddenly shuffled his feet, his voice concerned. "You're not... uh, you're not suddenly suspecting Angie, are you?"

Lane straightened, her hands finding her lower back as she stretched, answering, "I should, but..." She lifted the comforter and tossed it back onto the bed with a grunt. "I don't see a motive."

"You don't?" Philip's voice climbed an octave in surprise. For as long as he had known Lane, she had the uncanny ability of coming up with unseen or unsuspecting motives for people considered, otherwise, above suspicion. She called it being objective, and he was frankly surprised she was sparing Angie her suspicious speculations.

"Well, no." Lane tucked a wayward pillow under her chin and started to shimmy on the sheeted casing she had torn off. "If Angie inherited her father's money, there's no motive there, and according to Angie, Nancy was the one who encouraged her to start this horse-riding retreat. I mean..." Lane tossed the pillow down onto the mattress. "If you lived in fear of someone, would you hire them to teach your five-year-old to ride a horse?" Lane shook her head. "I don't see it, and I'm not saying she's not on the list of suspects, she's just way down at the bottom."

"Speaking of suspects... I see everyone is gathered in the mess tent, and none are looking too happy about it." Philip twisted around, peering back at the lit pavilion, the campers seated at a long table, plates of untouched food set before them. "They not allowed to leave camp yet?"

"On the contrary, I told them they were free to go. They can return to town or the mainland whenever they want." Lane suddenly gave a wicked smile. "And... as soon as I finish searching their tents and vehicles, they'll be able to take their belongings with them."

Philip chuckled. "They're sticking around for you to release their stuff."

"I'm about done. I tackled Angie and Tanya's yurt while Caleb searched the vehicles. We're working our way through the remaining tents now, and we've already been through the Mason's and Coletta's. I'm finished here. Hopefully, Caleb is almost done with the Reyerson's, and then we can all head back together."

"I'm assuming you've not found the smoking gun?"

"I wish!" She tucked a stray hair behind her ear and tossed the last pillow onto the bed. "But we've found plenty of other bits of possible evidence."

"Such as?"

"Well, for starters, an orange Denver Broncos hat was buried at the bottom of Aaron Coletta's suitcase."

"Never knew Aaron to be a Broncos fan."

"Which might explain why he says it's not his." Lane dusted her hands on her thighs and squeezed past Philip out into the open air, the night sky sparkling above. "And why Sandi says she didn't pack it."

"Interesting... Anything else?"

"Found a crumpled note in the pocket of a pair of discarded jeans belonging to Nick Mason. It was requesting a rendezvous outside of camp. Unsigned."

Philip raised an eyebrow. "Witt's handwriting?"

"Haven't been able to compare yet, but it was likely written by a man due to the cramped writing style." Lane shrugged. "And then there are the casino receipts stuffed in the glovebox of the Mason's car."

"That's Cami and Clint, right? What was so suspicious about that?"

"The casino receipts were paper clipped to Nancy Reyerson's credit card."

Philip let out a low whistle.

"Oh, I'm not done." Lane gave him a pleased smile. "Witt handed his cell phone over."

"Anything juicy?"

"I'd say so. His phone was littered with pantless selfies."

Lane gave a brief shiver. "Paired with promises to

leave his wife."

"So, he's got himself a lover."

"Try two. From what I can gather, a regular and a newbie..." Lane took a deep breath. "And neither woman seems to know about the other."

"What a heel."

"Hey, Sheriff?" Caleb's upraised voice broke across the camp, excited, "I got something!"

"Move it, Ranger." Lane lightly pushed Philip aside and headed for Witt and Nancy's tent, where Caleb stood at the entrance, a plastic gun case in hand, flopped open and lined with grey polyure-thane foam, a box of bullets nestled inside.

"Found this crammed under the bed." Caleb beamed from ear to ear as Lane pulled off her latex gloves and reached for her duty belt.

"And the gun?" she asked as she snapped on a new pair.

Caleb handed the case over with a shake of his head. "No luck, and I've torn this place apart."

"Looks it." She peered past him into the Reyerson's tent before turning the case over and closing it shut, the words "Smith & Wesson" em-bedded in the plastic cover. "Good work, Deputy. Chances are, you just found the case for our murder weapon."

CHAPTER 10

"Sheriff, you can't possibly be serious!" Clint Carson protested, the whole of the camp following close behind as Caleb escorted Witt to his patrol car. "There has to be a reasonable explanation!"

There was a rally of agreement, and Maddie's voice rose above the crowd, panicked, "Is this really necessary, Sheriff? The man just lost his wife!"

Raised grunts of approval and protest were echoed as Aaron pushed passed everyone, his voice lifted to be heard above the ramble, "Should I call you a lawyer, Witt?"

"Yes! Law offices of Heitman, Hiles, and Sh—" Witt was cut off as Caleb placed a gentle hand atop his head and eased him into the back seat of the patrol car, shutting the door.

"Now, be reasonable!" Cami elbowed her way up front. "Can't one of us go with him?" Her eyes were set on her husband as she urged him in the direction of the patrol car with a curt nod. "Clint, why don't you ride with the sheriff into town, and then you can—"

"Folks!" Lane turned on her heels with an arresting hand held high, quailing their objections and barricading the group from going any further. "We're only taking him down for questioning." She raised her voice and emphasized, "He's not under arrest."

"See, I told you!" Nick Mason, an annoyed frown in place, interjected. "If he were in real trouble, they would have handcuffed him." He stepped closer to Lane, his voice eager, "Does this mean we're all free to go?"

"Hold on a sec, Nick." Aaron Coletta placed a firm hand on his shoulder, silently declaring himself the spokesperson of the group. "Sheriff, will you please let Witt know I will be contacting his lawyer in the morning, but for now, I'll arrange for Mike Allister to meet you down at the station once we get into town."

"I'll pass the word on, Aaron." Lane succeeded in keeping her expression neutral, not thrilled with the idea of having to deal with the island's crotchety, semi-retired lawyer. "And to answer your question, Mr. Mason, you're all free to leave with your possessions."

"Off the island?" Nick challenged.

"No way, Sheriff. We're not going anywhere!" Clint glared at Nick before turning his attention back to Lane, his arms folded across his chest, his legs parted in a stance of defiance. "Is there a motel on the island?"

"Speak for yourself!" Nick Mason edged closer, side-stepping both Clint and Aaron. "Sheriff, when does the last ferry leave?"

"You can't be serious, Nick!" Clint turned, incredulous. "Witt needs our support, and you're leaving him in the lurch?"

"Hey, man... Aaron said he's getting him a lawyer. I don't see what I can do, or frankly, what you can do by sticking around here."

"We can give our friend support! A united front!"

"Then give it! You can hang out with Ranger Joe here, and... and..." Nick helplessly waved in Lane's direction, his eyes still set on Clint. "Sheriff Whats-her-name... Mine will be relayed from the comfort of my home back in Bellevue!"

"Nick..." Maddie offered the group an apologetic wince as she yanked her husband aside, her eyes frantically searching their reactions. "Sweetheart, I think it would be best if we stayed." She shot the sheriff a nervous smile before turning back to her husband, her intent stare conveying a deeper meaning than her words, her teeth gritted in a plastered smile. "After all, we are invested in what happens to Witt, are we not?"

Nick stared blankly at his wife and then huffed in frustration as she squeezed his arm, giving him a reassuring nod.

"Fine." He turned back to Lane with a subtle shake of his head. "Where did you say the hotel was?"

Aaron chimed in before Sheriff Lane could answer.

"There isn't one. Our island is too tiny. But you're all more than welcome to lodge with—"

Sandi suddenly appeared at his elbow, slipping her hand through Aaron's arm, her grip as tight as her smile, her voice a little louder than necessary, "We'd let you stay with us, but there's not enough room." She snuck a nervous glance at Aaron, who looked surprised. "Um, what about the apartment above Hattie's, Sheriff? It might be available."

"That is an option, but it's really only a studio with a twin bed. Not ideal for two couples," Lane explained, the tiny apartment above the general store having been her abode when she first arrived on the island. "In all honesty, there's not really any place for you all to board. It would be best if you headed—"

Philip joined the group and raised his hand, asking pardon for his interruption.

"This, uh, this might be a little unorthodox." He beamed at Lane as he rocked back on his heels. "But one couple could stay at my house. It's not huge, but it's got plenty of space."

"Then where will you be staying?" Sandi seemed almost annoyed at his hospitable offer.

"Oh, I'll just stay with—" Philip hitched a thumb in Lane's direction, but seeing her steely glare, instead cleared his throat and dropped his hand to his side. "Um, with my buddy, Harry. His couch will do me fine for a day or two."

Aaron nodded his approval. "Appreciate that, Phil. But... where will Witt stay once he's released from questioning?"

"OH,..." Sandi yanked on her husband's arm at the same time as she stepped forward, a bright smile lighting her face. "We have enough room for just Witt. He'll stay with us, of course."

"Then it's settled!" Aaron gently shook Sandi from his arm and turned to the group, seemingly unaware of the consensus of dirty glares. "Now. Let's all head back into town."

CHAPTER 11

Lane's headlights swept into her designated parking spot in front of the Sheriff's office, the dual beams centering on Mike Allister, the semi-retired lawyer waiting outside the station, an attaché case gripped tightly in his gloved hand. Despite the time of night, he looked bright-eyed and bushy-tailed, dressed in a crease-free suit with a heavy winter jacket worn over top. On his feet, a pair of comfy house slippers.

Shielding his eyes with a Rolexed wrist, Allister lowered his arm, a scowl firmly in place as Lane cut the engine and yanked the keys from the ignition, Caleb's patrol car pulling up beside her, Witt riding in the backseat.

"Sheriff, Aaron called me," Allister's gruff voice called out the second her boots hit the sidewalk.

"I'm here to meet with your detainee. I am officially representing Witt Reyerson and would like to speak with my client immediately."

"Evening, Mr. Allister," Lane greeted politely, minus a smile, since one was not offered, and slipped her key into the lock, wrenching it to the left before pulling the glass door wide and extending the invitation to enter.

"As I am sure you are already aware, Sheriff, I'll be advising him to hold his peace until he can convene with his mainland lawyers." Mr. Allister entered and paused as she brushed past, outpacing him to the locked lobby, it usually left open during the day. "I don't expect us to be here for long."

"No, of course, you don't," Lane sniped as she unlocked and pushed the door open, surprised when a witch's ear-piercing cackle broke the stillness of the dark lobby.

Startled, Lane instinctively stepped back and placed an outstretched arm protectively across Mike Allister's chest, the lawyer already striding forward to go through the door.

On Martha's desk sat a white skull, glowing bright orange, its mouth opening and closing in glee as a series of giggles, hideous in nature, issued from its toothy grin before abruptly going dark, the teeth chomping together in a finality of silence.

Lane pursed her lips and tentatively waved a

hand in the air, the skull once again coming to life, a built-in motion detector sensing her movement.

She was going to kill Martha.

"What the hell was that?" Caleb came up from behind with Witt Reyerson, a firm hand gripped around the older man's bicep.

"That..." Lane flipped on the lights as she marched over to the skull, its mouth snapping closed, the maniacal laughter coming to an end, "is one of Martha's Halloween decorations." She swiped up the plastic skull and yanked out the batteries, slamming it down. "Sorry, Gentleman. I'm afraid my dispatcher has gone a little overboard with the decorations. If you don't mind, I'll have Deputy Pickens direct you to our back conference roo—" Lane's eyes grew wide.

A full-length burial casket was propped in the corner of her office, clearly visible through the glass partition. At least now, she'd have a box to bury Martha in.

"Why am I not surprised you run this place like a funhouse?" Mike Allister, his frown somehow deepening, bristled before turning on his heels, not expectant of an answer, and extended his hand to his new client. "I apologize, Mr. Reyerson. I'm your lawyer, Mike Allister. I received a call from Aaron Coletta, who has retained me for the time being." He turned and addressed Caleb. "I'm ready to consult with my client, Deputy. If there is somewhere we can talk... Preferably, not with a coffin in the room?"

"Uh, sure thing, Mr. Allister." Caleb gave the lawyer a crooked smile, surprisingly receiving one in return, and led the two men down the short hallway, the three occasionally having to dodge a dangling ghost hanging from the ceiling tiles.

Opening the door to the first interrogation room, Caleb ushered them in, his voice carrying down the hall to Lane. "I'll put some coffee on and... I think we have some crackers or cookies in the breakroom if you're hungry, Mr. Reyerson. No?... All right, I'll be back in a few minutes."

At the sound of Caleb's boots traveling down the hall toward the lobby, Lane waited for his reappearance, "I'll get a pot going," she offered as he came into view, her deputy not bothering to stifle a yawn as he hiked a thumb in the direction of the street.

"Great... I'll grab the evidence bags from the car. Be right back."

"Thanks, Dep..." Lane yawned as well, hers triggered by Caleb's own gaping sigh. She didn't bother to finish speaking, as he was already out the door and instead, as promised, moved to the coffee station, where she impatiently shoved the life-size scarecrow to the side, mumbling death wishes upon Martha under her breath.

Minutes later, with a full pot percolated and

a cup of coffee for herself and Caleb already hastily downed, Lane headed toward the interrogation room with her deputy a few steps behind. She rapped on the door and waited for the beckoning call of "Come in," before swinging it open.

"Sheriff," Mike Allister started as soon as she stepped inside, placing two mugs and a coffee carafe on the table, along with a handful of sugar packets and small creamers. "My client is open to being questioned with myself present. However, he does have one stipulation."

Lane cocked a questioning brow, surprised at Witt's willingness to cooperate, confident that his new lawyer had advised him to remain silent.

"And what would that be?" She sat down, her eyes zeroing in on her number one suspect, still dressed in the same black clothing, his wife's dried blood under his fingernails.

"That you allow him to spend the night in one of your cells." Seeing Lane's stunned expression, the lawyer continued, "That, or release him into my care without telling the others in his group." Mike Allister reached for the carafe and poured himself a cup. "In the morning, he will take the first ferry out and head straight home. If you have more questions later, you can contact the law offices of Hiles, Heitman, and Shiels."

"That's an odd request, considering at the campsite, he seemed to soak up the group's tokens of comfort and well wishes." Lane pulled out her notepad and placed it on the table, tapping the end of her pen against the dark wood. "I'm curious. What's changed, Mr. Reyerson?"

"Everything has!" Witt snatched a sugar packet and gave it a vigorous shake. Ripping it open, he leaned over and whispered in Allister's ear, "Can you hurry this along? I need to call my P.R. guy so we can strategize—"

"Strategize?" Lane cut him off. "Exactly, what do you mean by—"

"Sheriff, please," Allister interrupted, his hand squeezing Witt's shoulder in solidarity. "We all handle grief differently." He leveled Lane with a disappointed stare, his tone chiding, "Try to keep in mind that my client is in mourning. There are two little girls he needs to get home to so he can break the sad news of their mother's passing."

Lane, feeling surprisingly convicted, politely nodded. "I'm sorry. I am sure that won't be easy. And I have no problem releasing you into Mr. Allister's care. This should go quickly with your cooperation." She plastered on what she hoped was a patient and warm smile, internally praying for a confession. "Let's start with the gun case found in your tent. At the campsite, you admitted the missing gun and the corresponding case both belonged to your wife?"

"Yes, but as I said, I had no idea..."

Mike Allister placed a restraining hand on Witt's arm. "Let me, Mr. Reyerson." He gave Lane a wolfish smile. "My client admits to recognizing the pistol case, as stated in his previous discussion with you at the campgrounds, but he had no knowledge that his wife brought the item along nor that it was being stored in their tent. By the way..." He glanced down at his Rolex, noting the time on his yellow legal pad. "I hope you didn't happen to search the Reyerson's tent without a warrant?"

"Of course not," Lane snapped, knowing Allister was looking for an easy out.

"Can you prove that you, or your deputy, didn't find the empty case BEFORE applying for the warrant? Because it would be rather awkward if we were to find out that it was discovered beforehand. You sure you didn't step inside any of the tents?" He turned to Caleb, addressing the deputy, "Did Angie, perhaps, give you permission to look? Allow you to pop your head in for a quick peek?"

"No, sir," Caleb answered, bending forward, his elbows resting on his knees, meeting Allister's gaze. "Rented tents or not, those campers are covered by the Fourth Amendment. That's why we requested and were granted the warrants."

"Well, I'm glad to hear it." Allister broke eye contact, his pen scratching across the legal pad. "But you'll understand if I don't take your word for it."

Lane gave her deputy a wink of approval, impressed by his solid response.

"Mr. Reyerson..." She suppressed a smile, returning her attention to Witt. "My deputy found your gun case crammed under the bed, almost out of arms reach, which is odd, don't you think?"

"Very odd, indeed," Allister piped up, choosing again to answer for his client. "Considering Mr. Reyerson has informed me that he was wholly surprised when you showed him the case. It was his belief the item was still locked up in their safe at home." Allister pushed away his legal pad and leaned back, his face smug. "I want to make it clear that Mr. Reyerson being honest, and claiming the gun case as his property, is not an omission of guilt."

Lane gave him a wolfish smile of her own. "Then can he account as to why the gun case was in his tent..." She cocked her head, her smile widening. "And not at home in the safe?"

"Easy. His wife brought it without his knowledge! She was the one who did all the packing for the trip."

"Any idea why she felt the need to bring a gun on a horse-riding retreat?" Lane asked, the question directed at Witt, his lawyer answering in his steed.

"It's common for riders to bring a weapon when they ride."

"But the gun wasn't on her person... on the ride."

Allister shrugged. "I didn't say she took it with her on that particular venture. I only speculated as to why she may have packed the weapon for their trip." He once again placed a consoling hand on his client's shoulder. "And you're making an assumption that there was a gun in the pistol case. For all we know, she packed it, believing the weapon was inside. There is a strong possibility that the gun is, in fact, locked in their safe back home." The lawyer held up his hand, halting Lane's counter. "But if the gun isn't at home, well then, one might also assume, after these sad events, that she didn't feel safe among her fellow campers and brought it for protection."

"Protection?"

"I would think it's obvious, Sheriff. One of their fellow campers is at fault." Lane's eyes whittled into slits, realizing the lawyer's clever approach, the older man taking a lecturer's tone, "Clearly, one of their guests, someone with access to the Reyerson's tent, which was left unsupervised and open for hours, knew Mrs. Reyerson had brought along a firearm and removed the gun for their own means." He took a hurried sip of coffee and added, "It is assumed they didn't have time to return the gun, or possibly, in a direct effort to implicate my client, purposely did not return the weapon, knowing you would find the empty case and blame him for his wife's shooting...

which is exactly what you've done, treating this poor man as a suspect instead of a victim, and they, the actual culprit, is now roaming our island free, while my client is being peppered with accusing questions during his darkest time. I hope you don't have serious aspirations of winning the next election, Sheriff, because I am here to tell you—"

Lane cut the lawyer off, ignoring his veiled threat, "Excuse me." She eagerly leaned forward, her chair scraping against the floor as she addressed Witt. "Mr. Reyerson, is this the real reason you're wanting to avoid your group?" She inched closer. "You believe one of them is the shooter?"

With a solid bob of his head, Witt swallowed and straightened his shoulders. "After speaking with Mr. Allister, here. I am only now realizing how lucky I am, riding off when I did!" He slammed a finger down on the table, punctuating his next sentence. "I could have been the one killed!"

Lane bit the inside of her lip, fighting the urge to roll her eyes. It was clear the lawyer had offered Mr. Reyerson a defensive lifeline to cling to. One, in all honestly, she had thought of herself, but only in the sense that one of his fellow campers was an accomplice. Was she looking at this in the wrong light? Maybe he was, after all, lucky to be alive? Lane dismissed the idea. It was more likely that he was stalling and trying to throw blame, possibly putting her on a false trail. He didn't strike her as being that clever... in fact, would he be able to point the finger at one of his fellow campers without accidentally giving motive against himself as well?

"Mr. Reyerson, why would one of your guests want to murder your wife?"

"You can't possibly expect him to know the mind of a murderer, Sheriff!" Mike Allister blustered. "The man was almost a victim himself! And here we are in the middle of the night... the man is exhausted, hungry... and... You do realize that he's lost his wife? His children have lost their mother, and the world has lost a—"

She once again cut Allister off, too exhausted to put up with the semi-retired lawyer's courtroom theatrics. "Mr. Reyerson, did your wife have an issue with anyone in particular?"

He gave out a bitter laugh. "She had an issue with everyone."

"Considering your wife was the head of a successful, multi-level internet business based on winning people over, I find that a bit surprising." Lane arched an eyebrow. "I would think she'd have to be quite the people person to pull that off."

"Oh, she could schmooze with the best! Had an extraordinary talent of making you feel like the greatest thing since sliced bread." Witt shook his head, his mouth twisted in a sneer. "But when that feeling wore off, or you displeased her in any little way, she could make life a living hell."

"And was there anyone in particular in your group that she made life... as you put it, a living hell?"

"Excuse me, Sheriff." Allister cleared his throat as he ripped out a page from the legal pad and folded it in half. "These are some of the issues Mrs. Reyerson had with her employees, slash, guests." He handed the yellow sheet to Lane. "As you can see, Nancy Reyerson was a prickly woman."

Lane took the paper, her brows knitted, and glanced down at the sheet, reading out loud, "Cami Carson, accounting discrepancies. Clint Carson, inventory and supply issues. Nick Mason, disputes over commission payouts. Maddie Mason, threatening to expose an affair?" Lane looked up and handed the sheet to her deputy. "Whose affair?"

"That you'll have to ask Mrs. Mason," Allister answered, waving for his client to remain quiet.

"And I will." Lane took back the folded sheet from Caleb and tucked it into her notepad, knowing Allister would not let his client elaborate unless he felt it was beneficial to his defense. "Speaking of Nick Mason, this note was found in his tent. Is this your handwriting, Mr. Reyerson?" Lane turned to her deputy and held out her hand, accepting a clear plastic bag, a torn note sitting inside, and placed it on the table. "It's requesting a meeting in the woods? Were you and Nick planning something?"

Both Witt and Mr. Allister leaned forward, the latter sliding the bag closer, his brow furrowed, clearly curious as Witt sat back, shaking his head side to side, the corners of his mouth quirking.

"No, Sheriff. I can confidently tell you. That is not my handwriting, and I did not have a meeting with Nick Mason."

"Do you recognize the handwriting? Perhaps, you know who wrote this note?"

Allister held up his hand, silencing his client's answer as he glanced down at his own yellow legal pad, scanning the long sheet, before answering for Witt, "Sheriff, he's not a handwriting analyst."

"I wasn't asking him—"

"Move on, Sheriff."

It was time for a change of subject.

"Okay... Mr. Reyerson, whose idea was it for the horseback riding retreat? You or your wife's?"

"It was his wife's idea." Allister smiled, making it clear he would continue to speak for his client regardless of whom she addressed. "Nancy had wanted to support Angie Bennett in her new business venture. It was her idea to have their corporate event on the island."

"I understand several people who were invited canceled at the last minute. Why was that?"

"If that is so, I don't know how those individuals, not on the island at the time of the sad event, can be of any consequence at this time. Please, Sheriff. It has been a long day, and Mr. Reyerson would like to get some rest."

Lane bit off a smart retort, surprised when Witt spoke up, "They didn't come because they couldn't stand her!" Witt gave an annoyed shake of his head, adding, "Nancy could be difficult. Headstrong. Liked things done a particular way, her way, to be precise. She demanded perfection, and that could grate on people's nerves."

"Sounds like it grated on yours."

"Sheriff, please," Allister huffed.

"I get the feeling your marriage wasn't a happy one," Lane prompted. "Were you only together for the business?"

Witt let out a heavy sigh and nodded, Allister, cutting in, "And for his children." The lawyer gave Witt a warning glance. "You were making the best of a difficult situation for your family."

"Then... divorce wasn't on the table?" Lane flipped back through her notebook. "Because Angie stated she overheard your wife Nancy threatening you financially if you two were to go separate ways."

"Threatened? Angie couldn't've heard..." Witt suddenly turned to his lawyer. "Do I have to answer that question?"

Allister shook his head, barking, "Sheriff, that is complete hearsay."

"It points to a possible motive," Lane argued.

"Hardly! Money is common leverage in marital issues. She just as easily could have said she'd take the children away."

"Oh?" Lane's eyebrows went up. "And did she?" She turned to Witt. "Did your wife threaten to take your kids?"

Maybe there was more than one motive for murder to be considered.

"Never." Witt shook his head, his thin lips pursed together. "And she didn't want a divorce. Neither of us did."

"See, there? No motive." Allister gave his client a firm nod and an approving wink before turning back to Lane. "Can we please move this along?"

Lane bristled but complied, referring to her notes.

"Mr. Reyerson, you were explaining that your wife being an unpleasant person was reason enough for someone to want her dead?" Allister sighed heavily as he refilled his mug. "The man was simply painting you a picture."

"I understand that, however, it's not matching with what we've been told from other witnesses." Lane nodded toward Caleb, who straightened and recited from his notepad.

"Your wife was referred to as energetic, encouraging, inspirational, motherly. One person even described her as an emotional cheerleader. Patient and kind. They also reported her to be having a good time and enjoying the retreat." Caleb flipped his notepad closed. "There seemed to be no indication she was afraid or wanted to leave."

"Doesn't sound to me as if your wife was concerned about her well-being." Lane tilted her head, waiting for an explanation. "Rather contrary to someone supposedly bringing a firearm along for protection, as Mr. Allister has suggested."

"As far as you or I know, Sheriff," Allister countered, sitting forward. "Keep in mind, this was a business event. She would need to put on a brave face as the founder of Vita Mineralium. We can't possibly know what she may have feared or, exactly, even who. All we know is the possibility is there."

He gave her a Cheshire smile, and Lane wondered, not for the first time, what Allister had been like in front of a packed courtroom in his hay day. She decided to try a different line of questioning.

"Were you aware, Mr. Reyerson, that your wife resided on Rockfish Island for a small period of time, roughly six or seven years ago? She was married, I believe, to Buck Bennett?"

"Yes. Buck is how we met. I was employed through the wealth management company that was handling his investments. I was his financial advisor."

"Oh, so you and the widow grew close after her husband's death?" Witt avoided her eyes, and Lane took a guess, "You were involved while she was married."

Allister crossed his arms. "Can I ask why this line of questioning is relevant?"

Lane didn't answer but asked instead, "Mr. Reyerson, according to Angie and Tanya, your wife insisted you come along on the horse ride this morning. You didn't want to go? Why?"

"It was the crack of dawn!" Witt wearily put his coffee mug down, cream-colored liquid sloping over the side. "And frankly, I was hung over with a pounding headache."

"As was the whole camp. Why did your wife insist you both still go on the ride?"

"I'd like to say torture, but it was really for appearance's sake." He straightened in his chair and sopped up the small spill using a tissue. "It wouldn't do for the company owners to be laid up in bed from partying too hard the night before."

"I see." Lane again referred to her notes, wanting to circle back. "Angie also stated that you and Nancy bickered the whole time on the ride up. What were you arguing about?"

"We weren't bickering, we were discussing."

"Discussing what?"

"Normal husband and wife things."

"Such as?"

Witt let out a loud huff with a corresponding shrug. "The kids, money, business decisions..."

"What about sexual affairs?" Lane smiled, clarifying, "Yours, primarily."

Witt shot a panicked look at his lawyer, clearly concerned, and seeing the reaction, Lane pushed on before Allister could intercede.

"Mr. Reyerson, we found, uh..." She cleared her throat, a sly smile crossing her lips. "Numerous text conversations with various women, who were not your wife, all accompanied with racy photos. It appears you have quite the full schedule throughout the week. Was Nancy aware of your weekly activities?"

Witt had the decency to look embarrassed as his lawyer cut in, his tone blasé, "Spouses have affairs all the time, Sheriff. This is nothing new under the sun." He nodded toward his client. "And yes, his wife was aware of his..." He paused to search for the right word. "Other engagements, being, he and she were no longer intimate. It was understood he would seek comfort and release elsewhere."

"Doesn't mean she liked it."

"I dare say she didn't. But there's no motive there. Unhappiness? Sure. Murder? No."

"But you'd agree, Mr. Reyerson..." Lane ignored Allister and, once again, addressed Witt directly, her eyes pinning him to his chair. "It was a point of contention in your marriage. Something that, if brought up, would be sure to get her goat? Ensure a fight? Harsh words?"

"What exactly are you getting at, Sheriff?" Mike Allister leaned forward, his elbows resting on the table, eyes squinted in suspicion.

"Well, it seems rather convenient, as Mr. Reyerson himself pointed out earlier, that he wasn't in the line of fire, or even in the area, when his wife was shot. One might speculate that he purposely tried to avoid going on the morning ride, and when that failed, intentionally picked a fight with his wife, separating himself from the situation." Lane tapped her pen point against the tabletop, garnering Witt's attention, his wide eyes swiveling to her in awe. "Possibly to get in position to fire the shot himself and dispose of the weapon before riding back upon the scene?" Lane sat back in her chair, pleased with the color of red seeping up Witt's neck and invading his receding hairline. "Or, he needed to get clear of the area, knowing full well someone would be taking a shot at his wife."

"Are you seriously accusing him of being the gunman?" Mike Allister inched closer to the table, almost amused. "Or even more ludicrous, hiring someone to kill his spouse?"

Lane shrugged. "I see this going down one of two

ways." She held up her index finger. "Mr. Reyerson shot his wife himself, from the safety of the trees, using the pretense of an argument to ride his horse into the woods..." She flipped up the second finger, her lips twitching into a smirk. "Or he knew his wife was going to be shot at, and he vacated the area, using the argument as a means to leave her behind, like a sitting duck. Which was it, Mr. Reyerson?" Lane leaned forward, her tone no longer light and casual. "Myself, personally, am leaning towards option one. You see, I find it interesting that you chose to wear entirely all black today. Was that to help you blend into the surroundings?"

"You're passing judgment on the man's clothes!" Allister scoffed, Lane's eyes continuing to bore into Witt, the man squirming under her scrutiny.

"It's only a matter of time before we find the ditched murder weapon, Mr. Reyerson. We have several volunteers out searching right now and another group set for early tomorrow morning," Lane lied smoothly, almost surprised when the island lawyer didn't jump in to dispute her claim.

"I didn't kill my wife!" Witt pushed his mug aside, his face an angry red. "And I didn't hire anybody." He pointed to his chest, his voice rising. "I may be a selfish jackass and an adulterer, but I'd never take my girl's mother away from them. Not to mention the business!" He suddenly pounded the table, his temper good and gone. "Don't you understand? Nancy's death ruins everything! I'll be lucky to salvage—." He suddenly grabbed Allister's arm. "Listen, we're wasting time here. I'll need you to get a hold of my publicity agent. Have him put a spin on this. Something like..."

"Yeah, that's probably a good idea, Mr. Reyerson," Lane cut him off, her own temper rising. "I can't imagine housewives and yoga instructors are going to want to buy vitamins from a cheating husband accused of murdering his wife." She looked at Caleb and leaned over, half whispering, "It's not a good look for a company about to go public."

"Exactly! This is will be a media nightmare!" Witt ran his fingers through his hair and turned to Allister. "Can we go now? I have phone calls to make."

"I think we're done here." Allister abruptly stood up, his own face red, embarrassed by his client's outburst. "Since you have no grounds to hold Mr. Reyerson, I don't see any reason to—"

"There were traces of gunpowder residue on his clothing." Lane stood with him as Caleb edged in front of the door, blocking their path.

"Inconclusive! Easily picked up from clutching his dead wife to his chest!" Allister raised his voice, his irritation coming through as he waved Caleb aside. "You're grasping at straws, Sheriff."

"Am I? Mr. Reyerson has several motives to murder his wife." She listed them off, "Control of the business, money, their children, divorce, his extra martial affairs... and yet, he's not been able to offer a logical motive for anyone else to kill his wife." She motioned to the yellow piece of paper sticking out of her notepad. "Except for some vague suggestions that you refuse to elaborate on. I can't help but feel he's simply parroting the excuses you've given him."

"As I said, we're done here, Mr. Reyerson." Allister grabbed Witt's elbow, urging him to stand. "The sheriff obviously has some more investigating to do."

"Mr. Allister, I'd advise you..." Lane put her hand out, stopping the lawyer and his client from barging past, Caleb still blocking the doorway. "To keep an eye on your house guest. This is my official request for Mr. Reyerson to remain on the island, preferably in your constant company." She dropped her arm and nodded for Caleb to move aside, addressing the back of Witt as he left the room, following his lawyer. "We'll chat again, Mr. Reyerson... after I've spoken with the coroner in the morning."

CHAPTER 12

"Hands full and too stubborn to make an extra trip to the truck, Philip fought with Lane's cottage door as he stumbled into her darkened kitchen, a stuffed duffle bag slung over his shoulder. Jockeying for the light switch with his elbow, he made the connection, flicking the power on and stopping short at the unexpected presence in the room. Rightly so, since finding a startled skunk with its tail straight in the air hissing a menacing warning would, to most people, be a cause for alarm.

"Hey, Stinker!" Philip dumped the duffle bag onto the kitchen table, the skunk's tail still at full staff as it stomped forward in three quick little hops. "You sure make one heck of a guard dog."

The skunk had come with the cottage.

Philip's uncle, a rich yet eccentric man, had saved

the little critter, his mama and siblings picked off by mother nature, with the full intention of releasing the skunk back into the wild.

Instead, growing fond of the little guy and giving him the moniker of "Stinker," Philip's uncle decided, though illegal in Washington state, to keep the striped fuzzball as a pet. Knowing how to throw money at a problem, his uncle managed (through the donation of a new x-ray machine) to convince Jerry Holmes, the island veterinarian, to de-scent the little guy and make him an official house pet.

The two lived happily together until old age caught up with Uncle Chuck, and he decided it would be best to move to the mainland and live with his daughter, whose condo did not allow pets. As it would happen, Sheriff Lane was living in the minuscule apartment above Hattie's and was desperate to find another place to live. Philip, seeing a solution to both his uncle's and the new sheriff's housing problem, suggested that at a greatly discounted rate, Lane rent his uncle's charming cottage... except, he hadn't mentioned Stinker until... well, a few weeks later... after she moved in. To his defense, she'd had her hands full solving a murder and dealing with the corresponding trial afterward.

When Phillip finally dropped the animal off on her doorstep, it had taken a bit of convincing and reassurance that due to old age, Stinker wasn't long for this world, and it would be considered a kindness to his uncle... and Philip... if she let the skunk live out his remaining days with her, here at the cottage, the only home he'd ever known. Admittedly, Philip had laid it on pretty thick, and he did feel guilty about it, but... she had been thinking of getting a cat, so...

"You hungry, little guy?" Philip swiped up Stinker and cradled him in his arms as he headed straight for the refrigerator, grabbing a baby carrot for the skunk and an ice-cold beer for himself. Thumbing off the bottle cap, he hooked a chair with his foot and plopped down at the kitchen table, an exhausted sigh puffing out his cheeks.

It had been a long day, what with his shift starting at five a.m.

He glanced at his watch and did the mental math, thinking himself lucky if he were able to grab a couple of hours of sleep before heading out again. Though tomorrow, or rather, today, was Saturday, Philip had promised Angie help packing up camp. He'd also managed to rope in Harry, in exchange for the small favor of meeting bright and early at Hattie's to unload a truck scheduled to arrive on the first ferry. He'd be dog-tired, but doing two good deeds would be beneficial for his soul. At least, that was what he was telling himself.

At the screech of the screen door opening, Stinker hopped down and scampered under the kitchen table as Philip slowly got up and opened the backdoor, Lane standing on the other side, her keys dangling in her hand.

"Hey." She gave him a weary smile and stepped inside, Philip shutting the door behind her and turning the deadbolt. "I assumed you'd be asleep."

"Only just got here. Took a bit to get the Masons set up at Harry's apartment, and then the Carsons settled into my place." He helped her shimmy out of her jacket and then headed for the fridge, asking, "You want a beer?"

Lane smiled at his offer, but she shook her head as she sat down, unbuckling her duty belt and lightly tossing it next to Philip's duffle bag on the table.

"So, how did it go then?" Deserting his route to the fridge, he circled around and placed one hand on her shoulder, the other at the base of her neck, running his thumb up and down her spine. "Did he confess?"

"Not even close," Lane sighed, tugging her bun free, her blonde hair tumbling past her shoulders.

"What happened?"

"Mike Allister, that's what happened." She paused, pulling away from Philip's kneading fingers to pick up Stinker. She placed the skunk gently on her lap. "All he did was put up roadblocks! Blustering about circumstantial evidence and how everyone at the campsite had free access to Nancy and Witt's tent."

"Eh... He's not wrong."

"Yeah, I know," she admitted bitterly, then cooed at Stinker, giving him a loving rub under the chin. "That, and between his half-hearted allegations of an illegal search, which was nothing but a stalling tactic, and his taunting that a gun case does not equal an actual gun..."

"Yikes. Not wrong again."

"I know! He's damn good at his job Phil, but frustrating as all get out. The only saving grace of the whole exchange was he actually did me a favor."

"On purpose?"

She twisted to the side, and peered back, her lips quirked. "What do you think?"

"Not on purpose." Philip firmly straightened Lane forward and continued to massage her shoulders. "How did that come about?"

"Witt has decided to avoid his fellow campers like the plague. Asked to sleep in one of our cells at the station and be allowed to return to Seattle without the others being informed of his departure." She yawned, Stinker jumping down to the floor and skittering under the table for his half-eaten carrot. "If Allister hadn't volunteered to vouch for Witt and invite him to stay at his house, I would have been sleeping at the office tonight."

"Sounds like Mr. Allister did both of us a favor,"

Philip teased, bending down and placing a soft kiss at the base of Lane's neck earning him a light smack upside the head and a tired smile.

"Well, it's clear Witt is trying to distance himself from the group. He claims, or rather, Allister put it in his head, that one of the others tried to kill him alongside his wife. I believe he knows better and is attempting to separate himself from an accomplice."

"You really think he did it?"

"He's the one with the strongest motive and the most to gain." Lane tugged her notepad from her back pocket and placed it on the table, yanking out a yellow piece of paper. Unfolding the sheet, she held it up for Philip to read. "He had Allister provide this vague list of possible motives for the others and then clammed up about it." She shook her head. "All clever subterfuge, if you ask me."

"I see Tanya, Angie, and the Colettas didn't make the list." Philip peered over her shoulder, slightly bent at the waist. "Seems to be pointing the finger at only the mainlanders."

"Which I find suspicious." She folded the list, tucking it back into her notepad.

"You suspect Aaron or Sandi? I can't picture either of them taking a potshot at her."

"But it wasn't some random potshot, Phil. This was a setup. Witt and his partner, whomever they may be, planned all of this... And keep in mind, he wouldn't point a finger at his own accomplice. Which makes it all the more plausible." She fought through a yawn. "Thankfully, Caleb has volunteered to search for the weapon come morning. He's convinced the gun was ditched since it wasn't found on Witt or back at the camp during our search."

"And you really don't think Witt's in any danger?" He gave her shoulders a final squeeze before rounding the table and sitting down, picking up his beer. "I mean, Allister could be right. Maybe the plan was to take out both Witt and Nancy. Or, at the very minimum, have Witt take the blame."

Lane shook her head. "If the shooter wanted both husband and wife dead, they could've easily picked them off side by side. Not to mention, if Witt riding off ruined the attempt, there was always an opportunity to try again on the trip back down from the sunrise point."

"Unless everyone would notice the shooter's absence from the camp. Maybe it wasn't a target issue, but rather, a time issue?"

Lane shook a finger at him, impressed. "Good point, Ranger." She picked up her notepad and began flipping through the pages, searching. "Here, Caleb made a list of who was in camp and where they were at the time of the shot."

"Oooo." Philip eagerly scooted his chair around the table and inched closer, craning his neck to read

Lane's notes. "This should be interesting."

Lane gave a quick smile, enjoying his excitement, and then referenced her scribbled notes.

"At the time of the gunshot, Clint Carson was passed out in his tent, and his wife, who he thought was inside the tent, stated she was actually sitting in front of the campfire sketching."

"Believable."

"Yeah, except Sandi Coletta, who was reading inside of her own tent, said when she came out to stretch her legs and visit the horses, there was no sign of Cami anywhere."

"Suspicious."

"True, but then, no one can vouch for Sandi either. Her husband was out chopping wood and—"

"Wait, Aaron was chopping wood?" Philip craned his neck even more, trying to read Lane's notes for himself.

"Yeah, that's what he said."

Philip scoffed. "Angie already had a full cord of wood. I should know, Kody cut while I stacked, and that was only three weeks ago."

"Well, maybe they had a bonfire?" Lane shrugged. "I mean, they were celebrating the night before. Could they have burnt through all that wood?"

"No way." Philip shook his head. "First off, Angie knows better. Bonfires are never allowed. Second, that would have been one hell of a fire if they had used a full cord. Lane, that much wood usually lasts people an entire winter."

"So, Aaron lied about cutting more firewood." She put a tick by the bank manager's name. "Then there is the Masons. Maddie and Nick. Both claimed to be down by the creek. Maddie on the bank doing her morning yoga, and Nick trying his hand at some fly fishing."

"Convenient that they can vouch for each other."

"Oh, but they can't. Neither recall seeing the other."

"Seriously?"

Lane nodded. "Either they honestly didn't see each other..."

"Fat chance. The creek is low this time of year until the fall rains arrive. Nick would have had to stand smack in the middle, in clear view. Unless he walked down a ways..."

"I'm of the mind that Caleb got to them before they could stick their heads together and come up with better stories."

"Which is odd, don't you think?"

"What do you mean?"

"Well, if you're planning to murder someone, wouldn't you make sure you had a solid alibi, especially from your spouse? I mean, seriously. I'd think you'd have that hammered out before talking to the authorities."

"Unless this was a crime of opportunity? Maybe one of them saw their chance and took it?"

"You mean feigned a hangover... purposely stayed behind?"

"Not necessarily. The hangover might have been legit."

"But they see a chance to sneak away from camp." Philip suddenly shook his head. "However, if that were the case—"

"Then they're probably not in cahoots with Witt." Lane frowned as she scribbled down, "Opportunist crime?" and added an arrow pointing toward Nick and Maddie's names. "Then, last but not least, is Tanya. She was in the mess tent clearing breakfast and prepping for lunch. She claims not to have seen anyone while inside, so she can't vouch for anybody."

"And no one can vouch for her." Philip flopped back in his chair, beer bottle in hand. "Not that she needs vouching for."

Lane gave him a quizzical look. "Why's that?"

"She's a nineteen-year-old kid."

"Phil..." Lane sighed, as they'd had this conversation before. "Age doesn't matter when it comes to murder."

"I know, I know. Youth does not equate to innocence when it comes to a homicide investigation. But!" He held up a finger. "She's a good kid. Really. I've gotten to know her a little bit over the summer."

He leaned forward, giving Lane a crooked smile. "And Kody's sweet on her."

She returned his grin. "Is he? How bad?"

"Head over heels bad." Philip chuckled. "Though I think she's been too busy helping Angie to notice. She's a hard little worker. Loves those horses... and her cousin. I think they're the only family each other has."

"Oh?" Lane frowned. "She an orphan?"

"I don't know the whole story, but her parents are out of the picture. If it's from a loss or a difference of opinion, I couldn't say. What I do know is when Angie asked for help for the summer, Tanya dropped everything and moved to the island." Philip smiled again, his eyes crinkling. "Kody sure hopes she plans on staying over the winter."

"I bet he does." Lane fought off another yawn and lightly slapped her notepad against the table, pulling a pen from the leather casing. "Okay, lovebirds aside. Let's look at this in a different light. They all had the opportunity to sneak from camp unseen, but would they have been able to get into Nancy and Witt's tent unnoticed to grab the gun? Now... if Clint Carson was asleep in his tent—"

"Oh, no, you don't." Philip stood, his chair screeching across the floor as he held out his hand. "It's almost two in the morning, and you need some shut-eye. You can tackle this line of reasoning in a few hours over coffee and eggs He dipped his chin to meet her gaze and then wiggled his fingers. "Come on... Let's get you tucked into bed."

Lane arched an eyebrow. "Yeah, about that. What was with you offering your place tonight?" She left his extended hand untouched and, instead, gave a pointed glance at the oversized duffle bag sitting on the kitchen table. "You do realize you can't actually stay here."

Philip dropped his arm and laughed. "Why not? I stay the night all the time!"

"Yes, and I enjoy having you over." She gave him a playful smile as she crossed her arms. "But it doesn't look like you packed for just an overnighter."

"Well... no." Philip's smile faltered slightly. "I thought I might as well keep some things here. You know, a change of clothes, a few favorite books, an extra shaving kit, maybe a..."

"Toothbrush?" Lane finished for him.

"Yeah, why not?" Philip lugged the duffle bag to the floor. "We've been dating for a year now, and we've not had any issues. I love you. You love me. Don't you think it's time we start looking toward the future?"

"By living together?" Lane looked around the tiny kitchen, her voice skeptical. "Here, at the cottage?"

"Yeah, here. Or my place... or anywhere on the island." He gave her a playful smile leaning forward.

"Or off? Wherever you want to live." Philip abruptly straightened, his head cocked to the side, suddenly concerned. "Unless... you don't want to?"

"Phil, have you ever heard of the saying, why buy the cow when you can get the milk for free?"

"Hey, now!" He pawed at her arm, his fingers trailing down and grabbing her hand, giving it a light shake. "It's not like that!"

"But it is!"

"No, it isn't!" Philip returned her insistent tone. "I don't want to play house, Lane. I want to expand our relationship. Move to the next level."

"What, shacking up? The next level, Phil, is marriage. At least, it is for me." She gave him a timid smile. "I know that might not make sense, being we share a bed together from time to time, but—"

"From time to time?" Philip shook his head, miffed. "More like any chance we can get! I'm not understanding where this is coming from. I'm trying to—"

"I know." Lane placed a hand on top of his. "I know your heart, Phil. But..." She paused, taking a deep breath. "I think living together would make things messy if we..." She shrugged. "If you... changed your mind."

"Why do you always go there?" Philip asked, an edge to his voice. "If you're worried about Allister and your job,... You know if you end up having to leave the island, I'm coming with you. Doesn't matter where we land." He shook his head, his tone hurt. "I've told you this a million times!"

"Yes, you have." She closed her eyes, her shoulders dropping. "And I know you say—"

Philip cut her off. "Then, why? Is it because of what happened with your mom?"

At the mention of her mother, Lane visibly bristled and turned away, her mouth set in a thin line.

"Hey, now listen." He gently shook her hand, trying to pull her eyes back to his. "I know your mom leaving your dad and you, kids... it was... well... That's not going to happen with us. I'd never abandon—"

"You know, Phil..." Lane suddenly stood, pulling her hand from his. "Why don't we put a pin in this for later? Morning will be here before we know it." She placed a hand on his shoulder and stepped over his duffle bag. "And you might as well put that in the guestroom."

CHAPTER 13

Arriving at Hattie's General later than promised, Philip gave way to a jaw-dropping yawn and rapped against the glass entrance as the sunrise, all pinks, and purples, brilliantly reflected off the store's front windows.

"You're late," Harry half-whispered as he yanked the door open, the golden bell atop ringing in unison with his jangling store keys still dangling from the lock. "And you look like hell."

"Feel it too." Philip walked through, offering his friend a tired smile as the door was locked behind him. "Coffee?"

"Help yourself." Harry pocketed his keys with a jerk of his chin. "First cup is on me."

"Wasn't planning on paying," Philip mumbled as he tip-toed past a snoozing Miss Hattie, the little old lady fast asleep in her rocking chair, snoring lightly, her chin resting on her chest.

"I know, and you can show your gratitude by buying the first round of beers tonight." Harry circled behind the front counter, a blue deposit bag tucked under his arm, and popped open the till, the ancient register chiming in protest. "It's the least you can do after last week's performance. Bowling a 220?" he tsked, "Embarrassing."

"Hey, that last frame was not my fault," Philip argued, snatching up the coffee pot and pulling a cup from the dispenser. "And bowling a 220 is still respectable."

"If you're playing with amateurs!" Harry dropped the deposit bag onto the counter and placed both hands on his hips, his tone serious. "If we lose again this week, you know we'll never hear the end of it!"

"Hey, that last frame was a fluke. Picking up a 7-10 split? Pure luck!"

"Ya, well, don't let Mollie hear you say that!" A smile suddenly broke across Harry's face, his chest puffing as he turned back to the register, placing the deposit bag under the tray. "You have to admit, my gal has got one hell of a hook!" He lightly closed the register drawer. "She picked up five spares last week!"

Philip arched an eyebrow as he snapped the lid onto his cup, his coffee perfectly sugared and creamed to his liking. "Five, you say?"

"According to Lane's scorekeeping." Harry suddenly frowned, an intrusive thought coming to mind. "You don't think the girls are cheating, do you?" The frown deepened, and his eyebrows practically met in the middle. "Think I should keep score tonight? Just to make sure?"

Philip shook his head bemused.

"Lane keeps score just fine, Har, and the girls won fair and square." He edged around Hattie's rocking chair, smiling at her light snores, and placed his coffee on the picnic table. "By the way, Lane might be a no-show tonight."

"I was wondering. What with everything that happened yesterday."

"Well, it's not only the new case..." Philip paused to straighten the blanket on Hattie's lap and remove the half-drunken cup of cocoa held loosely in her wrinkled hand. He carefully placed it on the table beside his own and plopped down on the bench with a heavy sigh, "Mind if I bend your ear a minute, Har?"

"Sure, but, uh..." Harry rounded the counter, tilting his head towards the stockroom. "Can't you bend it while we unload the truck?"

Philip ignored him and stayed seated, his smile dropping. "I really stuck my foot in it with Lane last night."

"Ha! That's nothing new," Harry smirked and

headed for the table. "You're always saying the wrong thing."

"Yeah, well. This was worse than usual." Philip fumbled with the cup's cardboard sleeve and avoided Harry's puzzled stare. "I, uh... I brought up the idea of us moving in together. Lane didn't think it was—"

"She said no?" Harry settled down on the bench, stunned. "I thought things were going good with you guys. I mean, she's always telling Mollie how great—"

"They are... They are great!" Philip brought a hand to his forehead, pinching his fingers together. "It's just... she wants a solid commitment before moving in together and—"

"Ohhhh..." Harry bobbed his head sagely. "Why buy the cow when..."

"You can get the milk for free!" Philip gestured into the air. "Exactly!" He shook his head, miffed, "I told her it wasn't like that!"

"Well, then buy her a ring and get your knees dusty! Propose already!" Harry swung his leg over the bench and half stood, considering his pal's problem solved. "We both know she's it for you, Phil. Now, let's go unload—"

"I'm not convinced she'd say yes if I asked!" Philip didn't budge from his seat. "At least, not now! I opened my big mouth, and well... I crossed a line."

He met Harry's eye, his face stern. "But it needed crossing! All I did was simply point out..." He shook his head, suddenly unsure. "Which maybe I shouldn't have... I mean, I knew it was a sensitive subject, and for good reason, but..." Philip's doubt disappeared. "We should be able to talk these things through! Work them out!" He pounded a fist on the wooden tabletop and then cringed, his regret instant as Miss Hattie stirred, her runny blue eyes briefly fluttering open. He waited for her to settle as she snuggled deeper into her chair and continued in a hush, "The thing is, I was attempting to reassure her, and, instead, I ended up throwing all of Lane's insecurities in her face. I don't know what I was thinking... and here I was, planning to ask —"

"Whoa, hold on." Harry slowly sank back down to the bench, his eyes wide. "You've already bought a ring, haven't you?"

"And called her dad, asking for her hand. But now... I thought if I suggested living together, that would prep her for the big question. You know, give her a month or so to wrap her head around the idea of a life together, and then..."

"Live happily ever after?"

"That was the idea."

Harry rapped his knuckles against the wooden tabletop, a broad smile spreading across his face. "And one I hardily approve!" He suddenly straightened and attempted to climb out from the picnic table. "Now, if you don't mind, we have a truck to unload."

At the sound of knocking, Miss Hattie startled awake, and her blue eyes popped open, focusing on Philip, a bright denatured smile springing to life.

"Oh,... I thought I heard the bell chime. Morning, Phil!" She raised a delicate hand and patted her white curls in place as she straightened in her rocking chair, adding, "It is still morning, isn't it? I haven't slept the day away, have I?"

"No, you're fine, Miss Hattie. It's only a little bit past sunrise," Philip reassured, shooting her a warm smile of his own as he started to heft himself up from the table. "I'd like to stay and visit..." He stopped short, mid-twist, finding Hattie eagerly scooting to the edge of her seat, still beaming at him, her cheeks rosy with excitement.

"Now, tell me." She gave his knee a solid tap, her blue eyes practically dancing. "Buck Bennett's widow. Who do you think shot her? One of them or one of us?"

Harry's voice suddenly floated the length of aisle one, already halfway to the stock room. "I better not be stuck unloading this truck alone, Phil!"

Ignoring Harry's bark, Philip inched closer, a slightly confused smile spreading across his face, baffled by Hattie's pointed separation.

"Who would be them, and exactly, who is us,

Miss Hattie?"

She batted an impatient hand, finding her meaning clear. "I'm praying it's one of them and not one of us. Though, if it is one of us... Well, I'm sure they thought they had plenty a reason." She sniffed, pulling a tissue from her sleeve, her head slowly moving side to side. "Their head filled with lies, no doubt."

"Well, I can't imagine anybody from here—"

"I'd like to think the same, Phil. But you can't fix the present without first dealing with the past." She sighed, stuffing the tissue back. "I suppose that's what she was trying to do."

"Who, Nancy? You mean, fix the present?" Philip frowned, as always, a little lost in the conversation. "I know folks didn't think much of her leaving so soon after Buck's passing, but I can't imagine somebody holding a grudge to the point of —"

"Passing?" Hattie's blue eyes grew wide, giving his knee a punctuating tap. "You mean murdered."

Philip's mouth dropped open, not expecting such a declaration despite never knowing what Hattie might say.

Buck Bennett, as far as he knew, had lived life on a steady diet of cigarettes, beer, and bacon. Dying from a heart attack in his early fifties, though tragic, had not been terribly shocking but, rather, expected. Granted, later than sooner, but still, it had not been a huge surprise.

The idea of Buck Bennett being murdered never crossed Philip's mind.

"Oh, well, I can see that was a bit of a surprise. Sorry about that, Phil." She pointed toward the entrance, the open sign facing their direction. "I don't suspect the tittle-tattle that comes through those doors ever makes it up to the ranger's station." She suddenly leaned in, her voice dropping to a conspirator whisper, "You do know she had a lover, don't ya?"

"More than one was my understanding," Philip admitted, recalling the rumors of the time. Despite Hattie's assumption, town gossip had no problem reaching the ranger station due in part to Martha Barnes and her home two-way radio.

"Well, then you can see what I'm saying!" Hattie sat back with a pleased smile. "It's as plain as the nose on my face."

Philip chuckled, not seeing at all.

"I'm sorry, Miss Hattie, but I can't figure..."

"Bless your soul, I can see you don't." She blinked at him fondly, her rocking chair falling into a steady rhythm. "And count that as a blessing. As for me, I've seen my fill of evil, a good deal of it done on this very island, and I know what walks this earth." Her eyes drifted to the simple gold band on her ring finger. "I worry that it's taking me so long to die that I imagine my poor Earl probably thinks I've gone to hell..." She suddenly leaned forward, giving his knee a hard slap, the corners of her eyes crinkling. "Won't he be surprised when I pop up in heaven!"

"I'm sure he'll have the red carpet rolled out." Philip returned her smile, his heart panging at the thought of Miss Hattie passing beyond the veil.

"Yes, when the time comes." Her smile dropped as she clutched her sweater closer, her knuckles white with the effort. "I can honestly say I've lived the best life I could, Phil. Though, I'm sure I used more than my fair share of grace in doing so!" She suddenly shook a crooked finger. "Grace is a necessity in life, and I judge it plain evil to deny someone the chance to right their wrongs." She gave her head a hard nod. "And the Good Lord knows that Nancy woman had a multitude!"

"Of wrongs? Oh, you mean with Angie." Philip tilted his head to the side in contemplation as he leaned back, arms crossed. "Well, I think Nancy was trying to do just that. I mean, right a wrong. She was the one who encouraged Angie to start this new business venture. You know, sort of took her under her wing. Even tried to bring business her way and put some money in her pocket."

"Pah! Money." Hattie sat back heavily, the force launching the rocking chair backward. "Angie never used to have to worry about money! Buck Bennett's heart was as big as his belt buckle!"

"I'd say she worries about it now." Philip placed the tip of his boot against the chair's rocker, assuring himself that Miss Hattie wouldn't topple backward. "She's up to her eyeballs in debt."

"Not surprising! That girl was way too young and foolish to be given all that money once her daddy was gone."

"Well, it's not like she had a choice. It was hers, free and clear." Philip frowned, his brow wrinkling. "But I am surprised Angie's inheritance wasn't put in a trust for when she was a bit older and wiser. As executor, I'd have thought Nancy would have—"

"See, there. That goes to show Buck hadn't planned on poppin' off so fast." Hattie gave a hard nod, her hands still clutching her sweater. "Sadly, the choice didn't end up being his, did it?"

"No," Philip agreed, subconsciously tapping his slight beer belly and thinking of the bacon he'd had for breakfast.

"A pretty-faced young bride and all that money sitting there for the taking?" Hattie's mouth turned down at the edges, her runny blue eyes sad. "Way too much temptation and no thought given to Angie losing her daddy!" Hattie smacked her hand against the chair arm. "Selfish and evil!"

Philip shook his head, his tone cautious, "You make it sound as if you think Nancy killed Buck."

Hattie's white eyebrows arched in surprise. "How

in the world did you come up with that, Phil?" She shook her head, frowning. "No, no. That's not what I'm saying at all!"

"Well, then... if you don't think Nancy did away with Buck, then who?"

"Well, that's simple enough to answer. Her lover!"

Philip gave Hattie a patient smile, his tone dubious, "And how would this mysterious lover make Buck's death look like a heart attack?"

"Oh..." Hattie shrugged her pink-shrouded shoulders, her eyes closing, tired from the excitement of their conversation. "Probably messed with his medication or slipped something into one of his beers. It would have been easy enough." She pulled her sweater closer, her blue eyes struggling to stay open. "Coveting thy neighbor..." She yawned, her words slightly muffled. "It's why Buck banked with the mainland."

"Sorry?" Philip asked softly, seeing Hattie's eyelids growing heavy. "What about a bank?"

"Well, folks always wondered why Buck kept his money with the mainland lenders." She closed her eyes completely, a slow smile spreading. "People can be so dense."

Philip was feeling pretty dense himself.

"Why would it matter to anybody where Buck Bennett kept his money?"

"Oh, it didn't matter. Except to Aaron Coletta."

CHAPTER 14

George Barnes wheeled a squeaky hand cart through the doors of the sheriff's office, his large boots clomping past Martha's desk, where Lane currently sat, leveling him with a disapproving glare. Already in a foul mood, she had called him at the crack of dawn, threatening hell and all of damnation if he didn't get to the station first thing and remove the coffin from her office, Saturday morning be damned.

"I'm sorry. Can you repeat that, Ralph?" Lane's eyes followed George across the lobby as she pressed the phone tighter to her ear, the squeal of the handcart's tires growing and fading as he passed.

"I said... the bullet nicked the victim's RCA causing massive blood loss. It would have taken a few minutes for her to bleed out. So, I'd guesstimate, she was probably conscious for at least—"

"Uh, RCA?"

"Right coronary artery."

"And death wasn't instantaneous?" Lane asked, distracted, the phone cord pulling tight against her chest as she craned her neck, her anxious eyes following George as she twisted in Martha's chair, the funeral director shouldering his way into her tiny office. She was more than curious as to how he was going to fit the life-size coffin onto the small hand truck and slightly panicked, her head flooding with visions of a flying casket crashing through the window-paneled wall.

"Not likely. Contrary to popular belief, shooting someone in the heart doesn't equate to immediate death." The sound of shuffling paperwork followed the coroner's declaration. "She also sustained a head injury."

"From falling off the horse?"

"Might have been the drop. Possibly had her skull stepped on... or someone took a rock to her head."

"A rock?" Lane swiveled forward, her attention no longer on George Barnes or his coffin. "Are you saying—"

"I'm only relaying that she had a brain injury on top of being shot. I found a deep cut on the side of her head." There was a slight pause, followed by hurried munching, and then, barely audible through a full mouth, "It was crescent-shaped."

"So, like a horseshoe."

Lane envisioned the thin coroner in his customary goose-down jacket, worn to fight off the polar vortex of the morgue, the odd little man sitting at his desk, a cookie hanging from his mouth.

"Could have been, but there were large broken bits of shale in the wound."

"Then you are telling me Nancy was brained over the head with a rock."

"No. I'm only telling you what I found." There was more munching. "Though, if someone thought she was in pain, they might have considered it a kindness."

"But the bullet to the heart is what actually killed her?" Lane moved a pile of clear evidence bags from one side of the desk to the other, trying to unbury her notepad and reports.

"Ultimately, yes." He cleared his throat. "A 9mm bullet, to be precise. I've already sent it over to ballistics."

"9mm, huh? Then that officially puts Angie Bennett in the clear." Lane scratched the girl's name from her notepad with a wave of relief.

"What was that?"

He hadn't heard her over his own chewing.

"Our main witness had a .22 Magnum revolver on her hip at the time of the shooting."

"Unfired?"

"And no gun residue on her hands." Lane tapped the tip of her pen against her notepad. "She stated the shot came from within the pines surrounding the meadow."

"Within the pines... that sounds ominous." Once again, the sound of shuffling papers came over the line. "I like it. It has a sense of foreboding."

Lane imagined the coroner, with his habit of naming cases, quickly scribbling the words down onto the tab of a manilla folder. She continued, as if he'd not spoken,

"Unless it was a random shot, a misfire." She paused, contemplating, "Maybe this is an accidental shooting after all? If the shooter was indeed a hunter, they might have been carrying a 9mm carbine rifle."

"Those are pretty nifty. Depending on the brand, you can find ones that fold in half and fit nicely in a hiking knapsack."

"Easy to conceal and transport."

"More than ideal for an ambush... But didn't you say you thought a handgun was used?"

"We found an empty 9mm Glock gun case in the vic's tent." Lane rubbed her temple. "I'm trying to keep an open mind."

"You mean cover your tush."

"Exactly. Anything else—"

The sound of squeaky tires drew near.

"Uh, Sheriff? Sorry to interrupt..." George's dolly abruptly clunked to the floor, his elbow holding it steady as he leaned against the propped coffin. "The wife wanted to make sure you knew this here casket, well... it's only a floor model. There's never been a body inside... dead, that is."

Lane gave him an arched eyebrow and placed a hand over the mouthpiece.

"I beg your pardon?"

"I'm only saying..." George nervously straightened, the coffin rocking slightly. "It's a completely unused casket. There's no need to be upset or—."

"George..." Lane blinked, her voice amazed, "Whatever possessed you to let Martha, floor model or not, put a coffin in my office? What were you two thinking?"

"Well... Thought it would be a bit of free advertising!" George gave the top of the casket a solid pat, a broad smile breaking out. "People like yourself don't realize it's never too early to start planning, and if you make arrangements now, your loved ones will—"

"Out, George." Lane pointed a finger towards the lobby exit, not interested in his sales pitch, and returned to her phone call, her tone apologetic, "Sorry about that, Ralph. Um, was there anything else?"

"There was, and I think you'll find this interesting, considering the victim's business is in dietary and nutritional supplements."

"Oh?"

"When taking samples, I noticed ridges running the length of her nailbeds, and then, examining the head wound, I discovered small patches of seborrheic dermatitis,... uh, basically dry, itchy skin, along with sections where her hair had begun thinning. To be honest, I might not have thought anything odd in these findings, that is, in a general sense, if I hadn't been thinking about what she did for a living. Promoting a vitamin line."

"Are you suggesting a poisoning?"

"No. Not in the sense you think. What came to mind was that she might have been suffering from a nutritional deficiency, primarily low in minerals like potassium and zinc, vitamins B and D. So, I ran some tests and confirmed my theory. Turns out, that was exactly the case on top of being extremely low in iron and borderline anemic."

"Vitamin deficient? That's odd because Nancy used her own products." Lane sorted through the evidence bags, finding and examining the discarded foil imprinted with the Vita Mineralium logo. "We even found empty pill pouches in her tent."

"Oh, I'm sure she did... and maybe in all good faith. But I advise sending the product line off for testing. My guess? It'll come back as subpar supplements. I'm talking super cheap vitamins."

"Well, they don't sell them for cheap!" Lane griped, remembering her sticker shock and the free samples still sitting in her office. She'd take his advice and request a courier from the WSP toxicology lab.

"That's not surprising. Vitamin supplements are big business, Sheriff, and unfortunately, there are some unscrupulous manufacturers out there who don't hold to our US guidelines, selling their product at a substantial discount."

"Produced in other countries?"

"Yes, and some brought here illegally. They're typically manufactured using high amounts of fillers, mostly sugar, with unhealthy dyes and all sorts of nonsense, contrary to the point of replenishing the body's nutrients. I'd be curious to see what actual nutritional value those pills held... if any."

"Basically, they could be selling vitamin placebos." Lane shoved the evidence bag to the side and plucked Mike Allister's folded note from her notepad. "Making Vita Mineralium a scam." Her finger traced the yellow-lined paper, stopping on the second name listed, her mouth twitching as she read. "Clint Carson, Inventory and Supply Issues."

"Well, it's pure speculation until the product is tested, but I wouldn't be surprised if the listed packaging doesn't match the actual ingredients." He cleared his throat again, adding apologetically, "If that's the case, the feds will need to get involved."

"Then it's a good thing I know somebody in the DEA," Lane muttered, referring to her brother Kent. "This is a big help, Ralph." She folded and returned the list to her notepad, her eyes landing on the Ziplock evidence bag holding the crinkled paper found in the pocket of Nick Mason's jeans.

"I'm glad, and I'll have my official report ready come Monday."

"Appreciate that, and thanks again for taking my call on a Saturday."

"As if I had a choice!" The coroner, his mouth full once again, mumbled, "And don't forget to bring some of your baked goodies as promised. Preferably something chocolate!"

"Dark, white, or semi-sweet?"

"Surprise me."

CHAPTER 15

Rolling to an abrupt stop, Caleb lurched forward in a hard jerk as he cut the ATV's engine, a massive fallen log blocking his way. "My kingdom for a horse."

It was not the first time he'd made such a declaration, as more than once that morning he'd been forced to backtrack, losing precious time as he followed the rutted trail, the worn path bordered by timber too thick for the quad to maneuver through. If he had a horse, such as in this instance, he'd be able to needle into the neighboring trees and stay on the original track, which apparently was the call of action, indicated by a side trail circling around the timbered cedar.

However, Caleb didn't have a horse, nor a kingdom for that matter, and he sat, undecided, his options limited. Retreating the way he'd come would take an hour and back across sections he'd already searched, his mission so far futile. He wasn't ready to give up, not yet, though he did desire to be closer to Angie's camp, the energy drink he'd had for breakfast pressing hard upon his bladder, and the persistent grumble of his stomach reminding him lunch was required.

His day had started with the sun, having arrived at the campsite with an optimistic assumption that he'd be able to borrow a trail horse to scour the forest and adjacent meadow. His enthusiasm quickly waned when he discovered Angie wasn't even in camp, having left an hour earlier, returning a good portion of the horses to Ol'man Jamison's homestead. Determined to be undeterred, he inquired about the remaining ponies, was informed that their tack had already been packed and that if he wanted a horse to ride, he'd need to wait for the horse guide's return.

The prospect of biding his time until Angie's reappearance had not been so bleak at first. Tanya, her auburn hair pulled into a French braid and wearing painted-on Levi's, posed to be a pleasant distraction. That was until Kody had shown up, the junior park ranger riding in on a rumbling ATV that looked like it had seen better days.

With golden retriever energy, Kody had bounded over, explaining he'd come to volunteer his services and help tear down the camp. The offer was welcomed, and soon the three were discussing the sad events of the day before. When Caleb revealed his intentions of finding the missing murder weapon, explaining his theory that Witt had shot Nancy and had chucked the gun before joining Angie at his wife's importune deathbed, Tanya became upset. Insistent that Witt was innocent, incapable of doing something so horrible, and that they simply didn't understand what a good man he was. If they'd known Nancy, they might even have sympathy for him.

At Caleb's rebuttal that the man was a selfish prick, tears began tracking down Tanya's freckled cheeks, and Kody quickly draped a protective arm over her slim shoulders, making it clear that "three" was a crowd. Caleb took the hint and, deciding to make himself scarce, accepted Kody's offer to borrow the ranger station's bunged-up quad.

Normally, he would have stood his ground, even purposely continuing to poke the bear, but he and Kody had recently struck up a delicate friendship. The year prior, the young deputy and park ranger had been at odds with one another, fighting for the affections of the same girl and both suffering the fate of being dumped, their mutual love interest, Amy Holmes, the red-headed bombshell, newly engaged to Kevin Givens.

Both jilted, he and Kody had licked their wounds,

bonding over a pitcher of beer, and had decided to call a truce. The island, with its shallow dating pool, was small enough. There was no point in making things worse with a rivalry. Seeing Kody's frown and his puppy dog eyes zeroed in on Tanya, Caleb decided he didn't want to burn the bridge they'd just built.

So, instead, he'd straddled the dented ATV and rumbled his way across the low creek, riding up the backside to Crescent Meadow, where he passed the Jamison's cabin, their corral full of Angie's horses. He decided not to stop, figuring Angie was probably on her way back to camp, and continued on, only to come upon a tethered horse. The big Bay, looking a lot like the mare Angie had ridden the day before, grazing peacefully, unbothered by the leather-worked saddle and rust-colored saddle bags still on its back.

Hoping to exchange mounts, Caleb had hopped off his borrowed ride in search of Angie. Instead, he'd stumbled across Jay Jamison, spotting the big man among the tall timber, a cap of bright hunter's orange crammed upon his head. The younger Jamison stood just outside the meadow, eyes downcast to the ground, a small burlap bag in hand. Caleb watched as he circled each tree, examining the ground closely before moving on to the next.

With a polite clearing of his throat, Caleb made his presence known, causing Jay to startle, his face flushing bright red as he straightened to his full height. Apologies were quickly made for the intrusion, and when asked what Jay was up to, the big man explained he was out hunting for mushrooms. He also let Caleb know that Angie was still at his cabin, visiting with his father, the old man probably chatting her ear off.

Much like earlier, the subject of the day before came up, and Jay gossiped that he and his father had recognized the victim as Buck Bennett's widow, though they hadn't mentioned the fact to her. With no further insight to gain, Caleb said his goodbyes and spent the next four hours searching the sunrise point and the vast wilderness surrounding Crescent Meadow with no luck.

And now, here he sat with his borrowed quad, wondering how hard it would be to drive over the log, traversing the cedar instead of backtracking through the meadow. With his off-roading skills being zero to none, Caleb thought better of it and decided he'd return the way he came, resigned to continuing the search after lunch.

The hunt for the murder weapon would have to wait.

His bladder, however, was not willing.

Climbing off the ATV, he jerked down on his zipper and stepped off the trail, not bothering to walk into the tree line to relieve himself, his head tilted back in relief. With a loud sigh, Caleb emptied his bladder and, when finished, opened his eyes as he jostled everything into place. He paused midzip. Above his head, snagged on a bare branch, was a leather riding glove.

"How did that get up there?"

Scanning the rest of the branches, he found them bare and, with a frown, followed the length of the tree to the rooted ground, the forest floor covered in moss and feathered ferns. He took a cautious step and noted the lack of prints, neither man or horse, his curiosity growing.

"Is there just the one?"

Eyes peeled, he trekked across the undisturbed covering, a litany of dried needles and cones crunching underfoot, finally coming upon the second glove several feet from the trail.

Pleased at his find, he bent down to retrieve the wayward glove, his hand extended, fingers barely brushing the worn leather, when he stopped short and straightened. Twisting at the waist, he peered back at the trail, his gaze floating from the dirt path to the above barren branches of the sparse cedar, calculating the distance between the two.

Someone, for reasons unknown, had thrown their riding gloves, one landing in the tree's branches, the other on the ground. But why?

He had a good guess.

Turning, Caleb eagerly swept his eyes downward and scanned the mossy undergrowth, his heart practically thumping out of his chest when, only a foot away, he discovered what he was searching for.

A Smith & Wesson 9 mm Glock.

CHAPTER 16

Pulling off to the side of the road, Harry squeezed his brown beast of a pickup between two large white pines and parked, their destination just on the other side of his bug-splotched windshield, the place looking deserted.

Outside, cream-colored splashes of canvas littered the ground, the yurt-like tents collapsed, their wooden poles piled to the side or left erect, Italian solar lights still hanging, dipping loosely to the ground. A jumble of furnishings and storage boxes, compiled in a disorganized mound, lay next to the unlit fire pit. The mess tent was only structure still standing, Angie's own rig and trailer parked in front, the backdoors open, the bumper empty.

"Seems we weren't the only ones who thought Angie needed help." Harry yanked his truck keys from the ignition and pointed out Caleb's patrol car and Jerry Holmes's dual cab. The latter hitched to a gooseneck horse trailer doubling as a moving van, the inside stuffed full of mattresses and folded tent canvases. "They've got quite a head start on us."

"Looks it." Philip shouldered the passenger door open, his coffee thermos loudly clanking against the side as he hopped out and slammed the door shut.

"Hey, man! Watch the paint!" Harry gave the rusted hood a loving pat as he circled the front fender and suddenly stopped short, giving out a yelp. "Ow!" He grimaced as he arched his back and stretched, his hands on his hips. "I think I may have pulled a muscle!" He carefully twisted side to side, eyeing Philip as he finished rounding the front of the rig. "I hope you know, unloading that truck all by myself was no easy feat!"

"But you're all muscle." Philip tapped the back of his hand against Harry's beer belly and chuckled, "Come on there, Hercules. We're late."

Walking into the grounds, the two were drawn to the pine corral, its fences harboring a handful of horses, Jerry Holmes inside, the veterinarian examining the feet of the speckled grey Philip had ridden the day before.

"Hiya, Jerry!" Harry bellowed, pressing his fingers to his lips and issuing a sharp whistle, the high-pitch noise accidentally startling the mare. "Over here!"

"I see ya!" Jerry batted an arm in the air, his curled mustache hiding an annoyed frown as he gave the grey horse a light smack and headed for the side of the corral, his free hand pinning his baseball cap to his head as he bowed low and slid through the bars.

"We meant to be here sooner," Philip apologized once Jerry was in earshot, the veterinarian offering a friendly nod as he dusted his palms against his leather chaps and accepted Philip's extended hand.

"Fellas." He let go and gave them a gritty smile. "I hope you're ready for bowling tonight." Jerry removed his baseball hat and used the back of his arm to wipe his brow, eyeing them both. "I don't think I can handle another week of losing, what with the way Heather rubs it in."

"Hey!" Harry gaffed, "Don't look at me! I'm not the one with a rubber arm!" He gave Philip's shoulder a playful punch. "Besides, Mollie has been bustin' my chops as well."

"Whoa, now. I've been reminded a time or two myself," Philip downplayed, having been ribbed mercilessly, Lane's competitive streak a mile wide. What had started out as a weekly date night for the three couples, and at first a friendly competition, had turned into an all-and-out battle of the sexes. And the women were winning. "Where are the rest of the horses, Jer?"

"Oh, most of them belonged to Mark Jamison. Angie returned them earlier this morning." He anchored his cap onto his head with a tug. "Those five are the only rideable ones Angie has left." Jerry nodded toward the pen, the horses staring back. "Lane was under the impression they were lame and asked me to give'em a once over as a favor. Guess someone told her one had a stone bruise and the little grey..." He pointed out the horse he'd been examining. "She'd thought it had thrown a shoe. Thankfully, all of them are fine. No bruises, and all shoes still attached." He turned slightly, ensuring they were alone, and lowered his voice, "Last week, I had to threaten Angie I'd cut off veterinarian services unless she paid her bill down. I hated to do it, but she was so behind. I was worried she'd never catch up. Luckily, the season is over..." He tilted his chin towards the filled horse trailer. "I think every last red cent that girl had, has gone into making this place work, and I don't believe she's gotten a return for all her efforts. I figure the least I can do, besides the favor to Lane, is help Angie pack this place up."

"Yeah, we had the same thought," Harry pipped in with a pleased smile. "Didn't we, Phil, buddy?"

Philip ignored him and pointed at the corral.

"You know, I borrowed that little grey yesterday. She wasn't missing a shoe when I took her out or brought her in. You sure it was the grey?"

"Pretty sure." Jerry waved a hand in the general direction of the horse pen. "I checked them all to be on the safe side. Everyone was shoed."

"Hmm... guess it doesn't matter." Philip looked at the empty bumper parked in front of the mess tent and asked, "How does Angie seem today?"

"She's been buzzin' around here so much I haven't gotten a chance to ask." Jerry twisted, indicating the pile of furnishings and stacked boxes. "If I didn't know better, I'd say she's trying mighty hard not to think about yesterday."

"Can you blame her?" Harry asked, rolling up his shirt sleeves. "It's bad enough there was an accident, let alone a shooting, but then a death? And the person killed is your own stepmom? If you ask me—" Harry stopped, Angie suddenly appearing at the entrance of the mess tent, her hair in a high ponytail with her arms wrapped around two large boxes, her face red with the strain.

"Hey, now!" Philip broke from the trio. "Those look heavy!" Angie slowed her pace as he came within reach. "Here. I'll take those."

"Thanks. You can just throw them in the bumper." She gave him a grateful yet frail smile, her eyes red-rimmed as she greeted Harry, her tone warm but unenthusiastic. "Appreciate you coming to help out, Mr. Vickers."

"Of course! Only too happy." Harry gave her a kind smile, then peered over his shoulder at the disassembled camp, searching for life. "We the only ones around?"

"Uh, Tanya and Kody should be here some-where. They're supposed to be loading Jerry's trail-er." She hitched a thumb towards the large pavilion. "I've been busy packing up the pots and pans."

"They're probably taking a breather down by the stream." Jerry tossed his head in the direction of the creek and then gave a slow smile, wiggling his eye-brows. "I get the feeling they like each other."

"Oh, I sure hope so." Angie cinched her ponytail tighter, then let her hands flop to her side, sighing, "Tanya has a thing for bad boys and even badder de-cisions." She swiveled towards the mess tent. "You fellas want something to drink? I've got some—"

"Was wondering... is Deputy Pickens in the camp-ground?" Philip, not hearing her offer, stepped from the trailer and joined the conversation.

"Caleb? Oh, I don't think he's back yet. He came up wanting to borrow a horse, but we'd packed all the tack and..." She gave Jerry a grateful smile. "Doc hadn't gotten a chance to look these hags over yet, so Kody ended up loaning Caleb his bunged-up ATV. I imagine he's giving Crescent Meadow another once over."

"Yeah, well... he's been up there for a few hours."

Jerry squinted an eye at the sun and then peered down at his watch. "Even missed lunch."

"Tanya said he took one of our radios with him." Angie tapped the two-way sticking out of her back pocket. "I'm sure he's fine."

"Let's hope so. It'd be lousy luck to have another accident," Harry chuckled, his smile dropping along with Angie's, her eyes instantly brimming.

"Well... uh... If you fellas don't mind, I'm gonna get back to work." She pointed towards the jumbled furnishings and began walking backward. "Feel free to start loading up furniture or—"

"Um, Harry...," Philip cut in, "Would you and Jerry mind tracking down the two budding love-birds and meet us over at the corral? Then we can all put our heads together and figure out what's left to be done." He turned to Angie, putting up a halting hand. "Get ourselves organized."

"Can do! Come on, Jer." Harry elbowed the vet in the ribs, a sly smile emerging. "Let's go ruin Kody's afternoon." With a reluctant nod, Jerry followed.

"Well, then." Philip turned and graced Angie with a toothy grin. "While those two are gone..." He paused to place a fatherly hand on her shoulder. "Why don't you and I hang out with the horses for a bit? I bet you could use a break." He tilted his head and met her eye, his eyebrows arching. "You holdin' up okay, young lady?"

Angie's brimming tears tumbled over as she shook her head. "No. I, uh..." She bit her lower lip and dropped her eyes. "I can't say I am."

"Ah, Ang." Philip wrapped an arm around her trembling shoulders as a small sob escaped, the young horse guide leaning into his chest.

"I feel so guilty, Phil. It was so awful and now her little girls —"

"There, now. There's nothing to feel guilty about!" He gave her a quick squeeze, unsurprised by her empathy, having lost her own parents at a young age. "All of this was out of your control." He started herding them towards the corral, his voice casual, "You know, I never realized the Nancy you'd been telling me about all summer was... well, your stepmom NANCY." He let her go and leaned against the pen, slinging his arm over the top rung, the horses moseying towards them. "You two kept in touch after your dad's passing?"

"Not at all." Angie's mouth quirked down at the corners, the dapple-grey nosing her shoulder. "The day after my eighteenth birthday... that was the last time I'd seen her until we bumped into each other, oh... about six months ago."

"I wondered where you got the idea to combine glamping and horseback riding."

"Oh, it was always my idea!" Angie insisted, running a hand down the length of the mare's neck. "She just... refined it. Truth is, I wish I'd never listened to her." She turned, her red-rimmed eyes meeting his. "I almost lost it all, Phil. The farm, the land, my horses... everything."

"I heard money was kind of tight."

Angie's face flushed as she swept a hand towards the camp. "I'm giving this up. I'll sell what I can and try to recoup my losses." She shook her head, turning back to the grey. "Can't imagine anyone is going to want to go glamping where a guest was shot and killed in an accidental shooting." She gave the horse a solid pat, pushing it away, the grey leaning hard against her palm. "Is Witt... is Witt off the island?"

"No. He's staying—"

"No?" She swiftly turned, her mouth dropping open. "Why isn't he with his girls? I would have thought he'd gone home to comfort them."

"Seems more concerned about his PR imagine from what I hear." Philip shrugged. "He's staying with Mike Allister for the time being. Plus, Lane's not done asking him questions."

"Questions?" Angie's brows crossed. "Why is she asking him stuff? He didn't shoot Nancy."

"Well... he might not have, but there's nothing to say he didn't arrange for her to be shot."

"No. He's not the one who..." Angie vehemently shook her head and stepped back from the pen, her voice insistent, "Phil, I'm sure it was a hunter. I... I saw the orange." She placed her hands on her hips. "And I told Lane all of this! I don't understand what she's trying to do."

"She's TRYING to do her job and look at this from every angle." Philip placed a gentle hand on Angie's shoulder, the girl relaxing at his touch with her arms dropping to her side, her temper spent. "If Witt's an innocent victim in this, Lane will ferret out the truth. If he's not, she'll nail him to the wall." Angie gave him a curt nod of understanding, her frown still in place, and turned back to the mare. Philip nudged her, his tone light, "What about the rest of the group? You think any of them could have had something to do with it?"

Biding for attention, the appaloosa edged the grey to the side, and Philip gave his chin a scratch.

"I don't know. They were all there..." Angie bit her lip as her gaze veered to the ground, lost in thought. "When I raced into camp. Everyone was accounted for." She looked up, meeting his eye. "I counted."

"Well, it was no secret where you guys were heading. Any one of them on foot could have double-timed it and followed the creek up to the meadow." Philip faced her, his elbow resting on the top rung. "At least, that's what I would have done." He gave her a shrug, cracking a smile. "That is if I wasn't scared stiff of trespassing on old Jamison's property."

"Oh, he's a lot of bluff," Angie laughed, turning

her attention to her beloved Appaloosa. "I've known him since I was a little girl. He'd sooner give you the shirt off his back than put a bullet in yours."

"That may be so, but he seemed pretty pleased to find out that Nancy had met her maker." He took a deep breath and exhaled, shaking his head. "Seems he didn't hold a very high opinion."

"Well, he wouldn't, would he?" Angie bent down and picked up a grooming brush, then squeezed between the pen's bars, stepping into the corral. "He was my dad's best friend. Everyone knew Nance was running around on pops before he died. Mr. Jamison holds a grudge because my dad can't. That's all."

"And you didn't hold one against her?"

"Oh, I did." She ran the brush down Tamarack's back, a cloud of hair and dust flying from the bristles. "That is, I had. When I bumped into Nance, I could see she'd grown up." She paused, mid-brush. "I started to think of her as two people. Nancy before kids and Nancy after kids." Angie shrugged. "I was hoping that 'the Nancy after kids' and I could be friends."

"Weren't you?"

"I think she tried in her own way. But then Witt got handsy with me, and well... things went pretty lukewarm fast. It was ridiculous how grateful I was when she approached me to host their business trip." She stopped brushing and gave Philip a hard look.

"At a grand discount, of course." She shrugged again, letting out a huff of pent-up air. "That woman was a user through and through. No amount of money, makeup, or snobby airs could change that."

"How was the dynamic with the rest of the camp?"

"Ha! That bunch of two-tongued vipers?" She lightly tossed the brush to the ground, the stallion trotting off. "All of them are so thirsty for success they lapped up every false promise as if it were holy water. Same as me."

"What do you mean by that?"

"All she... THEY... ever did was lie about money." Angie cinched her ponytail tighter and sighed, "Their check bounced."

"What?"

"The check Nancy wrote for a deposit. It bounced." Angie flopped a hand towards the camp. "And all either of them ever talked about was how great the business was doing and how everyone needed to invest more time and money for a higher return. A bunch of horse pucky."

"What did Nancy say about the bounced check?"

"She told me to talk to Cami. Uh, that's Mrs. Carson, who would write me a new check. Said she must have grabbed the wrong checkbook."

"And did you? Talk to Cami?" Philip looked toward the pavilion and the filled trailers, mentally adding up the cost of such a venture.

"Ended up being no need. Clint, that's Cami's husband, he had dropped the girls off for a riding lesson, and we got to chatting. I asked him to mention it to Cami for me, and right then and there, he wrote me a check from their personal account." She gave Philip a slow smile. "And then last night, he paid me cash for the whole amount owed, plus extra for the inconvenience. Thanks to him, I got every penny coming to me."

CHAPTER 17

Dried leaves fluttered across the sidewalk as Lane strolled the three blocks to the Gelato Deli, smiling at the lamp posts dotting main street as she went, all spiraled in orange twinkle lights, enjoying the storefront stoops adorned in corn stalks and carved pumpkins.

Autumn had befallen downtown, apparent by the random bales of hay lining the sidewalks and the vintage Ford in front of Hattie's, the pickup filled with pumpkins and gourds for sale. A large banner still hung at the street entrance, declaring the coming and going of the Harvest Parade, the weather-worn announcement destined to hang until Thanksgiving, when it would be unstrung and replaced with the signage for the Christmas season.

Such was small-town life. And Lane loved it.

From the monthly town meetings to the church bakes and social banquets to the high school football games and sports fundraisers. She had grown fond of the little town and fiercely protective of its residents... Even stodgy old Mike Allister.

The thought of someday no longer being the sheriff of Rockfish Island broke her heart.

The fact was, the old lawyer carried a lot of weight in the small town's politics, and though Lane felt the majority of the residents liked her and felt secure under her watch, there was always the possibility that strings might be pulled from the mainland to remove her from office. It was something to be mindful of... though it wouldn't change the way she did her job.

If the day came and she was given no choice but to leave Rockfish Island... Philip had offered to follow. He'd told her time and time again that he'd leave his career, which he loved, along with his friends and hometown to follow her, no matter where she landed.

The thought thrilled her heart but soured her stomach. Believing that Philip was willing to turn his life upside down petrified Lane. But then again, love was scary... and she did love him.

Though Philip, after last night, probably had his doubts, and Lane couldn't blame him. She'd overreacted when he brought up her mother, a sensitive subject on a normal day, but after the earlier events, and her heated conversation with Allister only an hour prior, she'd simply shut down, her insecurities taking over.

She would need to apologize... but he still wasn't going to move in. She'd meant what she said, and if the idea of marriage caused him to bolt, it was better to know now.

Lane's worrisome thoughts vanished at the deli's storefront window.

She'd spotted Cami Carson on the other side, her head bent to her cell phone, deep in a text conversation, sitting with a half-drunk cup of cappuccino and a biscotti balanced on the rim, an unoccupied chair tucked under the table, her only company.

With the coroner bringing up potential motives, undiscovered and somewhat substantiated by the list volunteered by Allister, Lane had questions for the Carsons, and Cami was a good start.

Quickly swinging the door open, Lane hastily gave the owner, Stephano, a friendly wave in answer to his question, "The usual, Sheriff?" and made for Cami's table, greeting her with a cheerful, "I see you've discovered the best cappuccino this side of the sound."

Thumbs still flying across the phone's keyboard, Cami gave a disinterested, "Hmm, Hmm," and then edged her coffee cup forward for a refill, still glued to her screen.

Mistaken for a waitress, Lane cleared her throat and spoke in an authoritative tone, "Mrs. Carson, mind if I join you?"

At the unexpected question, Cami's head popped up, and upon recognition of the speaker, darted a glance past the sheriff's shoulder toward the door before snapping back and mustering a pleasant smile.

"Unless... you're expecting someone?" Lane offered cautiously, her hand on the back of the chair. "I'm not interrupting a lunch date, am I?"

"Not at all," Cami reassured, nodding for Lane to take the seat as she placed her cell phone face down on the table. "I'm just wasting time. My husband is out running." She waved a hand in the general direction of the sidewalk. "Clint's a jogger, and rain or shine, he's got to get a run in." She picked up her cup and took a delicate sip before running it the length of her chubby form, "As you can tell, I am not a jogger."

Lane smiled politely at the self-deprecation and pressed, "Well, I was thinking more of Sandi Coletta or Maddie Mason joining you. I thought maybe you were meeting together for coffee or lunch to console each other over yesterday's sad events?"

"Oh." Cami nodded her head, then immediately shook it side to side. "No, that's not likely." At Lane's confused frown, she hurried on, "We're not friends... outside of Nancy." She lowered the cup, rattling it against the saucer, and picked up the biscotti with a heavy sigh. "And now there is no Nancy. So, there's no point in pretending otherwise."

"I see." Lane slowly took out her notepad and placed it on the table. "Then, would that maybe explain why Sandi stated she hadn't seen you sitting by the fire sketching when the shot was heard yesterday afternoon?" Lane decided she'd try to poke a hole in either Sandi or Cami's alibi.

"Didn't see me?" Cami tried to look appalled, but it fell flat. "She was in her tent reading! Unless she has x-ray vision, she wouldn't see me."

"According to Sandi's statement, she was actually outside by the horse corral." Lane referred to her notepad. "Facing the fire." She pretended to scan the page. "And... she definitely said you were not there." Lane fingered the edge of her notepad. "But she did note that your sketchbook was left behind, sitting in the chair."

"Oh... um." Cami's nostrils flared, and she reached out, straightening her cup. "I did run down to the creek for a bit. I wanted to capture how the morning light danced on the water."

"With your sketch pad left behind?" Lane didn't give her time to counter. "I suppose while you were at the stream, you saw Maddie or Nick, possibly both?"

"No. Neither." Cami frowned and then leaned forward, a slow smile sliding across her lips. "I did, however, see Aaron Coletta."

"Did you stop and talk?"

"No. It wasn't me he was looking for," Cami hinted and then abruptly returned to Lane's original question. "And regardless of what Sandi claims, I WAS sitting at the fire when I heard the shot. She's either remembering wrong or lying." Cami dipped the biscotti cookie into her coffee. "Sandi, would you know. Lie, that is? She has never cared for me... or Nancy." She took a bite and quickly swallowed to add, "She and Maddie are probably celebrating... the heifers."

"Uh..." Lane's eyebrow shot up, her mouth quirking at the unexpected animosity. "Celebrating? Would you mind clarifying that statement?"

Cami dunked the remaining cookie in time with the bob of her head, her eyes once again casting towards the front door.

"They only pretended to look up to Nancy. In truth, they were scared stiff of her." She took a quick bite, holding a hand under her chin to catch any wayward drips or crumbles. "And for good reason."

Lane's curiosity was piqued, and she was about to ask Cami to elaborate once again when there was a sudden knuckle rap on the storefront window beside their table. Clint Carson, his hair plastered to his forehead, stood with a fist against the window wearing a sweat-soaked gray t-shirt and black shorts with a padded fanny pack around his waist. His expression at first seemed to say, "What the hell?" as he shook his head at Cami, but as he caught a glimpse of Lane out of the corner of his eye, his frown morphed into a charming smile.

He quickly signaled he'd come inside, and both followed his progress as he made for the front of the deli, swinging the door wide and pointing to their table as he tossed over his shoulder to Stephano a desire for a dry cappuccino.

At his grand entrance, Lane faced forward and casually closed her notepad from prying eyes and noted Cami's grim expression as she hurriedly glanced back through the window, down the sidewalk, towards the bank. By her worried appearance, it was clear her husband had not been the person she'd been waiting for...

"Why, hello!" Clint greeted as he grabbed a chair from the neighboring table and bent down to his wife's offered cheek, her nose wrinkling at his sweat-patched armpits. He placed a feather-light kiss upon her blushed skin, the display of affection tolerated. "Sorry, Love," he casually apologized as he sat. "I wasn't expecting to find you here. I thought we were meeting later. Did plans change?"

"No, I... I got bored, and..." She turned to him. "And thought I'd check out the antique shop." She ran her eyes down his ruddy cheeks and drenched hair. "What'd you do? Run a whole marathon?"

Clint chuckled, giving a polite nod as Stephano placed his cappuccino down and handed Lane a wrapped sandwich before moving back to the deli counter, two tourists walking in. Lane noted Cami's breath hitch and then release, not recognizing the newcomers.

"Not quite. This town is minuscule, so I headed into the park. Found a great running trail, along with some beautiful sights." This last comment was directed toward Lane, who was getting bored with the niceties. "We'd planned on stopping by your office to see Witt—"

"That would have been a short trip. Mr. Reyerson is no longer in my custody."

"Oh, I know." Clint gave her a wide smile as he brought the cup to his lips, beaming over the brim. "Aaron called us this morning. Glad to know he's a free man."

Lane resisted the urge to counter with, "For now," and instead said, "I do have some follow-up questions about yesterday." She pushed her wrapped sandwich to the side and re-opened her notepad, the leather top slapping against the table. "I wanted to ask about the credit card and casino receipts found in your vehicle during the warrant search."

"Sure, Sheriff. We can only imagine how that looked," Clint said with a sage nod, quickly exchanging a knowing glance with Cami, his demeanor a drastic change from the challenging bravado of the night before. "But there is a logical explanation."

Lane, skeptical, looked from husband to wife and then prompted, "Which is?"

"Witt has a gambling problem." Clint put his cup down and straightened in his chair, Lane's focus narrowing on him. "He's struggled with it for as long as we've known him." He glanced over at his wife, who sat deathly silent, her face unamused. "Cami and I met Witt while working at a wealth management company in Seattle. This was prior to his marriage to Nancy. He had been—"

Cami placed a pausing hand on her husband's forearm, her voice tight, "We'd just started dating. I was a junior accountant in the fixed income section, and Clint was retirement funds."

She gave his arm a light tap, permission to continue.

"Witt had been transferred to our office as an advisor, working with what we call in the finance business, whales."

"He means people with five million or more," Cami interjected, taking another sip of her coffee. "That's how Witt ended up landing the Bennett account and meeting Nancy."

"And ultimately, how they started dating," Clint added, his eyebrows rising with the words.

"I'm sure that was awkward, being Nancy was married to his client," Lane deadpanned.

"It did cause some issues. He was in the process of—," Clint started.

"We tried our best to discourage it at the time," Cami interrupted, exchanging an embarrassed look with Clint. "We thought Nancy wasn't quite the right fit for Witt... But they were infatuated with each other." She shrugged with a reminiscent shake of her head. "He looked upon himself as a hero. Saving this attractive girl, married to an old rodeo hand almost twice her age, and trapped on a nowhere island." Cami suddenly grimaced. "Sorry, but that's what it seemed like at the time. Anyway, she always regretted how their relationship started. You need to know, Sheriff. Nancy frowned heavily upon infidelity." Cami shot her husband a side-eye glance as she placed a tentative hand on his arm. "In fact, she did her best to discourage those types of interactions within our group. Just the day before—"

"Cami," Clint sighed, lightly shaking off his wife's touch. "Please, let's stay on point." He scooted to the edge of his chair and leaned upon the table, cupping his cappuccino. "Once his and Nancy's affair was disclosed to management, Witt was immediately removed from the Bennett's account. Sadly... well, depending on your point of view, Mr. Bennett died soon after, and the two were able to marry."

"You said the affair caused issues with the employer? Who brought the affair to light?" Lane had plucked her pen from her front pocket, her thumb depressing the top with a loud click.

Clint shrugged. "Probably Buck Bennett himself."

"Okay? And where does the gambling come into play?"

"Ah, well. Anytime an associate is forcefully removed from a client's account, an audit is conducted."

"And I take it they found funds missing?" Lane looked from one to the other, deriving the answer.

Clint nodded as Cami joined along, the two looking more and more like bobbleheads. "Witt admitted to embezzling some of the Bennett's funds to fuel his gambling habit. Luckily, he was able to pay back the account and was given the option to resign."

"And because Nancy was the executor of Buck's estate," Lane speculated. "She didn't file charges?"

"Bingo!" Clint pointed a finger at the sheriff, impressed. "Witt was able to avoid prosecution and keep his record intact."

"Did he continue to work in wealth management?"

Once again, Cami placed a restraining hand, speaking first, "Yes, and he did quite well. Very successful."

Lane waited and, when Cami didn't elaborate, turned a questioning glance toward Clint, who obliged, "Witt was making money hand over fist, and because of his success, his gambling worsened. He never, as far as I know, dived into his client's piggy banks again, but he did clean out his own savings and credit cards upon hitting a terrible losing streak. Next thing we knew..." He pointed between himself and his wife. "Their house was in foreclosure, and he'd been let go from his job, unable to get another because—"

"Of a low credit score." Lane leaned back, crossing her arms. "You can't manage other people's wealth if you're incapable of managing your own."

"Exactly." Clint shot Lane another bright smile.

"But then Nancy...," Cami chimed in with a smile that rivaled her husband's. "Oh, she was so smart! To keep them from going under, she started a small business from their garage, and it took off, morphing into Vita Mineralium!"

"And Witt, being a brilliant strategist, took the brand to the web! Before they knew it, their mom-and-pop business exploded." Clint reached over and took Cami's hand, the two surprisingly beaming at each other like a hallmark card. "We consider ourselves fortunate that they asked us to join along for the ride."

"And what does that exactly entail? Are you employees of their business or..." Lane dropped her arms and reached for her notepad, nodding at Cami.

"Do you sell their product? Are you part of the up-line?"

"Upline? No. I was her personal assistant." Cami straightened and pushed her shoulders back. "That is, I do sell on the side, but I primarily handle... or should say, I used to handle Nancy's schedule. I assisted her in anything she needed, from running errands, returning phone calls, tracking expenses... that sort of thing." Cami tilted her head towards Clint. "In the early days, he used to help with their distribution, but—"

"I didn't do it for long." Clint let go of his wife's hand, feigning humility. "The business grew so quickly that it was wiser to have an actual distribution company handle everything."

"Oh, but you did a great deal!" Cami gripped his upper arm, giving it a squeeze with a slight shake. "He's being modest, Sheriff. He handled all the custom broker paperwork and vendors, plus international relations."

Lane shifted her focus from Cami to her husband. "Customs? Exporting goods or receiving imported items?"

"A little bit of both, right, babe?" Cami questioned, answering for him, her tone tinged with meaning.

"Honey." Clint's smile turned brittle. "We're getting away from our subject, and the Sheriff does have other things to do."

"It's okay. I have time," Lane assured, pleased the conversation was going in this particular direction. "Tell me, Mr. Carson, who produces the vitamins for the Reyerson's company?"

"Um... I have no idea." Clint noted the sheriff's dubious expression. "Not now, at least."

"None?" Lane arched an eyebrow, her eyes still on Clint. "I ask because, on the vitamin packaging, it states, 'Made in the USA' and lists an address..." She referred to her notepad. "To a warehouse in Tacoma. Actually, it's only a large storage unit." She leaned back with a shrug. "That is, according to Google Maps and the pictures I found online. Would you be able to shed some light on that? I mean, the Reyersons aren't still working out of their garage, are they?" She gave a light chuckle to match her humored smile, though if one knew Lane well, they'd recognize the dangerous glint in her eye.

"No, they've definitely moved past the garage days." Clint matched her humored grin, his attention centered on her scribbled notepad, noting the yellow legal note and a Vita Mineralium brochure tucked within the pages. "But as for how they are handling things nowadays, you'd have to ask Witt." He gave a casual shrug of his own. "After a disagreement, I stepped back from the business and decided to focus on our family."

"He's a modern stay-at-home dad now." Cami's smile looked as rigid as her husband's. "He totes the kids all over the place in his fancy minivan, hangs out with all the other stay-at-home mothers. A regular kid taxi service, while I—"

"Disagreement?" Lane cut in, wanting to stay on point. If it be faithfulness to Witt as accomplices or vengeance of their own for a committed wrong, she was still searching for a motive that would involve the Carsons.

"Yes, a very minor one." Clint sighed heavily before proceeding, "Originally, when Nancy started this vitamin venture, her product was imported from Canada. She'd stumbled across a supplement company that was going out of business and was able to buy their stock for a song. Filled her garage up to the brim." Clint chuckled with a shake of his head. "After doing some research, Nancy decided she'd re-package the pills. Clever, really. Basically, created her own vitamin packet combination and put them up for sale." He shrugged, a smile of remembrance budding. "I don't think she ever dreamed it would catch on like it did. But once it took off, Witt and she asked for my help. To be honest, I didn't know what I was getting myself into." He took Cami's hand, stalling her from speaking out of turn, her body language leaned forward, her mouth dropping open. "But when the inventory from the Canada warehouse ran dry, Nancy asked me to start looking elsewhere, suggesting companies in India and China. I was successful in finding eager partners within our budget, but all were, in my opinion, low quality and very shady. When I reported my findings to Nancy and Witt, they wanted to move forward, not seeing my concerns. Things got a bit heated, and I told them that simply repacking pills from who knows where, holding who knows what, could not be considered 'Made in the USA.' Not to mention walking a very fine ethical line with customs and FDA regulations. I wanted no part of it."

Cami, not willing to be sidelined any longer, piped in, "And thank goodness Witt listened to Clint! He took his suggestion to heart and contacted a manufacturing company here in the USA. Even had a new logo and packaging designed." She nodded at the Vita Mineralium brochure sticking out of Lane's notepad. "Really a vast improvement."

"Then why, after they followed your advice, did you not continue to stay in charge of distribution?" Lane ignored Cami, her eyes not leaving Clint.

"When sharing my concerns, I'm afraid harsh words were exchanged. For the sake of our friendship and our kids..."

He glanced at his wife, who solemnly nodded along, Cami expounding, "Their girls and ours are very close."

"I stepped down, and as Cami said, they brought in proper help, and everything is now on the up and up." Clint broke eye contact and turned to his wife, lowering his voice, "Don't forget we're meeting the Coletta's for a bite. We should probably go so I can shower and change." He peered over at Lane and explained, "Sort of having a meeting of the minds on how to help Witt clear this mess up with the media." He turned back to Cami, his voice lifting in tone, along with his eyebrows. "I think we should maybe get back to the credit card receipts?"

Cami frowned but twisted forward and faced Lane. "Yes, so sorry. Uh, you probably assumed the gambling receipts were from one of us using Nancy's card?"

"Long story short, I'd given Witt a ride," Clint took over. "He'd tossed the card and receipts in my glove box for me to give to Cami later. But I'd completely forgotten." He started to stand and took the final sip of his coffee, placing the small cup on the saucer with a clink. "That's the long and short of it. Nothing too exciting, I'm afraid."

Lane put up a pausing hand, shaking her head. "And Cami, you track Witt's casino expenditures?"

"I do! Nancy wanted to make sure he stayed within his budget."

"Budget?"

"He has a monthly gambling allowance," Clint

explained, rolling his eyes.

"Does that actually work?" Lane found it hard to believe a gambler, brave enough to steal from his millionaire clients and now flush with cash, would have the ability to show restraint. "He hasn't found a workaround. Say,... opening a secret account or hoarding cash?"

"There have been a few times he's gone over budget, but I was able to do some... fancy... calculations." Cami's words dribbled to a halt at Clint's disapproving scowl. "Oh, not in the sense you're thinking! I simply shuffle funds from various accounts so that the quarterly auditor doesn't notice the winnings..."

"Or losses?" Lane tilted her head, frowning.

"Something like that," Cami hurried on, "But it's all proper and legal, I can assure you, um... all taxes are paid, everything in order. Honest." She glanced at her husband, his frown deepening. She returned to their original subject, "Anyway, I keep track of Witt's spending." She turned to Clint. "Ready to go?"

"One more question," Lane stalled, finding the Carsons quite obliging. "Were either of you aware Witt was having an affair?"

The couple quickly exchanged a look, Clint remaining stoic with no added commentary as Cami, her eyes a little too wide, vehemently shook her head in the negative, answering, "I think if Witt were having an affair, Nancy would have told me... or at least shared her suspicions." She straightened her shoulders as she stood from her chair, her chin tilted, peering down her nose at Lane. "As her best friend, I can tell you, she would not have shied away from confronting Witt or his... his..." Cami stepped behind her husband and waved a frantic hand, struggling for the last word, "lover."

"Well, then you'll be surprised to find out this is not mere speculation. There is ample proof of his infidelity and—"

A trilling melody interrupted Lane, and Clint winced an apology as he quickly held up a finger, at the same time pulling a cell phone from his front pocket and glancing down at the caller ID.

"Sorry, but this is Aaron." He held up the phone and added, "You'll have to excuse me for a moment. I'll go ahead and take this outside." He squeezed past his wife, the phone still chirping in his hand as he made for the exit.

Cami, in turn, waited until Clint reached the front counter before quickly swiveling back to Lane, her face flushed. "I'm sorry... How do you know he's been unfaithful? You said something about proof?"

"Compromising photos on his cell phone," Lane answered as Clint paused to ask Stephano a question, his phone held against his chest. Receiving a hurried nod from the deli owner, he tapped his own wristwatch and held up two fingers, eliciting another nod of understanding on Stephano's part. Satisfied with the reassuring head bob, Clint resumed his phone call and headed out the door.

"Uh... the photos you're talking about..."

Lane pretended not to notice Cami's hurried glance toward the entrance, making sure her husband was out of earshot.

"Was the woman... could you see... I mean... is her face?" Cami inched closer, her painted nails digging into her palm.

"Visible?" Lane provided and then leaned in, wondering if Cami's concern was due to the possible media implosion the scandalous photos could cause or the possibility that Cami herself was in said photos. "And don't you mean which woman?"

Cami blanched, her lips paling despite her bright red lipstick.

"It seems impulse control is not one of Witt's stronger suits," Lane continued, keeping her voice neutral. "I mean, between the gambling, the affairs, stealing from his past clients..." She tilted her head, catching the other woman's eye. "You and your husband have known Witt a long time. You're not concerned he might drive Vita Mineralium into the ground now that Nancy isn't here to balance him out?"

"Witt, regardless of some of his actions, has great business sense. Nancy didn't always appreciate—"

"Did they often argue about the business?" Lane tapped her pen against the table, Cami's eyes focused on the door, waiting for Clint to walk back through.

"Well, yes. Commission payouts were a big point of contention between them." Cami suddenly sat back down, her concerned expression slipping into a sly smile. "Actually, it caused a big blowout between Nancy and the Masons... You know, Nick and Maddie."

"When was this?"

"Oh..." Cami's shoulders drooped in thought as her head tilted to peer at the ceiling. "Roughly two months ago. Nancy had lowered commission payouts and began collecting chargebacks for refunded product or inactive accounts. A penalty fee of sorts if your upline members weren't selling."

Lane frowned. "Are you saying if you signed someone up under your umbrella, and they weren't making sales, she was penalizing you? How much?"

"Twenty dollars a head, per weekly session."

"And were there any signup bonuses paid when you did recruit?"

"Well, there was never any pay-per-person bonus, but the more people added to your sales group, the higher your tier in commissions."

"But she did away with that as well?"

Cami nodded. "It wasn't until the big blowout with Nick that Witt got involved." She coyly leaned in as if relaying a secret. "Maddie has the largest up-line, and they consider themselves the superstars of the company." She leaned back, letting her hand fall on her lap. "They're also the biggest whinners, in my opinion. If it hadn't been for Nick causing a practical mutiny within the other districts... Witt ended up having to revamp the whole commission payout! Just for them! And yet, Nick isn't satisfied. He still finds it unfair..." Cami suddenly turned, her husband bursting through the deli door, his face lit with excitement.

"We've got to go!" Clint held up a friendly hand and nodded at Lane. "Sorry, Sheriff. I was just able to convince Witt to join us for a late lunch at Aaron and Sandi's. We're meeting in thirty minutes, and I still need to shower."

Cami bolted from her chair. "Witt will be there?"

"Yes, and the Masons. Now, come on." Clint waved her towards the door and then jutted his chin in Lane's direction. "Hope we were able to clear everything up for you, Sheriff. Thanks for your time!"

Lane gave him a casual wave in return as she closed her notepad, the couple venturing from the sidewalk and crossing the street to their vehicle parked on the other side. Cami lagged behind, a frown lining her lips, while Clint was all smiles, eagerly running ahead to open her car door once the taillights blinked, indicating the vehicle was unlocked. It was hard to tell if his chivalrous gesture was to flatter his spouse or simply get her into the car quicker.

A chirping melody exploded from Lane's shirt pocket, and she pulled out her phone, Philip's handsome face beaming up from the screen. She turned to sit back down and held her breath, her finger hovering over the accept button, debating if now would be a good time to issue that apology... But then Jay Jamison came into view. The giant of a man was coming from the direction of the bank, walking at a brisk pace, trying to force a wad of cash into his wallet. This might not have caught Lane's eye if not for the bright blue and orange baseball cap perched upon his head, the exact replica of the one found in Aaron Coletta's suitcase... The one he denied owning. What were the odds, especially in green and blue Seahawk country?

Jay, still walking at a steady pace, twisted his wrist to look at his watch before stuffing the thick wallet into his back pocket and scanning the buildings, his feet carrying him closer to the deli, his attention suddenly swiveling across the street towards the Carson's vehicle, its reverse lights on. Jay completely halted, his brow knitted, and Lane found herself turning in the same direction, curious and completely shocked to find Harry's brown beast of a truck barreling down the road, it barely missing the

Coletta's BMW as he whizzed past, his horn honking at a stray dog, the poor pup barely dodging the oversized knobby tires.

Lane's cell dinged in her hand, and she quickly glanced down.

This time, a text message.

From Philip.

It read, "Caleb. 9-1-1."

CHAPTER 18

"Lane, he's okay." Philip launched from the waiting room chair, a halting hand held up in the air as Lane crashed through the door of Dr. Hadley's office, concern etched on her face. "He's a bit bunged up, but he's fine." He countered Lane's side-step as she looked past his hulking frame and scanned the reception area. She found only Harry seated among the worn chairs with a scrunched up, brown paper bag in his lap, the rest of the medical facility empty. "He was on an ATV and rolled it. Got pinned underneath. He radioed for help, and we brought him in. Dr. Hadley is giving him the once over now." Philip stepped closer and bent to Lane's level, his voice soft and apologetic, "I didn't mean to scare you with the 9-1-1 text. I figured... maybe you weren't taking my call? I wanted to make sure you knew..."

Lane placed a hand on his upper arm, her concern transferring to him. "No, I'm sorry. That's not why I didn't answer..." She paused, frustrated at their lack of privacy, as Harry scooted to the edge of his chair, clearly eavesdropping, the wrinkled sack clutched to his chest, a lopsided smile forming.

"What...?" Philip gently prompted, trying to pull her focus back to him.

"You and I are...," she hesitated and pointed a frown in Harry's direction before meeting Philip's nervous stare. "We're fine." She gave him a quick peck on the lips and let her arm drop. "And you..." She poked a finger in Harry's direction. "I should give you a ticket for speeding, Mr. Vickers."

Harry's goofy smile dropped just as the door of the exam room opened and Dr. Hadley stepped out, the elderly physician's peppered hair standing up on end, his white coat strained over his broad belly.

"Well... your boy has a dislocated shoulder and a fractured distal radius.... er broken wrist," he grumbled, jerking his stethoscope from around his neck and plopping it down onto the reception desk. "As luck would have it, on the same arm. He'll need to wear a sling, and I'll cast his wrist, but other than a couple of bruises and a nasty burn on his lower leg, he's in excellent shape." The old man pointed to the sack in Harry's arm. "Is that what he was in such a big hurry to bring into town?"

"Sure, is!" Harry stood and offered Lane the crinkled bag. "It's sealed in a ziplock. I just put it in the sack so nobody else would see what it was."

Lane looked from Harry to Philip to Dr. Hadley, the older man just as curious, and then peered into the sack, her head popping up with a bright smile. "He found the gun!" Tilting her head, she opened the bag wider. "And a pair of gloves?"

"Humph." Dr. Hadley flung open the door to a large medicine cabinet stationed in the corner. "That wouldn't happen to be the weapon used in the "accidental" shooting from yesterday, would it?" He placed great emphasis on the word accidental. "Doesn't look like a hunting rifle to me."

Lane curled the top of the bag into a handle and placed it carefully on the chair. "With this being an active investigation—"

The doctor held up a pausing hand and then started to load rolls of cotton wool, gauze, and plaster bandaging into the crook of his free arm. "I know, I know. Open case, can't say anything, blah, blah, blah." He chuckled, shaking his head. "I'll just take that as a yes." He dropped the collected medical supplies into a small metal bowl and headed back to the cabinet, this time pulling out a pair of medical shears and neon bandaging. "Funny how things circle back on people."

"How so?" Philip asked, taking a seat next to Harry, Lane wondering the same.

"Well, it was Buck Bennett's widow that was shot, right? At least, that's what the gossip monger says..."

Everyone knew he was referring to Martha Barnes.

"It was." Lane frowned, curious to his point.

"Well, then, there you have it. Karma at work."

"How is that karma?" Philip suddenly stood and moved to the reception desk. "You hinting at something, Doc?" He leaned against the counter. "Like, maybe Buck's death wasn't natural?"

"No way!" Harry balked, his disbelief evident. "Buck croaked from a heart attack! In his easy chair! You can't get more natural than that!" He shook his head and shared a skeptical look with Lane, who appeared more than mildly surprised at Philip's suggestion, considering, just the day before, he had held the same opinion as Harry.

"Oh, his death was natural. There wasn't anything fishy..." The old doctor gave Philip a wink. "That is... that we had time to find." He inhaled through his nose, his round tummy stretching the fabric of his white coat. "The young missus forbade an autopsy and had him cremated in record time. I wouldn't be surprised if she hadn't handed the lit match herself to set him ablaze."

Lane joined Philip, her blue eyes steel. "So, you had unspoken suspicions? Why? Buck say something to you? Did he feel he was in danger?"

"Noooo." He shook his head, his face dropping. "Harry is correct. Buck wasn't in the best of shape to begin with. Suffered from high blood pressure, had a couple of stints already in place, and ate bacon and potato chips, though he was supposed to be working on keeping his cholesterol down." He shook his head. "Probably was one of the worst patients I had as far as not following directions."

"But," Philip prodded.

"But, it just all seemed a bit too convenient." He threw the pair of medical shears and bandaging into the bowl. "His young bride getting all that money, selling his assets, then not bothering to give him a proper burial."

"What money?" Lane asked, giving Philip an annoyed look. "I was told she didn't inherit from the will and was only the executor."

Dr. Hadley made a face. "What fool told you that?"

Philip cleared his throat, a red blush rising to his hairline. "That'd be me."

"Oh, well... you're mistaken. She got a nice chunk of change. Granted..." He held up a finger. "Not the whole kit and kaboodle. That went to his kid. But a chunk all the same. I don't doubt that was a big disappointment. I'm sure her boyfriend didn't like—"

"Boyfriend?" Lane cut in.

"I told you she... uh, got around," Philip reminded out of the corner of his mouth.

"Yeah!" Harry stood, now joining them at the counter. "Wasn't she seen with…" He scratched his head. "Aaron Coletta, right before Buck passed? I seemed to recall a big brouhaha between the two over her."

Doctor Hadley shrugged. "I thought it was a mainland fellow." He picked up the bowl and headed toward the exam room. "All I'm saying is, if she did take his life, then it is only fitting she lost hers here as well."

CHAPTER 19

"That should do it." Dr. Hadley stood back and admired his work, a freshly casted Deputy Pickens seated on the edge of his exam table. "That cast is gonna need a day or two to harden, so don't be karate chopping nothin." The old doc gruffly ordered as he turned and tossed a bowl full of milky water into the sink behind him, the bowl itself following after and clattering against the sides of the metal basin. "And don't get it wet." This mandate was followed by a severe, waving finger. "As for your shoulder, keep that sling on twenty-four-seven for the first full week. Even at night. We'll re-evaluate at your check-up next Friday." Grabbing a sheet from the paper dispenser, he dried his hands and turned to his patient, continuing, "The only time it comes off is for a shower. Now..." He pulled an Rx pad from his coat pocket and tore off the top sheet. "Here's a prescription for a couple days' worth of pain meds and some ointment for your burn. You'll need to get that filled on the mainland. Though... and you didn't hear this from me, Miss Hattie has a homemade salve that is better than anything on the market for burns." He took a deep breath and puffed out his chest. "She's got a bottle of it waiting for you over at the store."

"Thanks, Doc." Caleb took the handed prescription and hopped down from the exam table, wincing as his boots hit the floor.

"And don't jostle around! That shoulder can pop out as easily as I popped it in." He yanked the door open and held it wide. "Now, skedaddle. I've already missed half of the Huskies and Ducks game." He let Caleb limp towards the exit, following close behind. "And your ride is waiting for you."

Inching through the doorway, careful of his slinged arm, Caleb found the waiting room empty, with the exception of Lane, who sat with her notepad open, pouring over her notations.

"Well, Sheriff. He's all yours," Dr. Hadley announced loudly, wiggling out of his white coat. "I'll give you five minutes, and then I'm locking up." He then disappeared into his office, not waiting for a word of thanks or farewell, the door firmly shutting behind him.

"You've looked better," Lane observed as she flipped her notepad closed and stood up, giving her deputy a wry smile.

"I could say the same of you," Caleb countered, noting her tired eyes. "Where are Phil and Harry? I wanted to say thank you."

"Harry needed to relieve Len and Mollie from Hattie-sitting." She tucked her notepad in her back pocket and nodded towards the front door as she stepped up beside Caleb, who was already limping towards the exit. She hovered a guiding arm behind him and added with a pleased smile, "And Phil is running your evidence over to ballistics."

"Hope he asks them to put a rush on it."

"He will. Even told him to say pretty please." She stepped through the door and held it open as he maneuvered through. "Along with reminding Alicia in the crime lab that she owes me a favor. Now, where did you find the gun, Deputy? Don't tell me in that grove of pines because it wasn't there. Phil and I gave that place a thorough search."

"Found it on the opposite side of the meadow heading back to Angie's camp." He waited on the curb as Lane unlocked the passenger side of her rig and opened the door. "Spotted a glove up in the branches of a tree, then started looking for its match. Found it lying a few feet away from the discarded weapon."

Stepping off the sidewalk, Caleb slowly climbed inside, doing his best not to grimace at the pain, and settled in the passenger seat. "You mind stopping by Hattie's before taking me home? She's got some burn ointment for me."

"Sure. I'll run in and get it for you," Lane offered, noting his torn and dirty shirt as she pulled his seat belt from the side and stretched it across his chest. Doing her best not to bump his arm, she clicked it in place. "There. That comfortable?" She eyed him until he gave a curt nod, then closed the door and jogged to the driver's side. "By the way..." She crawled in beside him. "Does the sheriff's department owe the ranger station a new ATV?" She gave him a questioning frown as she snapped on her own seat belt. "Did you total the thing?"

Her deputy gave a lopsided smile for an answer. "Thought so."

He hurried on, wincing as he bumped his elbow against the door's armrest. "I know it was a stupid thing to do, but I was amped about finding the gun, and I didn't want to have to backtrack a whole hour. All I could think about was returning to camp so I could let you know and, more importantly, get my hands on Tanya so I could ask her a few questions."

"The cousin?" Lane punched her keys into the ignition, stopping short of cranking the engine. "Whatever for?"

Caleb did his best to turn and face her, his face lighting up.

"Okay... hear me out. Who would have had the perfect opportunity to hide the gun in a specified location so that Witt could find it and shoot his wife?" He waited a split second before eagerly answering his own question. "Tanya! She told me herself that she rode up the trail before anyone else that morning to set up the sunrise supplies." Seeing Lane's intrigued expression, he excitedly continued, "Witt could have snuck his wife's gun from their tent and given it to Tanya, who rides up as planned first thing in the morning. There's no one to see her, no one to question if she returns a little late. Then Witt, back at camp, stuffs the gun case way under the mattress, out of reach, and hopes his wife doesn't find it empty. And since she doesn't, they go on their ride as planned..."

"Where he picks the fight, rides off, locates the hidden gun, and uses it on his wife... Hmmm." Lane shook her head. "Then how did it end up on the other side of the meadow? I was right behind Witt on the ride down, I would've spotted him flinging a gun into the woods."

Caleb shrugged, instantly regretting it. "Maybe before he reappeared, he rode across the back side, threw the gun away, and then galloped back to the trial, where he pretended to hear the shot?"

"I like where your head is at, Deputy. Except, I'm starting to doubt Witt is our trigger man."

"What about him wearing all black? You, yourself, said it was like camouflage."

"I know I did... But."

"And he had full access to the weapon."

"Yes. IF it was the weapon that was used to shoot Nancy. Ballistics still needs—"

"Come on! What are the chances that the missing gun from the case, found not that far from the shooting site, wasn't the gun used? It's gotta be the murder weapon!"

"And it probably is, Deputy. It's just I can't see Witt getting his hands dirty himself. The way everyone fawns over him... psychologically... don't think he'd be the one to pull the trigger. Pulling the strings would be satisfaction, enough." Lane twisted the key and then pulled on the gear shift, reversing from the parking spot.

"Pulling strings? You're talking about an accomplice. Not an outsider, but someone from camp?"

"It makes more sense, especially if the missing gun is indeed our murder weapon. If our shooter was a hired gun from the outside, they'd use their own arsenal, which would have no ties to Witt or Nancy."

"I see what you mean. Being able to connect the gun to the victim and the possible shooter does seem rather unprofessional. More like a rookie's mistake."

"A sloppy one at that. Unless this was a crime of opportunity, and like Allister pitched last night, someone knew Nancy brought the gun and stole it from their tent before making their way up the meadow."

"Which would also bring us back to Witt's list of suspects that Allister gave you."

"Exactly," Lane huffed. "I've already spent a good portion of my day trying to pierce holes in everyone's alibi." She threw the truck into drive, her foot slowly pressing on the gas. "As I see it, we have three options to consider. The first, Witt went it alone. He plotted and executed his plan, all by his lonesome. The second, he had an accomplice. Someone he trusted wholeheartedly. Not only to pull the trigger but faithful enough not to spill the beans after the deed was done. And lastly, he's innocent. One of the seven either saw a window of opportunity or already had concocted a scheme, one which may have included Witt in the death count. As much as I hate to admit it, Allister brought up a good point last night. Guilty as Witt looks, and with as much motive stacked against him, there is a chance he could have been a victim himself, or at the very least..."

"Convicted for a crime he didn't commit." Caleb rolled his eyes, a smirk lining his lips. "I know you're always telling me I need to have an open mind and be objective, but don't you think we're just mudding the waters here?"

"Possibly," Lane admitted, stifling a yawn, her foot letting off the gas. "I'll concede, I'm more of the mind that Witt had an accomplice, but as we stated earlier if it wasn't a hired gun, what motive or reason would one of the seven have to participate in a homicide?"

"Well, just off the top of my head... money?" Caleb scoffed, bouncing a finger off his forehead.

It was Lane's turn to roll her eyes. "That is a given deputy and one I would consider more likely if everyone wasn't already well off."

"Except for Tanya."

"Yes, except for Tanya." He was like a dog with a bone.

"Blackmail might also be another option. I don't care how rich someone is, they always seem to want a bigger piece of the pie. Like, maybe Witt bought them with a promise of being placed on the board of Vita Mineralium?"

Lane frowned. "With Nancy gone, the company might falter altogether. She was the face, the driving factor, and why people signed up. The one who brought followers into the flock, so to speak. Witt might be a heartless ass, but he had a legit reason to be nervous about the business imploding." Lane gently pressed on the brake, a car inching out from a parking space and into the road. "The coroner suspects those vitamins are nothing but sugar fillers. I sent some samples over to the WSP lab. If proven, that will be the end of Vita Mineralium." She tapped a finger against the steering wheel and proceeded forward. "Oh, you'll find this interesting. Witt, after all that hoopla last night about wanting to stay away from his group? He had lunch with the lot of them over at the Coletta's."

"How'd you find that out?"

"Clint and Cami Carson." Lane glanced over at Caleb. "They were a wealth of information this afternoon. So much so, we can apparently add gambling to the list of Witt's vices. Oh, and embezzlement."

"Of his own company?"

"No. At least, not that's been discovered yet." She cracked the window and aired the cab. "Requesting a full financial audit for the business and their personal finances is on my to-do list. After we pick up your ointment, I'll tell you all the intel the Carsons shared." Lane shook her head. "Why they blindly follow that man is beyond me."

"That whole gang is just gaga for him." Caleb, his brow furrowed, flopped back into his seat. "Even Tanya! You know, Sheriff... She still could have hidden the gun AND been the shooter. She knows the terrain, and no one can verify she was in the mess tent all morning." He leaned forward, eager, twisting carefully. "Yeah... She rides up and hides the gun.

When the coast is clear, she sneaks out of the mess tent and high-tails it to the pine grove. Once Witt rides off as pre-planned, she shoots Nancy before tearing down the hillside, returning to camp on foot."

"Okay, sure. She could have," Lane admitted, "But what's her motive to help Witt? She doesn't strike me as a materialist girl."

"Me either, but it does seem like she'd do anything to help her cousin out, and it's no secret Angie needs money. I don't know..." Caleb made a face, shaking his head from side to side. "The way she spoke about him..." Caleb rubbed his temple, frustrated. "She gave me a tearful tirade this morning, crying about how Witt was an innocent and abused man by his wife. She had absolutely no sympathy for the dead woman. It was like she was taken in by him as much as the rest of the group."

"I suppose she could have developed a crush on Witt. A small infatuation with an older, established man...I have no doubt he tried his charms on her." Lane swung into the second spot in front of Hattie's General. "You might have a point, Deputy. Could be she's one of the girls he's been messing around with."

"Easy enough to find out if she's in his phone!" Caleb's tired face lit up. "I'll tackle that first thing in the morning."

"You bet you will!" Lane teased as she threw the truck into park. "I hope you don't think a broken wrist and dislocated shoulder are gonna get you out of working this case, Deputy."

"Oh, I know better," Caleb chuckled as she hopped out. "Tomorrow, I'll pour over Witt's phone and start dialing numbers from his contacts. See what I can find out, though I'll have to wait until Monday to request his call records and tower history." He suddenly asked, curious, "Hey, did you get a chance to go over that scribbled note we found in Nick Mason's jeans?"

"Yup." Lane grabbed her jacket from behind the seat, the sun starting its early descent.

"And? Who wanted to meet up with Nick?"

"Well... I'm no expert, but I compared our written statements with the note, and the handwriting seems to match up with Aaron Colletta's."

"Why would Aaron and Nick need to be having a secret meeting all by themselves?"

"I don't know, but I plan on asking."

"That reminds me, I still need to contact the rest of the group that no-showed for the camping event altogether. Which almost feels like a waste of time. Our killer was on the island."

"No stone unturned, Deputy."

"I know." Caleb's thoughts seemed to wander. "Sheriff, do you think a judge would give me a warrant for Tanya's cell phone records? If I told them my theory..." He paused, Lane no longer paying attention, her focus shifting past his shoulder to the vehicle pulling in beside them.

Sandi Colletta, giving the door to her Volvo a hard slam, threw her keys into her purse as she quickly strode past, not sparing a glance, a look of hurried determination creasing her Botoxed brow.

"Sheesh. Where's the fire?" Caleb joked as his eyes followed the woman past the front of the patrol truck and over to their driver's side, expecting Lane to agree. Instead, he found the driver's door ajar, and Lane, a few steps behind the bank manager's wife, Caleb, all but forgotten.

CHAPTER 20

The golden bell atop thrashed in protest as Lane cannoned through the door of Hattie's General and barreled into Dub and Glen, both too engrossed in their argument to notice the interruption. She hastily exhaled a breathless apology, the two old-timers muttering points about fly fishing, nymph vs. streamer, and managed to catch a glimpse of Sandi placing her purse in the front section of a wobbling cart and cornering aisle seven.

Lane swiped a wired basket from the metal stand and blew past the cashier, the young redhead, head buried in a bridal magazine, and swiftly stepped around Hattie's empty chair, entering the designated row.

The chance to question Sandi without her husband or her fellow cult-like Vita Mineralium family was too good to pass up, especially after learning that the woman's husband may have had romantic ties to the deceased. And then, of course, there was plain ol' curiosity. How had the importune lunch gone with Witt, and what had they discussed?

In hot pursuit and hoping to glean a clue from the luncheon discussion, Lane spotted her quarry at the end of the aisle. Easing around the end cap, she spied as Sandi pondered the Health & Wellness section, the other woman's nimble fingers walking the shelved merchandise, occasionally flicking a bottle or boxed item into her shopping cart, the medicinal products, primarily Pepto-Bismol, Tums, and Imodium, landing haphazardly beside a spray bottle of carpet cleaner and a large jug of bleach.

"Evening, Sandi." Lane approached, deceptively perusing the aspirin section before peering over and giving a casual smile, her glance dropping to the contents in Sandi's cart. "How was your day—Gee, are you feeling all right? Are the kids, okay?"

"The kids?" Sandi asked, momentarily confused as she tossed a box of Kaopectate onto the growing pile and swiveled towards Lane, her expression dawning. "Oh, no. I mean, yes, They're fine. Still at my mother's." She waved a nonchalant hand toward the shopping cart. "This is for our... guest."

"Who would that be?" Lane inched closer and peered directly into the metal carriage, adding with a light chuckle, "And do they need medical atten-tion?"

"No, but the new rug in my living room does." Sandi nodded towards the carpet cleaner and bleach. "We hosted lunch today at our house, and, well, not everyone was feeling so great afterward." She leaned in and dropped her tone, "I blame the late meal we had last night at camp. The hamburgers that Tanya served? Mine was virtually raw in the middle." She scanned the shelves again. "I refused to eat it, which is why I feel perfectly fine."

"And, who is unwell?" Lane grabbed a bottle of Advil and, just for show, added it to her carry basket.

"Poor Witt, for one, and both Cami and Clint are feeling under the weather. They went back to Phil's place to hopefully sleep it off, and then Maddie..." A huff of air flared from Sandi's nostrils. "She's stay-ing with us for the rest of the weekend. My thought-ful husband made the suggestion since Harry's up-stairs apartment is so tiny." Her eyes rolled to the store's ceiling, with an annoyed shake of her head. "Anyway, I plan on dropping some of this off at Mike Allister's for Witt. If I know Mike, everything in his medicine cabinet will be expired, the old bachelor." She stooped over the cart, separating her goods. "Though, rumor is Sue Carter has been keeping him company. They even went off to Europe for one of her treasure hunts. Doesn't surprise me after what those two went through... It probably drew them to-gether."

Lane shook her head, not because she disagreed but because she didn't want to be sidelined with local gossip. "And Aaron and Nick... how do they feel?"

"Oh, hunky dory, fine." Sandi sounded bitter as she returned to a standing position. "Some people seem to have a coating of metal lining their tummies."

Lane bobbed her head, wanting to move past the subject of sour stomachs. "So, Sandi, um... You never told me how you got involved with Vita Mineralium. Were you and Nancy, friends, back when she lived on the island?"

"No! In fact, I had no idea she had ever resid-ed here until Aaron brought it up. I guess she wasn't here very long. A non-islander like myself. Well, yourself as well!"

"Oh, I didn't realize you... where are you origi-nally from?"

"Renton."

"Oh, okay." Lane inched closer, her eyes scanning past Sandi as she lowered her voice, "Does it both-er you knowing Nancy and Aaron used to... um... go out?"

"What?" Sandi put a manicured hand to her chest, clearly surprised. "They dated?"

"He never mentioned it?"

"Not once." She frowned. "Was it serious?"

"Oh, I have no idea, but it's curious that neither told you." Lane eyed her for a moment before suddenly huffing, "Huh." She stuck out her bottom lip, the corners of her mouth drooping in mock stupefaction. "Well, maybe it was a short romance," she excused and then tilted her head, adding lightly, "So, you met Nancy, how?"

Sandi blinked at the change of subject, clearly distracted by Lane's recent revelation, but answered, "Through social media."

"Like through ads or a friend-of-a-friend connection?"

"Ads. Her face and product were everywhere! At first, I just scrolled by, but her enthusiasm was contagious, and then all these people were posting testimonials about how great they felt and the health benefits of her vitamins. I was sucked right in, along with the prospect of making a bit of extra money." Sandi's voice dipped in volume. "You'd think a bank manager would earn a great deal more than Aaron does."

"He doesn't make much?"

This was surprising since the Coletta's lived in a lovely three-story house, not too far from the point, their expensive cars parked in a three-car garage, the couple and their children always dressed to the nines in brand-name wares.

"Not compared to... others."

"So, you started selling Vita Mineralium to make

ends meet?"

"Ends meet? Well, I wouldn't go as far as that!" She gave out a defensive huff. "More to, you know, help out with the kid's sports, maybe, um... afford a nice trip somewhere. A little extra Christmas money."

"You must be doing good then." Lane peered at the other woman, who kept her eyes downcast. "You've probably sold to everyone on the island. Must get some pretty nice commission checks."

"I have." Sandi pushed a loose hair behind her ear, a polite smile stiff upon her lips. "I mean, I do."

"I understand that the Reyersons changed up the commission structure. Did that have a big effect on you and your upline?"

Sandi didn't answer but instead stared at Lane for a few seconds in contemplation before letting her strained smile drop with a heavy sigh.

"You know, don't you, Sheriff?" She didn't wait for Lane to respond, continuing as if speaking to herself, "Of course, you do." She exhaled through her nose and gave a regretful shake of her head. "I imagine you've dived into everyone's financial backgrounds for the investigation and have figured out that Aaron and I... we're flat broke."

Lane, in fact, did not know but stayed stone-faced as she gave a sympathetic nod, Sandi meeting her eye, almost defiant.

"I've done my best to keep appearances up...

for Aaron's sake. After all, who would entrust their money to a bank where the manager walks around with holes in his shoes? I've managed to do a good job of it, too! My handbag, for instance?" She tapped a manicured nail against the double G emblem on her purse. "It's a knockoff."

"You said for Aaron's sake?" Lane gripped Sandi's cart, ensuring the woman wouldn't have second thoughts on sharing, and wheel herself away. "Your money issues aren't his fault?"

"No. They're mine. All mine!" She unzipped her purse and fished for a tissue, her eyes starting to water. "At first, everything was fine. I was making money. Lots of money! But then, after a few months, sales slowed down, and Nancy started coaching me, advising that I needed to invest more capital in the higher packages and build up my inventory. So, I did…by using our savings, which wasn't an issue at first! Everything I was taking out, I was putting back in, and Aaron was none the wiser. In fact, I'd say, he was rather proud of me... and then... sales started declining, chargebacks starting happening, and people stopped referring the product." Lane didn't doubt her story. Sandi's soft sell approach had become more insistent in the latter months. "And then my upline partners started dropping out or not selling at all, which caused penalty fees!"

"Why do you think that was?" Lane leaned in,

hanging on her every word.

Sandi shrugged. "Complaints about bottles being shipped with fewer pills than they should, or bottles with the seal already broken. Packaging issues."

"Nothing about the vitamin's potency? No complaints there?"

"Well... some," Sandi admitted. "But that's why it is important to be completely balanced. Our Titan package, for instance. It covers all—"

Lane cut in, "So, how did you counter the drop in sales?"

"Oh. Well…as a temporary fix, I dipped into the kid's college funds, hoping things would improve."

"So, it's all gone?"

"Every penny."

"And Aaron has no clue?"

"None whatsoever." She sighed, straightening. "I've been lucky. He's so tired of looking at figures at the end of the day that I've always been the one to handle our home finances." She shamefully shook her head. "Each month, I proudly show him my commission checks because, at a glance, they look great... but when you compare how much product I had to buy for inventory…and was unable to sell... I'm in the hole. A bottomless pit, actually," She lightly groaned, her shoulders slumping. "I've got vitamin shakes, pill pouches, and bottles hidden all over the house."

"Why haven't you told him?"

"I've been trying to avoid it if I can. Joining Vita Mineralium had been all my idea. What with the weekend getaway, I'd planned to have a word with Witt... see if maybe I could get a reprieve, like maybe he'd buy the product back or... I don't know. Give me a personal loan?"

"Why, Witt? Why not approach Nancy?"

"Oh, well... turns out that Nance isn't... excuse me... wasn't a very approachable person. Her enthusiasm didn't always seem to extend past the camera, and her disappointment would have been palpable. I... I was in the inner circle, Sheriff. If I'd gone to her, she only would have made me an example of failure." She shivered, visibly upset.

"And you thought, or rather think, that Witt will help you?"

"I had... I had hoped, but then at camp, he started pushing hard on Aaron and Nick, advising, or rather, telling them they needed to invest heavily... even suggested sinking our kid's college funds directly into the business as future stockholders. Out of desperation, I mentioned it to Nancy, hoping she'd tell him to back off or drop the subject, I mean, that's a heavy commitment and asking a lot. But she just pushed me off."

"You're worried Aaron will actually do what Witt suggests, and then the cat would be out of the bag," Lane guessed, placing herself in Sandi's shoes. "Except with Nancy dying, it already is, isn't it?"

Sandi dabbed her eyes, staining the tissue with mascara. "I'm ashamed to confess, but Nancy being killed will bring everything to light. If the company falls apart, which Witt keeps claiming it won't,... but if it does, then there is no way for me to recoup my losses."

"The meeting you had today... what was discussed?"

"Witt seems to think we can ride out the bad press from the investigation and your..." She paused, giving Lane a grimaced apology. "Your accusations against him. He thinks if we throw enough money at the media, everything can be salvaged... and I hope he's right."

"What did the others think?" Lane prodded, "What are Aaron's thoughts?"

"Oh, he thinks Witt should liquidate and sell the business. Wait for everything to blow over and try again."

"Sell, huh?" Lane pondered if it was sound advice. "And the others? Anybody else have any ideas?"

"Oh, yes! Clint suggested Witt should temporarily step down until after the investigation and offered to take over. Surprisingly, Nick and Maddie backed him up." Sandi, tissue in hand, lightly touched the corner of her lashes. "Witt absolutely refused, and I think he was right to do so. He shouldn't give up the reins... not yet."

"You're still hoping he can help."

She nodded, giving one last sniffle. "I've been trying to catch him alone all weekend, but everyone is always around, and now he's not feeling well... I know that might seem callous, after everything with Nancy, but I'm desperate." She roughly threw the used tissue into her purse. "In fact, I only made the offer to pick up all of this as an excuse to see Witt..." She waved a hand over the cart's contents. "In hopes of appealing to his kindness in secret. With Maddie staying with us, it'll be my only chance, especially since I'll be stuck with her for the rest of the night while Aaron is out bowling."

"I forgot it was league night." Lane let go of Sandi's cart, her plans to veg out and binge true crime television while snuggling with Stinker now out the window. She'd be rushing home to change clothes and grab her bowling ball.

"Yeah, well, Aaron never forgets. Every Saturday, he's off with the guys down at the bowling alley." Sandi suddenly laughed and flapped a hand in Lane's direction. "Oh, you should know! You probably see him all the time there on league night!"

The thing was... Lane hadn't. Not once.

CHAPTER 21

Under the dim glow of parking lot lights, Philip slowly circled the cramped and crowded bowling alley in search of a vacant spot, only to be repeatedly taunted by "Compact Only" signs and idling cars that seemed in no rush to depart. Impatient, he found himself tempted to slip into one of the graveled spaces in front of the neighboring dive bar but wisely thought better of it, knowing Edgar Rowles and his tow truck would be on the prowl throughout the evening cruising for parked violators.

A pair of white reverse lights suddenly came to life, and like a vulture, Philip swooped into the freshly deserted slot, priding himself on his patience as he exited his rig to the sound of distant thunder, in actuality, the colliding of crashing pins and bowling balls echoing through the rectangular building's tin siding. Easily spotting Harry's brown beast of a truck and Jerry's quad cab, he was pressed to find Lane's pick-up, coming to the conclusion she was still with Caleb or, finally hitting exhaustion after the last two days, had decided to stay home, probably curled up on the couch. He, himself, was dragging, but due to his promise to his buddies, who were bound and determined to stage a comeback against their ladies' fair, he had arrived with a willing heart and bowling ball in hand.

Swinging the front door open, pop music flooded his senses, the sheer volume muffling the sound of laughter and crashing pins as he weaved his way to the front desk.

A cheer of "Hey, Phil made it!" carried over the chaos, and Philip raised an arm of greeting as he slid up to the shoe counter, slapping a hand against the outdated Formica and lightly yelling over the din, "Hey, Eric! How's your night? Can I get a Size 14 and a pitcher of beer, please?"

At the slight wave of acknowledgment that his request was heard, Philip's attention wandered towards the lanes and the various small groups, some in matching bowling shirts, others in casual wear, all cheering or jeering their neighbors under the large bannered slogan, "A community that bowls together, stays together. Welcome to Sasquatch Lanes!" The saying was followed by the alley's mascot, a large and goofy-looking Big Foot with oversized feet, its bare toes poking through the tips of bowling shoes, it offering the guests a large and toothy grin of welcome.

"Here you go, Phil. Beer coming up."

A pair of mismatched shoes were plopped down upon the yellowed laminate, and Philip twisted back around, stopping short as he recognized the two men standing further down the way, the shoe counter splitting off into a small concession bar. They were chatting up the pretty blonde behind the beer tap until Nick Mason veered off with a brimming pitcher of beer and headed for a designated lane. Aaron Coletta was left behind, still happily conversing as he handed over a credit card.

"Evening, Aaron!" Philip greeted a tad too loudly as he clamped a friendly hand upon Aaron's shoulder, the bank manager turning at the energetic greeting with startled surprise. "I didn't know you enjoyed bowling."

"Oh,... hey, Phil." Aaron took a step back to offer his hand, along with a generous smile, and nodded towards Nick, his bowling partner bent over the electronic touchscreen, laboriously punching in their names, his efforts displayed on the computerized scoreboard above. "Just showing some island hospitality." He gave Philip a wink before returning his focus to the buxom blonde swiping his credit card, her thin eyebrows furrowed as she read the small green screen.

"Something wrong?" Aaron asked, his hand pre-emptively wandering to his back pocket and wallet.

"Yeah, um... sorry." She offered an apologetic smile and handed him the card. "It came back declined."

Aaron bobbed his head as if he'd expected the issue and finished digging out his wallet, flipping it open and plucking out a different card. "Give this one a try," he directed and then turned to Philip with a shy smile. "I'd complain about the bank, but I happen to run it." He chuckled, further explaining, "Our metallic strips just don't seem to keep their charge."

"I'm so sorry..." The bartender held out the second card, looking miserable.

"Here, let me." Philip quickly yanked his wallet from his jeans pocket and gingerly pushed Aaron to the side, lightly adding, "And can you open a tab for me?" He then turned to Aaron, who was starting to protest. "Hey, I never got a chance to thank you for approving my boat loan. My way of saying thanks."

"Appreciate that, Phil, but I was just doing my job." He stuffed his declined card into his wallet red-faced and gave a grateful smile before turning on his heels to leave. "Well, have a good game."

"Did you fellas want something to eat as well? I was gonna order a few hot dogs," Philip offered, accepting his bank card back with no issues. "Has Nick eaten yet?"

Aaron shook his head, giving his stomach a solid pat. "I think we're both stuffed from the pizza we had for lunch, but thanks for offering." He tipped his head in appreciation and took a tentative step backward, Philip quickly filling the gap.

"I, um... I wanted to ask you... uh... since I've got you here," Philip started, their waitress sliding a pitcher of beer toward him. "How are you holdin' up with Nancy Reyerson's passing? I got to thinking about when you two dated..." He paused and tossed a few dollars into the tip jar before picking up the pitcher. "You know, back in the day, and I mean, obviously, you stayed close friends..." Philip's question petered off as Aaron's expression changed from mildly curious to befuddled.

"I never dated Nancy."

"Well..." Philip gave him a sly smile. "You might not have officially been a couple, but you were seeing her." He nudged Aaron's arm with his elbow. "Back when she was married to Buck?" Aaron's mouth dropped open in a stupefied expression, and Philip hurried on, "Of course, I'm not judging. We were all young and stupid once, and if the rumor mill of the time was to be believed, it wasn't you that did the pursuing."

"I'm trying to follow along, Phil." Aaron gave his

head a subtle shake, his tone uncertain. "Are you telling me you think Nancy and I were lovers?"

"I've been told—" Philip felt an unexpected slap against his back pocket and practically jumped out of his skin, a small body sliding up against him, Lane appearing at his elbow, cutting in,

"Hey, fellas! Sorry, I didn't catch all of that. You and Nancy weren't romantically involved?" She looked inquiring from Aaron to Philip. "Did he say they weren't lovers? I missed part of that."

Whether it was from Lane materializing out of nowhere, as if she'd been part of their conversation from the beginning, or simply that she was no longer wearing a bland, tan, and brown uniform but dressed in tight jeans and an oversized t-shirt which read: Big Foot, Hide and Seek Champion with her accustomed tight bun, loose and messy... Aaron seemed speechless. With his jaw hinged open and eyes somewhat bugged out, he stared at the petite blonde before him, expectant of an answer.

"Where... where did you hear that?" Aaron finally managed.

Philip suddenly looked sheepish, a guilty flush running up his neck as he admitted,

"Well, I'd heard you and Buck had come to blows over her."

"That wasn't... I mean, we did, but not because..." Aaron edged closer and grabbed Philip by the arm, practically towing the two away from the counter as Lane followed, the beer in Philip's pitcher slopping over the side. "Nancy and I were never involved romantically. Ever." He quickly scanned past their shoulders, finding that their group of friends were staring, waiting for Lane and Philip to join the party. He spoke quickly, "You've got the wrong end of the stick. Buck and I had ALMOST come to blows, and yes, it was over Nancy, but not because she and I were sleeping together."

"Then why?" Lane shouldered in front of Philip, accidentally jostling his arm, more golden liquid dribbling down the pitcher's side.

"I had shared my suspicions that Nancy was actually sleeping with Witt Reyerson, and Buck, the drunk fool, was trying to defend her honor. Though he knew damn well, I was telling the truth!" Aaron took a deep breath before continuing, "For this all to make sense, I've got to go back a bit. You see, Buck... You know he won the lottery, right?" This was directed towards Lane, who nodded. "Okay, well, Buck was a good friend of mine through the bank. Like a lot of people who've never had more than a few dollars to their name, he was burning through his winnings like wildfire, as if he'd never run out... and though he did have a ton, at the rate he was going, he'd be broke within two to three years. So, I advised him to work with a wealth management company.

Invest. Have his new funds work for him and build upon his fortune instead of squandering it on anything that caught his fancy."

"Sounds like sage advice."

"It was... until I found out Buck's wife was sleeping with his finance advisor and that the two were embezzling funds."

"How'd you figure that out?"

"By accident. Buck was studding one of his stallions to a high-end breeder and was having a hard time understanding all the legal jargon on the contract, so I offered to decipher. He'd dropped off the papers, and I found his financial records included in the pile."

"Might not have been accidental at all," Philip suggested, hinting that Buck may have already had suspicions but was too embarrassed to ask.

"Either way, the figures reported were all over the place, and if it wasn't embezzlement, it was a gross mishandling of Buck's finances. I started making more official inquiries. Wasn't long before I found out that Nancy and Witt were sharing the sheets. I warned Buck about it. Begged him to pull his money from the wealth management company and tried to encourage him to bring it all back to the island for safekeeping. At least, until I could figure something else out." Aaron, his expression forlorn, rocked back on his heels. "But Buck's pride got in the way and... well, then he died, and it was a moot point. Nancy got her allotment and Angie the lion's share. Sadly, she's just as careless as her old man with cash and has blown through her fortune with nothing to show for it."

"She's been able to keep the farm." Philip felt defensive on Angie's behalf, though he hadn't disagreed with a word Aaron had said.

"Not for long. IRS is about to swoop in due to back taxes and sell it from underneath her." Aaron's forehead wrinkled in true concern. "She's in a real pickle. I've been on her to sell her horses, all of them, just to buy her some more time." He shook his head. "Shame this camping retreat thing didn't work out. Sounds like she's going to have to accept Jay Jamison's offer to buy the place if she wants to stay— "

Not interested in Angie's financial woes, Lane interrupted, "I'm sorry... this isn't making sense. If you know Witt Reyerson to be an embezzler, why do you have your nose so far up his—"

Philip cleared his throat, interrupting, "What she means is, how can you be in business with this guy... and Nancy?" Philip offered him a crooked smile with a hapless shrug. "Knowing what you know?"

"You have to admit, Aaron, that is weird," Lane agreed. "The whole lot of you seem... well..."

"No, you're right." Aaron held up a hand, then

let it drop to his side, defeated. "And it's awkward as hell. A year ago, Sandi came to me about this vitamin company she wanted to get involved with, a way to make some extra pocket money. I thought it was a good idea. It wasn't long before she was bringing home pretty sizeable checks and being invited to fancy dinners and little side adventures, like wine tours or weekend spa trips." He crossed his arms and gave a slight shrug. "After a few good recruiting months, she'd reached the top level and was offered a seat at the big table." He tossed his head in Nick Mason's direction, still plunking away at the scoreboard. "Spouses are and were encouraged to join along, and we made... friends. That's when I discovered that the Reyersons of Vita Mineralium were, in fact, Buck Bennett's Witt and Nancy Reyerson."

"And that didn't have you running for the hills?" Lane asked, itching for her notepad.

"Oh, I wanted to tuck tail, all right," Aaron chuckled. "But... well, Sandi really enjoyed them, and people can change after all. It was clear they were on their way up the ladder of success, and being parents, it appeared they'd settled down. Nancy was nice to Sandi and even paid for our kids to take horse lessons with her girls. I don't know. Seemed like they'd grown up."

"Did they know you were the one to expose their affair?"

"Possibly? Nancy made a few comments that I took to be a little passive-aggressive, but nothing straight out. Could've been that Buck told her it was me. But if so, Witt didn't have an issue with it. I tell ya, that guy has got a sound financial mind."

Lane shook her head, still in disbelief. "I can't believe you actually trust him."

"Trust, Witt?" Aaron dropped his arms, warding off the suggestion. "Oh, not as far as I can throw him! You misunderstand me. Just because I think Witt is a financial genius doesn't mean I think he's got a great moral compass."

Lane gave him a slow smile, starting to understand. "You're still keeping an eye on him. Making sure he's on the up and up?"

"Trying my best." Aaron suddenly glanced over at Nick and, under his breath, muttered, "Keep your friends close and your enemies closer."

"Speaking of enemies..." Lane pounced at the opening. "You were quick to come to Witt's defense with a lawyer last night. Was that to protect your financial investment or because you think he's innocent?"

"Both. He's an ass in many ways, but I have a hard time picturing him taking his girl's mother away."

"Well, if not Witt... then who?"

"I'd like to suppose, as you originally suggested, it was a hunting misfire. A terrible accident."

Philip, his smile dropping, interjected, "Not likely, Aaron. Nancy's missing gun was found not too far from the meadow."

At this comment, Lane shot Philip a scathing look, her lips thinning as she pursed them together. She'd not wanted that made public. Not yet.

"You found it, huh?" Aaron raised an impressed eyebrow. "Well, then, it's only a matter of time before you identify fingerprints and DNA. That should clear up if Witt shot her or not."

"It might be that easy, and then it might not. We're leaning towards him having an accomplice."

"You mean one of us? Back at camp?"

"In your opinion, is there anyone who might be overly devoted to Witt... or possibly benefit from both of the Reyersons being eliminated?"

"Are you saying whoever shot Nancy may have been trying for Witt as well?"

"It's a working theory."

"Well, Sheriff, I hate to be unhelpful, but... in all honesty, everyone in camp, some more than others, their whole livelihood revolves around Vita Mineralium being profitable. To kill Nancy is awful, but taking Witt out... that'd be the final nail in the corporate coffin." Aaron cringed. "Sorry, that was a bad analogy."

"And if Witt wanted Nancy out of the way? Any takers there?"

"No. I just don't see it."

Lane frowned, suddenly thinking of Caleb's theory. "No romantic entanglements that might prompt—"

"Sorry, I can't think of anyone. Listen, I better get back to my guest, and it looks as if you're friends are getting impatient as well."

"Hold on." Lane put a restraining hand on Aaron's arm, stilling his motion to leave. "At the time of the shooting, you'd told my deputy that you were out cutting wood, but Phil here, he said that Angie already had a full cord."

"And there was plenty still up there yesterday," Philip chimed in, giving Lane a firm nod of solidarity.

"Which begs to be asked, what the heck were you really doing when Nancy Reyerson was shot?"

"Just what I said I was." Aaron shook off Lane's hand, his polite countenance a moment before disintegrating. "I was bored and decided to burn off some energy by throwing the axe around. There's nothing nefarious about that."

"I agree. It's just that I wondered if, maybe, you'd actually gone into the woods to meet someone. Possibly had a rendezvous, a meeting of the minds?" Lane nodded toward Nick, not having had the chance to ask him, herself, about the crumpled note found in his jean pocket, the scribbled request in Aaron's handwriting. "I get the feeling you're not the only member of the group that has had second thoughts about Nancy and Witt's leadership."

"I don't... No, there was no. I was out cutting wood." Aaron placed his hands in front of him and took a step back. "And I didn't see anybody."

"Not even your wife?" Lane stepped forward, her smile dropping.

"She was in our tent reading."

"Not the whole time. Not according to her or Cami Carson. Was she maybe out looking for you?"

Aaron, his color draining, hesitantly pondered, "No... she wouldn't have come looking for me." He suddenly nodded as if to reassure himself. "Not with her bad knee. Besides, she probably went to the outhouse, and Cami missed her."

"And you didn't see anyone else? Neither of the Masons? Nick or Maddie?"

"No. No one," Aaron answered tightlipped, his eyes roaming from Lane's face to over her shoulder, where his head tilted up, a bright smile replacing his soured expression. "Hey ya, Harry! Sorry to keep your bowling partners. I've been gabbing their ears off. You all have a good night!" He gave Philip a quick slap on the upper arm. "Thanks again, Philip, and good luck!"

CHAPTER 22

Perched on tiptoes, Lane stretched as her fingertips lightly brushed her desired object, a green thermos just out of reach, stationed on the top shelf of her kitchen cabinet. With a hop and a grunt of effort, she managed to knock the metal flask from its perch, the thermos tumbling down and clattering against the countertop, its lid bouncing into the sink.

"Dang it," she muttered and reached for the wayward cap, cocking an ear, fearful she'd managed to wake the dead, Philip still asleep.

At the sound of a jet landing and taking off, Philip's snores echoing down the hallway, Lane gratefully slid the length of the counter to the coffee pot, where she succumbed to a languished yawn and filled the hollow insides of the thermos with caffeinated goodness.

Philip, still thankfully slumbering in bed... in the guestroom, would be up soon and heading out the door to help Kody retrieve the decimated ATV. She'd decided to fix him lunch and fill his thermos, hoping to give him a few extra minutes of sleep before beckoning him down the stairs to start his day.

Setting the filled thermos beside the packed cooler, Lane poured herself a cup of coffee and swiped up Stinker, the skunk settled at her feet, and padded herself out onto the front porch. There, with the sun barely above the water, she attached her furry companion to a tether and let him out into the yard. She then sunk into one of the white rocking chairs and took a well-deserved sip before pulling out her cell phone.

A male voice, filled with gravel, answered, "Hey, kiddo. It's awfully early. Everything, okay?"

Lane bit her tongue, knowing from past pleas it would be fruitless to reiterate her dislike for the endearment "kiddo"... because her brother already knew. "I thought you'd be up with the chickens, Kent," she teased, knowing full well her elder sibling was far from an early riser. "Thought I should let you know I'm working a homicide, so I won't make it to dinner tonight."

"Another? Sheesh, kiddo. Cabot Cove is a safer place than your little island."

Lane rolled her eyes at the exaggeration and asked, "Have you ever heard of the company Vita Mineralium?"

"Vita, what?"

"Mineralium. They sell vitamins."

"Oh, wait. Yeah... Real big on social media." There was a sound of rustling sheets, and Lane assumed Kent was climbing out of bed. "They accidentally poison somebody?"

"Not exactly, but you might want to take some notes for your DEA bosses." Lane took a sip of her coffee. "The founding owner, Nancy Reyerson, was shot. When they conducted her autopsy, the coroner discovered she was suffering from several vitamin deficiencies."

"Odd for somebody that sells the stuff. She have a rare case, or doesn't use her own product?"

"I'm waiting for some testing to come back from the WSP lab, but the speculation is their vitamins are basically sugar pills."

"Well, now. That would interest my DEA bosses...especially the deputy general. Who is Vita Mineralium's manufacturer?"

"That's what I was hoping you could find out for me, big brother," Lane playfully snarked. "Might help me out with motive."

"You lacking one?"

"Far from it. I have too many, but this might be

an angle I need to investigate further."

Nancy Reyerson didn't strike Lane as the type of woman who would let a scandal destroy her business or reputation without a fight. Then again, neither would Witt, shown by the confidence he seemed to have in his P.R. agent's abilities. The question was, were Witt and his wife aware of the substitution in ingredients? If the coroner was correct, and the so-called vitamins were nothing more than sugared fillers, the Reyersons were conducting a fraudulent business... which was about to break nationwide. What would Witt... or someone else, whose financial existence depended on the company's success, do to keep that a secret?

"Alright, kiddo. I'll bring it up to my director and see if he'll let me look into it."

"Appreciate it, brother of mine."

"Anytime. By the way, chatted with Pops the other night. He tells me you're dating the park ranger AND..." he hurried on, keeping her from interrupting, "You two are getting pretty serious. Why haven't you brought him over for dinner? Mindy's cooking isn't that bad."

"Your wife's cooking is perfectly fine... most of the time."

"Yeah, those lessons have done wonders! So, what is it? He ugly or something?"

"No."

"Well, then bring him over next Sunday. Unless... he's... UGLY. Don't want to scare the kids."

"He's far from ugly," Lane laughed. "And we'll see."

"We'll see?" Kent sounded annoyed. "Seriously, kiddo! What's with all the secrecy? Did Dad get the wrong end of the stick? You not into this guy?"

"On the contrary, I'm into him a lot." Lane sighed, putting her coffee down. "And he's into me. Even wants to move in together."

"And that's an issue? Why?" Kent suddenly whispered into the phone, "He's not already married, is he?"

"No!" Lane huffed, "Nothing like that!"

"Man, he must be really ugly then."

"Kent, stop!" Lane lightly admonished, her smile dropping as she confessed, "It has nothing to do with him and everything to do with me... or rather... mom."

"Ah... kiddo." Kent's teasing tone dissolved, turning tender. "She ruined a good portion of our childhood. Don't let her spoil what's left of the years we have. Fall in love, stay in love, and if, by chance, love loses its luster, just remember you were happy for a while."

"Aren't you poetic?" Lane scoffed despite appreciating the sentiment. "Better to have loved and lost, than not to have loved at all. Is that what you're telling me?"

"Pretty much! It's not rocket science." Kent paused, Mindy's voice carrying from the other room and over the phone line. "Gotta go, the wife needs me. But you bring lover boy to supper next Sunday, okay? And if I find out anything illegal on your vitamin company, I'll ring you up."

"Sounds good and... Hey, Kent? Thanks."

"Hay is for horses. See you next Sunday, kiddo."

CHAPTER 23

"On the count of three then." Philip leaned into the tipped ATV and paused as Kody inexplicitly dusted his hands on the side of his jeans before gripping the muddy and dented back fender. "You ready, kid?" he asked, sharing an amused smile with Jay Jamison, who had stepped up and anchored onto the front tire for leverage.

"Ready," Kody answered with a curt nod, his face stern, eyes pinned to the fender, not picking up on their amusement as he ground his boots into the turf.

"One, two... three!" The directive was followed by a trio of grunts and an inappropriate curse, the quad bouncing back onto all fours.

"Best for it to sit there and let the oil settle," Jay suggested as Kody gripped a handlebar and launched a leg over the seat, surveying the damage. "Give it at least five minutes." Jay headed for his own quad and tossed his baseball cap down into the mounted open storage. "Then we'll see if it'll start up."

"Doubt it will." Ol'man Jameson pointed down to a dark pool of liquid, his horse shuffling to the side underneath him. "It's sprung a leak."

"Sure enough." Philip bent down and examined the growing oil slick. "Jay, you got a tow rope, or..."

"Right here." Jay held up a bright yellow strap. "I'll get it hooked up and towed to the gravel road. Edgar Rowles should be able to pick it up from there."

"He'll charge extra for driving that far out! Best take it all the way to the ranger station, son." The old man pointed a nicotine-stained finger towards Kody, who was now off the quad and stooped over, peering at the undercarriage. "He can ride on your rack. It'll be a bit bumpy, but if you run into any trouble, you'll have an extra pair of hands."

"I think that's a good plan," Philip concurred and eyed Jay, confirming he was in agreement as well, then added, "We appreciate all your help, fellas." He turned on his heel and gave the older man a courteous nod before facing back around to his young ranger and raising an eyebrow, a silent suggestion that a comment of gratitude was required.

"Yes. Thanks for your help, Jay... Mr. Jamison." Kody stood to his full height, his face crest-fallen, his knees dirty. "And I don't mind riding on the rack.

As long as I get this back to the station in one piece." He gave the front tire a solid kick.

"Then it's settled. Phil, you ride back with me." The old man jerked his head at the two horses Philip and Kody had ridden to the site, both tied to an old cedar, grazing on the short grass lining the trail. "My back is starting to ache, and this cold weather doesn't do me any favors. Come on, these two got it from here."

Receiving a salute of farewell from Jay, Philip gave Kody's shoulder a solid slap, the young ranger slumping forward with the hit. "Radio if you have trouble."

By the look on Kody's face, Philip concluded he wouldn't want to be in Deputy Picken's shoes the next time they saw each other. He bumped Kody's arm and leveled him with a look. "It was an accident."

"I know..."

"And Sheriff Lane has already promised her department will replace the quad."

"But she can't replace the memories, Phil." Kody rubbed his hand along the handlebars. "I've been all over the place on this thing."

"And it shows." Philip chuckled, pointing to the scrapped paint and old dents, the bumper askew, held together by bailing twine. "Now, cheer up, or I won't let you pick out the color for the next one."

"You mean it?" Kody's face lit up. "That would

be cool, Phil. I always thought neon green would be wicked!"

Philip didn't have the heart to tell him that no matter what color Kody picked, the quad would be repainted in a standard green and stenciled with the park's logo.

"See ya back at the station, kid."

Untying the tethers from the cedar, Philip gave a calming word to his mount and gripped the saddle horn, placing his boot into the stirrup and heaving himself up. Throwing his leg up and over, his old gunshot-wounded thigh protested, and he sat down with a grunt, a chuckle escaping from the older Jamison.

"Use to be a lot easier ten years ago, wasn't it?" The old man teased before clucking his tongue and nudging his horse's side with his heels, starting back home.

With Mark Jamison setting the pace, Philip brought his ride to a light canter, a painted mare ponied behind him, keeping up with no trouble as the two men rode single file. Above them, swirling clouds of dark mist urged them on, the prospect of a downpour visible on the horizon, enforced by the touch of a cool breeze at their back.

"I hear Jay is looking to buy Angie's place. I didn't know she was even considering selling?" Philip ventured, the trail starting to widen, Crescent Meadow looming ahead.

"I'm afraid she isn't," Mark Jamison answered over his shoulder as he readjusted, sitting back heavily in his saddle and letting out an exasperated sigh. "That girl is as obstinate and bulled-headed as her daddy."

"Not her fault that she's comes by it naturally," Philip smirked, remembering Buck Bennett and his stubborn streak. "Is Jay hoping she might have a change of heart now that she's closing the camp? I know she plans on selling off what she can, and I have it on good authority she'll need every penny she can get it..." Philip paused, the old man nodding along.

"Old Uncle Sam, wanting his cut." Mark Jamison spat to the side. "Damn taxes." He turned, twisting in the saddle to peer back at Philip. "I suppose you figured out Jay was planning on rescuing more than just the farm by buying it up."

"Your boy hoping that Angie and the farm might be a packaged deal?"

"He was." Mr. Jamison faced forward. "I can't figure out if she's just too proud to accept or—"

"I'd suspect, heartbroken. She and Kevin were together for several years."

"Little good he was having around the place. Never lifted a finger to help."

"That's true, but I do know he chipped in on the bills." Philip glanced up at the sky, the clouds having grown darker. "How did she go through her inheritance so fast?"

"Aww... well. The majority was spent on vet bills. That girl tried to save every hag she could from the slaughterhouse. Buying up or adopting unwanted horses…paying to get them fixed up or buried." He twisted back around and raised his voice so he could be heard. "Then she paid to have the place renovated with high-tech gadgets. You've seen that fancy RV horse trailer she's got parked behind the barn? Don't think she's taken it across the ferry once. It's just wasting away."

"I thought Angie was using it as an apartment for her cousin Tanya?"

"Maybe... but she won't want to stay in it come winter."

"You'd think, with all the money Buck had, that there would have been enough left over for—."

"Oh, there was! Plenty until that she-devil got her hands on it." The old man spat again, this time uttering a curse. "Conniving woman didn't even wait until his body was cold before she started selling stock, tracks of land he'd bought over in Montana." He shook his head. "Claimed she was doing it for Angie, yet... the girl never saw a dime."

"That so?" Philip inched forward, his mount eager to leave the trailing dust and lingering smell of cigarettes. "Angie never asked for an audit?"

"No. Like her father, she thought there was money a plenty and that it would last her forever. As if it grew on a tree out back!" The old man suddenly halted his horse and leaned forward, squinting into the distance.

Crescent Meadow was open wide before them, a parcel of black-tailed deer littered across the long grass, their heads popping up one by one at their intrusion. He jutted a chin in their direction and then turned to Philip, picking up where he had left off, "Aaron Coletta looked into Nancy's doings but said everything was above board, what with her being the executor and Angie on the verge of eighteen. Said what the widow did before she handed the reins over, well, she apparently had every legal right to do. But if you ask me, there was not a moral bone in that woman's body. Her abandoning Angie days after her eighteenth birthday says that alone."

"Yeah, that rubbed a lot of people the wrong way. But I got the feeling Angie was glad to be rid of her.

"They never hit it off. Timing might have played a factor in that, Buck remarrying so soon after losing Suzanne. Threw everyone for a loop, especially Angie." The old man seemed to shrink in his saddle, his voice soft. "You know, when Susie died, I begged him to skip the rodeo circuit and stay home. Take care of his daughter. But Buck was drowning in his sorrows, and I suppose... needed the distraction."

The deer scattered from the meadow into the woods, and he clucked his horse forward. "I know folks thought Buck was taken in by sweet words and tantalizing kisses, but what he really was after, I think, was a mother for Angie." The old man's tone turned bitter. "And what he got was a whore and a thief."

Philip's eyebrows raised at the statement, and he cautiously hazarded, "I'm not making excuses, but Nancy was a young girl herself. Enticed by literal millions, she was pulled into a whirlwind romance and made a mother overnight. With Buck passing so soon after their marriage, I doubt she had time to form an emotional tie to Angie or the island."

"You give her more credit than she deserves, Phil. She was a weak woman through and through. Easy fodder for the likes of Witt Reyerson, that devil." Ol'man Jamison pulled tight on the reins, his horse coming to a short stop, its hooves landing on the blood-stained trail where, two days before, Nancy Reyerson had taken her last breath. "I hope they both rot in hell."

"I doubt Witt will be seeing the underside of six feet any time soon." Philip tugged the painted mare, not wanting to linger, the first drops of rain pattering against their saddle bags.

"No?" The old man sniffed, his head swaying side to side in disgust. "Then three feet in a shallow grave will have to do."

CHAPTER 24

"Sorry, I'm late." Lane hastily pulled a chair from the gingham-dressed table and moved aside a teaming glass of ice water as she picked up a menu. "Have you two already ordered?"

She was met with silence, her companions focused on something of apparent interest, their gazes glued to the other side of the Royal Fork's dining room. Their curious expressions were hidden behind glossy menus, their eyes covertly hovering over the edges. "What are you two looking at?" Lane turned her head, her query a tad too loud, as she was instantly shhh'ed by Heather Holmes, who lowered her menu and tipped it toward a couple seated by the window.

Nick and Maddie Mason.

"Those two have been going at it hammer and

tongs since we sat down," Heather whispered, returning her menu to full staff like a shield.

Lane followed her darting gaze and found that the reportedly heated conversation had hit a lull. But by the rigidness of Nick's shoulders and the shade of Maddie's cheeks, fiery words had most definitely been exchanged.

Mollie dropped her own menu to take a sip of wine and smiled over the rim at Lane. "We've only been able to catch bits and pieces, but those have been pretty juicy."

"Yeah, talk about dinner with a show," Heather laughed, her eyes dropping down and actually pursuing the menu. "Did either of you notice what the lunch special was? I've plum forgot."

"French Dip and fries," Mollie answered, her head still tilted in the Mason's direction. "The main theme seems to be money and jealousy." She suddenly peered at Lane and leaned forward, setting her menu flat on the table. "It's interesting because I see that lady at the bank all the time." She quickly glanced over each shoulder before proceeding, her voice dropping to a hush, "Won't let anyone but the bank manager, Aaron, help her."

"Really?" Lane scooted her chair closer. "How often does she pop into the bank?"

"Oh, I'd say at least once a week."

"And is it the same day each visit?"

"Not that I've noticed." Mollie slouched in her chair and pondered, "No! Because she came in on a Monday two weeks ago, and last week, it was a Wednesday. So, not the same day!"

"Then... is it always at the same time? I mean, like a scheduled visit?" Heather joined the speculation, picking up on what Lane was alluding. "You think they might be having an affair?"

"What? Aaron cheat on Sandi?" Mollie shook her head, immediately dismissing the idea. "He's too much of a stuffed shirt to do anything like that."

Heather nodded, adding herself, "And I suppose he isn't foolish enough to meet with his mistress on the island. Not with Martha Barnes on the prowl. She would have sniffed out their affair already if that were the case."

Lane's eyebrow shot up at the thought, finding truth in the statement. But then again, Martha wasn't infallible.

Loud voices came from the Mason's table, their conversation once again escalating as Maddie shot up from her chair. "I've told you everything, Nick!" She tossed her napkin down, her bobbed hair swinging. "I shouldn't have to keep repeating myself."

Nick remained seated, his commanding voice reaching their table with little effort. "Madilyn, I'm getting fed up with these—."

"You're being ridiculous!" She pushed her chair

back, then held up a hand as Nick grabbed the sides of his own to lift himself up to a standing position. "No. Just stay and finish your meal. I need some air."

Nick, ignoring her request, began to stand, but Maddie pushed hard on his shoulder and bent to his ear, her tone a harsh whisper that, no matter how far Lane and the girls leaned in, were unable to hear.

As a response to whatever his wife conveyed, Nick heavily plopped back into his chair, and she gave his shoulder a firm squeeze before storming past their table and out the front door in the direction of Hattie's General, and in all likeliness, the apartment upstairs.

"It appears our entertainment is over." Heather dropped her menu as she sipped from her wine and exchanged a disappointed look with Mollie. "Wonder what it was all about?"

"Only one way to find out." Lane scooted her chair back and stood. "Order me the special when Lacey swings by. I won't be long."

Leaving Mollie and Heather to ogle after her, Lane crossed the dining room, eliciting a collective gasp from her prior table as she took the seat opposite Nick Mason.

"Why... have a seat, won't you, Sheriff?" Nick deadpanned, seeming unsurprised to find someone other than his wife sliding into her vacated seat.

"Thank you, Mr. Mason." Lane pushed Maddie's

abandoned plate to the side, noting that she had practically licked the dish clean and beamed a confident smile, unphased by Nick's condescending offer. "I noticed your wife left in a hurry and thought I'd come over and see if everything was okay?"

"It is. Thank you for your concern." He quickly glanced up from his plate, fleetingly meeting her eyes before dropping his gaze and shoveling a forkful of food into his mouth.

"It's only that your wife seemed unwell. Possibly suffering from a touch of food poisoning?"

"She's fine."

"Then she'll be coming back?"

Nick tossed his fork down with a clatter, his annoyance at her trespass obvious.

"My wife has gone back to that mouse hole of an apartment to lie down. Now, if you'll excuse me, I'll join her and see to our packing. We plan on leaving with the next ferry."

"The two p.m.? Oh, good luck. That ferry is always stuffed to the gills between day fishermen and tourists heading back mid-afternoon. You'd be smarter to wait for a later one." Lane graced him with an oblivious smile and reached for her notepad. "Now, I'd like to ask you a few questions, being this is the first chance I've had to chat with you alone. I'm sure you're eager to help me clear up a few things?"

"Well, since I now seem to have extra time on my hands..." Nick pushed back his plate, resigning to Lane's will. "What would you like to know?"

She recognized that the question was more of a challenge than an offer of assistance.

"Mr. Reyerson, during his interview, shared a few theories. Possible motives as to why someone may have wanted his wife dead." Lane plucked the yellow legal lined paper from her notepad and waved it in the air. "Your name came up, among others."

"You're joking."

"Not in the least. He's accused you of mounting a mutiny over bonus payouts, or rather, the change in the commission format. That true?"

Nick, a smirk lining his lips, crossed his arms. "Witt must be scared stiff if he's trying to point the finger at me."

"That sounds like a yes."

"Because it is. But that was months ago, and the issue was resolved."

"I take it ultimatums were made, say, if your demands weren't met?"

"You bet there were, but not by me!" Nick let his arms drop and leaned forward, his index finger crashing down onto the tabletop. "Nancy was the one tossing around veiled threats."

"What kind of threats?"

"Illegal ones."

"I'll need you to expand on that, Mr. Mason."

"Happily. I have no problem speaking ill of the dead."

"Good. Candor is always appreciated." Lane rolled her wrist, motioning for him to continue.

"When I voiced my displeasure with the new rollout, Nancy tried to reconstruct the districts to avoid paying commissions, re-assigning our top up-line members to other, lesser resellers. When that didn't scare us into submission, she flat out threatened to not pay another dime or relinquish the inventory we'd already purchased, claiming low stock."

"Her tactics worked?"

"Scared Maddie to death. I, however, decided to bring in reinforcements."

"The other members of Vita Mineralium." Lane smiled. "Is that when Witt got involved in the... negotiations?"

Nick nodded, picking the napkin out of his lap and tossing it on the table. "Witt is exaggerating to save his own skin. I, nor my wife, had a motive to kill Nancy. If anything, everything we've worked so hard for will go up in smoke, regardless of our best efforts."

"You don't support Witt keeping the business going?"

"I don't support Witt, period."

"Is that why Aaron asked to meet you in the

woods during your stay at the camp?" She reached back into her notepad and pulled out the encased scribbled note. "We retrieved this from your jeans pocket during the warrant search." She held the bag up and waved it side to side. "Planning a coup? I understand you lent your support to the idea of Witt stepping down from the business."

Nick gave a subtle nod but said nothing.

"Is that what Aaron wanted to talk to you about? In the woods? Was he curious as to where your loyalties lie?"

Nick rolled his eyes but stayed mute.

"Did the two of you meet while the Reyersons were out of camp? Possibly on their morning ride? The day of the shot?"

Nick sat up straight, his smirk dropping.

"As I already told your deputy, I was out fly fishing that morning, and I can honestly tell you, I didn't see Aaron Coletta, nor anyone else, for that matter."

"Including your wife, I understand."

"She was further down the stream."

"Doing morning yoga?"

"As she does every morning... and Saturday evenings."

"Evenings?"

"Yeah, late night hot yoga with guru somebody or another."

"I see. Well, if Maddie was doing her morning

yoga, should I assume she wasn't aware you were meeting—"

"Sheriff, I see you seem to think Aaron and I were in cahoots, but it couldn't be further from the truth. Now, if you'll excuse me." Nick stood, his face a dark plum color. "I'd like to check on how my wife is feeling." He pushed his chair back and reached for his wallet, throwing down two twenties. "And if you have any further questions about the Reyersons or Vita Mineralium, I suggest you contact the law office of Hiles, Heitman, and Shiels."

"They'd be the same lawyers representing Witt, correct?" Lane called out, Nick Mason's back offering no retort.

CHAPTER 25

"Hey!"

There was a hard rap against the glass entrance, the unexpected interruption surprising the room's occupants, Sheriff Lane standing by the station's coffee nook with coffee pot in hand, and Caleb seated at his desk, it covered in papers and evidence bags.

"Thought I'd find you two here." Philip's voice carried through the locked lobby door, offering them a broad smile as he held up two paper bags from the mini-mart, one of which was grease-stained. "I brought dinner!"

"Phil..." Lane lowered the carafe and put a gentle hand on Caleb's good shoulder, a silent command to stay seated, as she made her way across the lobby, turning the key. "Why aren't you crashed out in bed?

It's late!"

"Was wondering the same of you," Philip whispered as he brushed past, placing his food offerings on Caleb's desk and admiring Martha's Halloween decorations, his eyes widening at the life-sized scarecrow still propped by the coffee nook. "What cornfield did you pluck him out of?"

"Oh, that's all Martha's doing." Lane waved a dismissive hand as she opened the greased bag and frowned down at a selection of corn dogs and bean burritos. "She's gone a little overboard, to say the least."

"Nothing wrong with being festive." Philip wandered over to Martha's desk. "I think it's all kinds of fun!" He picked up the white skull and brought it up to eye level, matching its grin.

"That's because you're nothing but a big kid," Lane teased as she pulled an energy drink from the opposite sack and a six-pack of Coke. She placed them both on the desk, snagging a can for herself. "How did the ATV retrieval go?"

"Fine. Oh, almost forgot!" Philip put the skull down and reached into his jacket, handing her a ziplocked sandwich. "Turkey on Rye. I know you don't like gas station food."

Accepting her pleased smile of gratitude, he then turned to Caleb and sat down on the corner of Martha's desk. "The quad is sitting in Rowles's towing yard. Kody is going to see if we can sell it for scraps."

"He still sore at me?" Caleb asked, doing his best to unwrap a burrito one-handed.

"A little. Might give him a day or two to cool off." Philip smiled, swiping up the energy drink as Caleb reached for it, pulling the tab. "He loved zipping around on that thing, but Kody knows it was an accident." He handed Caleb the opened can. "Anything back yet from ballistics?"

"Too soon, even with calling in a favor." Lane pulled her sandwich apart as if cracking open a book and smiled at the lack of mustard. "I'm more interested in the lab results on the vitamin samples."

"You really think that's the motive for Nancy's death?"

Lane shrugged. "There's nothing saying we can't have more than one motive. For all we know, the potential exposure of fraud may have been what pushed Witt into motion."

"So, you've still got all your hopes pinned on the husband, huh?" Philip grabbed a chair and sat down, cracking open his own soda. "Nobody else is taking the lead?"

"You mean, operating outside of Witt?" Caleb straightened, glancing over his shoulder at Lane. "I can think of somebody who may have acted on their own... or with Witt."

"Deputy," Lane warned, her eyes darting from him over to the curious ranger. "It's all speculation, Phil."

"Not Angie?" Philip darted a panicked look between the two. "I thought she was cleared."

"She was... is, cleared," Lane clarified, frowning over at her deputy. "Caleb suspects that cousin Tanya may be Witt's accomplice. And..."

"You're not serious!" Philip laughed, tilting his can in Caleb's direction. "She's a hard-working kid! I can't picture—"

"Kid? Come on, Phil! She's at least nineteen or twenty, and she had the perfect opportunity to hide the gun for Witt... if he was the shooter." Caleb leaned forward, his tone earnest. "And being a horse girl, she's more than capable of shooting the dang thang herself!"

"That is a valid point." Lane stepped between the two, though their conversation wasn't heated. "She could have hidden the gun AND been the one to shoot it."

"Kind-hearted little Tanya?" Philip scoffed. "I don't believe it."

"Listen, man, I found flirtatious texts between Witt and her." Caleb snatched at a plastic bag, Witt's cell phone inside. "She's not as innocent as you may think." He tossed the bag aside and picked up a stack of papers, rifling through until he found what he wanted. "And by Angie's own statement... and I quote..." He read from the sheet. "Before we left camp, I overheard Witt and Nancy fighting in their tent. Nancy seemed upset about the way he was looking at someone and was accusing him of sleeping with that person. She didn't mention a name... unquote." Caleb tossed the paper down onto the desk. "Witt was messing with another woman. Someone he couldn't keep his eyes off... meaning someone in camp! What if Witt convinced Tanya that Nancy's death was the only way they could be together? Or... what if Tanya, on her own, decided to get rid of Nancy because she was afraid Witt would end things and stay with his wife and kids?"

"Are you really buying this?" Philip, his eyes wide, turned to Lane. "Have you questioned the kid?"

Lane shook her head. "We're still in the gathering stage. Until we get the ballistics report, along with the financials and the lab results on the samples, it is all conjecture."

Caleb swiped up his burrito, his tone leaning more conversational. "Yeah, spent most of my day delving into Witt's text messages and voicemails... along with calling the other members of the pill cult."

"Deputy..."

Caleb gave Lane a crooked smile and held up a defensive palm. "Not my words! It's what a Mr. Dugle..." He referred to his notepad, "in Idaho called them."

"What else did Mr. Dugle have to say?" Lane pulled a chair over by Philip and sat down, taking a bite of her turkey on rye.

"He and his wife had accepted the invitation to the retreat but then changed their mind once they received their latest commission check."

"Less than what they expected, I take it?"

"And by a lot. They weren't the only ones. Three other couples, the Berrys, the Nybergs, and the Palominos... all complained about severely cut commission checks based on supposed chargebacks. Oh, and then... " Caleb flipped a few pages. "There were additional complaints about product being received damaged, and when returned to corporate, their accounts went uncredited. That happened to the Wolfes, the Cobbs, and the Erkmans, along with the Nybergs."

"So, the long and short of it is that most of their top sellers were getting the shaft." Philip finished his pop and tossed the empty into the garbage can, smiling as it hit the rim and toppled in.

"And they probably all figured out that if they showed up to the corporate getaway, the Reyersons were going to put the screws to them to invest more money. I don't blame them for skipping the trip." Lane shook her sandwich in Caleb's direction. "In fact, I'd be pretty upset they were spending money on an all-inclusive holiday when they couldn't even pay their commissions correctly."

"That's probably how the Reyersons were even able to afford the event." Philip stood and circled his chair, leaning onto the back with his forearms. "Angie mentioned that even after giving them a huge discount, they'd written her a bad check."

"You're kidding?" Lane looked at him, her heart panging for Angie. "That poor gal. She just can't seem to catch a break."

"I was thinking the same. Luckily, Clint Carson came to the rescue. Wrote her a check for the whole dang thing, plus some."

"That was awfully nice of him." Lane's brows furrowed. "Seems the Carson's are in the habit of covering up Witt's shortcomings. Cami practically admitted to accounting fraud. All in an effort to keep Witt's nose clean with their auditor." Lane's brows went up, and she turned to her deputy. "Hey... on Witt's text messages... We'd figured out he had a steady affair going and then a new girl on the side, right?"

"Yeah, the new girl being Tanya."

Lane waved his comment away. "Who was the long-term partner? Whose number was that?"

"From what I can tell, a throwaway phone."

"Then whoever his mistress is, she's probably married."

"And covering her tracks, as well as Witt's," Philip

agreed, standing as he gripped the chair, stretching his thigh. "Are you now leaning towards this being a murder of passion... or murder for passion's sake?"

"I didn't say that," Lane pipped up, popping the last bite into her mouth. "I think it's all financial."

"Explain, please." Philip eased back into his chair and stifled a yawn. "If you don't mind."

"Well, what if this is an attempt at a corporate takeover? The brand name Vita Mineralium might crash and burn, but the structure is still there. You take over the existing upline sellers, change up the name and logo, and you keep going... but under new management."

"With a few tweaks, they'd be back in business without having to start from scratch." Caleb scribbled the theory onto his notepad, nodding along, "And if Witt was one of their targets, whoever stepped into his shoes could continue business as usual."

"And depending on if the vitamins come back as junk, the new owner could either correct the issue, making everything legit, or in theory, been successful of keeping it from coming to light and continuing on with the deception."

Philip held up his soda, begging pardon. "And who is in the running to take over the business?"

"My guess, Clint Carson, but I believe Aaron and Nick are making a power play."

"Aaron? I thought he was set on ensuring everything was on the straight and narrow?"

"So, he says." Lane shot Philip an exasperated look. "People lie, Phil, and some are really good at it. He and Sandi are invested in that vitamin company, though Aaron may not be aware of how invested. Sandi has sunk their money, savings and all, into Vita Mineralium."

Philip gave out a low whistle. "That's a shame."

Caleb straightened in his chair, carefully adjusting his shoulder as he placed his elbow on the desktop.

"I think we're going down too many rabbit holes. Whoever shot Nancy obviously wanted it to look like a hunting accident," Caleb protested, peering into the bag and grabbing a corn dog. "Which brings us back to Witt and an accomplice." Caleb's eyes suddenly grew wide, a new idea dawning. "What about life insurance? If there was a big policy on Nancy, maybe that was Witt's scheme for more gambling funds. Money he could spend without having to account for where it went."

"Way ahead of you, Deputy." Lane leaned back and propped her feet up onto the desk. "Her life insurance, which wasn't much, goes into a trust for her girls. Witt gets nothing... that is, according to Mr. Allister."

"You talk to him today?" Philip asked, surprised,

pulling out a corn dog of his own.

"I did. After I heard Witt was feeling under the weather, I called. Allister said he was doing much better, only a touch of food poisoning like the others, and that he'd be heading back to the mainland come Monday morning if I had no objections. I, of course, objected, and surprisingly enough, he remained forthcoming with a few of my questions, one of them the insurance query, before clamming up and referring me back to the mainland lawyers."

"That was very un-Allister-like."

"Agreed. I get the feeling he doesn't care for Witt all that much." Lane leaned to the side and started straightening Caleb's desk. "He's only handling this case as a favor to Aaron."

"Well, it's the neighborly thing to do." Philip smiled, knowing Lane still struggled with the concept of a close-knit community. "And speaking of neighbors, I have my own wild theory to throw into the mix."

"Oh?" Lane arched an eyebrow. "Do tell, Ranger."

"Now, don't get annoyed with me, I know I vouched for him earlier."

Lane dropped her feet to the ground and sat up. "Who?"

"Mark Jamison." Philip hurried on, glancing over at Caleb, who was just as intrigued. "I may have underestimated his dislike for the Reyersons. He still has a lot of hostility towards Nancy and Witt for the way they conducted themselves while she was married to Buck, and... well, I think the island consensus is that Witt and Nancy... may have found a way to kill Buck and make it look like an accident."

"Are you going off of what Dr. Hadley said yesterday? A belated revenge of some kind?"

"Miss Hattie thinks the same," Philip countered.

Lane bit her tongue, knowing everything the little old lady said was considered gospel in his eyes.

"Hey, now," Caleb interjected, flipping through his notepad towards the front. "That could actually make sense!" He stopped to lick his thumb, flipping a few more pages. "Yeah, right here. The old guy and son came across the group the day before the shooting. He probably recognized her and then, the next morning, went out, laid in wait, and shot her when she got into the clearing!"

"I hate to say it, but it could have been that way," Philip admitted, sheepishly peering over at Lane, who was shaking her head, disagreeing.

"You're both forgetting something. If the murder weapon does end up being the gun stolen from Nancy's tent, then Mr. Jamison didn't have access to it."

"Unless..." Caleb was warming up to the idea. "He saw Tanya hiding the gun, and he stole it—"

"You're back with the Tanya thing?" Philip interjected. "Come on, Caleb. She's a good kid and couldn't have had—"

The discussion was interrupted by Caleb's desk phone, the ring rattling above their conjectures.

Lane glanced at her wristwatch, surprised, being it was Sunday, the town typically tucked in and quiet after seven p.m. "It's after ten. Who would be calling?"

Caleb, his bottom lip stuck out, shrugged. "It's the emergency line." He picked up the phone. "Rockfish Island Sheriff's Department."

Philip and Lane inched closer, both straining to recognize the voice as Caleb asked the caller to hold and then extended his good arm, the handset offered to Lane. "It's Dr. Hadley."

She quickly snatched the handset from his hand and pressed it against her ear.

"Lane, here."

"Sheriff." The doctor's gruff voice came over the line. "Thought it would be best to let you know I just had Witt Reyerson and Cami Carson airlifted to Swedish Hospital."

"Whatever for?"

"Severe food poisoning by the looks of it."

"I thought he was feeling better?"

"A small intermission. Neither are doing well now."

"Then how are Cami's husband and Maddie

Mason feeling?" Lane bent down and quickly scribbled on Caleb's notepad, "Witt & Cami. Airlifted. Food poisoning. Hospital." She then glanced up at her companions, both nodding they understood.

"I don't have any knowledge of a Maddie, but Mr. Carson only had complaints of a minor tummy ache."

"What are the chances Witt and Cami are faking?"

"Sheriff, if you saw the state of my exam room, you wouldn't be suspicious," he huffed and then cleared his throat. "We're talking the burps and squirts in excess, along with dehydration and severe low blood pressure. Believe me, those two are very ill."

CHAPTER 26

At the literal crack of dawn, Harry's brown beast of a truck came to a rattling stop in front of Hattie's General, the driver cranking down the frost-covered window, surprised to find Sheriff Lane propped against the front door, her arms crossed with a welcoming smile.

"Well, mornin', Sheriff!" Harry called out, his truck door flying open. "You waiting on us?" He chuckled at his own joke and hopped out, heading to the back of his rig, grabbing Hattie's walker, and lugging it over the dented tailgate.

"I am," Lane admitted as she pushed off the door and stepped off the curb. "Need a few things before I head over on the early ferry." She strolled to the passenger side of Harry's pickup and gripped the cold metal handle, prying the heavy door open.

"Morning, Miss Hattie. Can I help you out?"

"Don't you have a coat that fits you, Sheriff?" Hattie teased, running an eye down Lane's frame. "You're always wearing your clothes too baggy. If I had your figure, and mind you, I used to, I'd be bursting at the seams!"

"Is that so?" Lane asked with a chuckle as she took Hattie's arm and helped her scoot to the edge of the bench seat until her feet dangled over the side.

"You betcha!"

Without warning, Hattie suddenly reached for Lane's hand and ran her thumb the length of her ring finger, her blue eyes squinting down at the bare knuckle. "Well, that's a shame."

Before Lane could ask what she meant, Harry had rolled up behind them with the walker, his voice overly cheerful,

"Thanks, but I've got her from here, Sheriff." Harry lightly elbowed Lane out of the way and jerked his head towards the door, his keys still dangling in the lock. "Feel free to go on in. I'll close up behind you."

Lane felt Hattie give her hand a gentle squeeze before letting go and sliding down to the asphalt, Harry assisting her as she grasped the handles of the walker.

Realizing she was more of a hamper than a help, Lane did as Harry asked and let herself into the store. By the time she was done shopping, placing her chosen items onto the front counter, Miss Hattie was comfortably seated in her rocking chair, Harry somewhere in the back.

"People don't have much patience these days, do they, Sheriff?" Hattie suddenly asked, her wrinkled hands smoothing out the heavy wool blanket on her lap, making sure it covered the length of her legs.

At the old woman's question, Lane immediately stopped drumming her nails against the countertop, her foot's impatient tap coming to a halt.

"I'm of the opinion that if they'd waited it out, the whole thing would have imploded on itself. They wouldn't have had to lift a finger." She sadly shook her head, her runny blue eyes blinking as she peered up at Lane. "For proper revenge, you must have patience. People typically do themselves more harm in the end than those wishing them ill intent. Human nature."

Intrigued, Lane inched away from the counter and closer to the rocking chair.

"Who wouldn't have had to lift a finger, Miss Hattie?"

"The shooter." She beamed up at Lane, who squatted down to meet her baby blues. "If they'd been patient. From what I hear, things were already falling apart."

"Things?"

"The marriage."

"Marriage?"

Lane was starting to feel like a parrot.

Hattie sagely nodded. "Money, you see."

"Mone—" Lane stopped herself just in time and stood up, completely confused, her cell phone suddenly coming to life in her pocket. "Sorry, one moment, Miss Hattie." She pulled it from her coat and glanced at the caller ID, swiftly bringing it to her ear.

"Hey, Martha. What's up?"

"Found your note that you're heading to the mainland first thing this morning."

"Wow. You're at the office early."

"I had George drop me off so he could help me put up a few things."

"Not more decorations?"

"But that's not why I called." Martha sidestepped the question. "When I got here, the phone was ringing off the hook." The line went quiet, muffled, before Martha came back on, her voice in a whisper. "NO, I said over there, George. By the window!"

"Martha, who called?" Lane asked, growing impatient. "Ballistics, WSP lab, forensic accounting?"

"No, it was Maddie Mason calling from Swedish Hospital. She wanted to let you know that Cami Carson has been put on life support and—"

"Life support!"

"Organ failure. From the sounds of it, Witt

Reyerson isn't too far behind."

"And how did she sound?"

"Other than emotional? Fine. Why?"

"A hunch." Lane glanced at her watch. "Martha, I gotta go if I'm going to catch the ferry. I'll touch base when I can." Lane stuffed her phone back into her coat pocket. "Sorry, Miss Hattie. Can you let Harry know I'll be back for those items? I've got to make sure I don't miss the ferry."

"Sure, I can, Dear." Hattie swiftly reached out and grabbed Lane's hand, once again running her thumb over her bare ring finger, her bright blue eyes pinning Lane in her spot. "Betrayal is hard to overcome, as you know. But it can be." The little old lady held her grip, her eyes intent on Lane's. "Phil is a good example. There is somebody who has been betrayed at the most intimate level and left in a hideous manner, yet he still ventures to love with his whole heart." She gave Lane's hand a gentle shake, then dropped it, her voice cheerful, "Take your things." She nodded towards the groceries sitting on the counter. "I'll have Harry start you a tab. I'm sure you're good for it."

CHAPTER 27

"If you could sign in here, Sheriff, and then have a seat with the family? I'll let the doctor know you're waiting."

Lane scribbled her name on the indicated sheet, then turned her back to the U-shaped ICU reception desk, the nurse's sneakers already squeaking down the hallway. She quickly scanned the immediate row of plastic chairs anchored to the wall and, not spying anyone familiar, moved further down the hall to a T-juncture, where she paused at the warning signs, all declaring no admittance.

"Sheriff Lane?" A familiar voice carried from the left hall. "Over here." Lane turned and found Maddie Mason rising from a plush chair as Clint stood beside her, his arms crossed, eyes red-rimmed. "You got my message?"

"I did." Lane took a seat beside her, her expression wary. "Any changes?" She leaned forward, catching Clint's eye, the man seeming despondent. "How are you holding up, Mr. Carson?"

Clint gave a shake of his head and wandered a few chairs down, sitting by the window, his lost gaze falling to the plaza below.

"He's not," Maddie whispered. "Cami is in full renal failure. They're simply making her comfortable." She wiggled in her chair to inch closer to Lane, keeping her voice respectfully low. "He hasn't left her side. He's only out here waiting for his in-laws to arrive..." Maddie paused, her eyes brimming. "They just flew in from California."

"And Witt?"

"We haven't had word yet. But I can't imagine any better, from what Clint described." She tucked a hair behind her ear and whispered, "Said he was as yellow as a lemon."

"He'd gone jaundice?" Lane hadn't bothered to whisper, causing Clint to look over and give a curt nod of confirmation.

"And how are you two feeling?" Lane pointedly looked at Clint, who had suddenly stood up.

"Fine. Um... Sheriff, please tell your Ranger friend that I'll return to pick up our luggage from his house as soon as I can... today. Maybe tomorrow or the next day, depending on..."

"Oh, well, I can do that for you," Lane offered, giving him a sad smile. "Myself or my deputy could drop off—"

"Everything still needs to be packed, and I'd prefer to do it myself. Cami is a stickler..." Clint trailed off, then seemed to rally, "Listen, I'm going to wait downstairs. Make sure her parents find their way up here with no issues." He padded past Maddie and placed a hand on her shoulder, giving it a squeeze. "Call me if... if anything changes."

Maddie, in turn, gave a quick nod, her eyes following him down the hall, only returning to Lane once he'd cornered the hallway out of sight. "Poor guy."

"And you, Maddie? How are you feeling?"

"Oh, well, that's why I called." She bit her lip and slunk back into her chair. "I thought I better be up-front since I would imagine you'll have to look into what made Cami and Witt so ill." Maddie suddenly took a deep breath as if bracing herself. "Sheriff, I was never sick."

"Excuse me?"

"I was faking."

"For what reason?"

"To be near Aaron." She suddenly sat up, her bobbed hair swinging forward as she jutted out her chin. "We've been having an affair for the last three months." She stole a quick peek at Lane, her defiant expression turning confused. "You don't look surprised."

"That's because I'm not." Lane tilted her head and gave Maddie a level look. "Saturday night hot yoga?" She flipped back through her notepad. "Aaron telling Sandi he's bowling every Saturday? When he's not even in a league. Your weekly visits to Aaron's bank?"

"You know about that?"

"I do. Does Sandi?"

"I doubt it." Maddie gave a subtle shake of her head. "At least, I hope not. For Aaron's sake... and hers."

"And hers? Why?" Lane crossed her arms, settling into her chair, giving Maddie a disapproving frown. "Aren't you two leaving your spouses?

"No." Maddie rested her elbows on her knees and began picking at her nails. "No, we're not. Saturday night was our final... our last time together." She brought her thumb to her mouth and began gnawing on the edge. "Pretty despicable, having to do it in his own house with his wife asleep down the hall."

Lane didn't argue.

"That's indeed bold. Weren't you worried about being caught?"

"Oh, we already had been. By Nancy."

"While in the act?" Lane asked, appalled.

"No." Maddie chuckled, scooting to the edge of her chair. "Sorry, way before Saturday... and thank goodness, not in the flesh. No, Nancy had pieced it together somehow, probably the same way you had." She shrugged, her eyes whittling down to slits. "Or... maybe Cami told her? She was always trying to keep close tabs on everyone. Loved sharing anything about anyone that would put them in a disparaging light with Nancy." Maddie sighed, shaking the thought away. "Anyway, shortly after arriving at Angie's camp, Nancy pulled me aside and threatened to expose Aaron and I's affair to Nick if I didn't end things."

"Why would she care if you two were involved?"

"She felt it put our little vitamin family at risk, or at least, that's how she spun it. In truth, it was ammo she could use to keep me in line and hold Nick in place so he wouldn't continue to make waves." She leaned in, explaining, "Nancy and my husband had bumped heads over commission payouts, and he'd won the first round." She looked up, the edges of her lips curling. "Nance was bound and determined he not win another. So, I did as I was told and ended things with Aaron."

"And how did that go?"

"He was upset, as was I, and in denial. Tried to talk me into leaving Nick, which is a conversation we've had a thousand times."

"You don't want to leave your husband?"

"No, that is, not until our kids are grown." She

shook her head. "Oh, saying that out loud... it just sounds awful." Lane, once again, did not argue.

"And this conversation with Aaron, you ending things... When was this? That night? Next morning?"

"First night of camp. It was hard to keep up a smiling façade for everyone. Needless to say, I had more than my fair share of hot toddies, and thankfully, Clint had a heavy hand with the liquor, so no one noticed me drowning my sorrows. Believe me, we were all regretting it the next morning. Especially him."

"So, I heard. How about the next day? Were you really down at the stream doing yoga bright and early?"

"No, and Aaron wasn't chopping wood if that is your next question."

It had been.

"We had snuck out of camp." Maddie, drawing blood from her thumb, dropped her hand and placed it under her thigh. "He had slipped me a note asking to talk, and I—"

"Uh, this note?" Lane plucked a sealed Ziplock from her notepad.

"Yes!" Maddie took it in hand and squinted through the plastic. "I thought I had lost it walking back to camp."

"You had. This was discovered in your husband's jeans pocket during our warrant search of your tent."

"Nick, had it?" Maddie's face blanched.

"Afraid, so."

"I should have guessed. He's been so..." Maddie handed back the bag. "I better find myself a damn good divorce attorney."

Lane cleared her throat, not having a sympathetic word to give.

"Um... on your... nature walk with Aaron." Lane doubted there had been any walking involved, having recalled Caleb's notes stating Maddie had been seen returning to camp, tying up her yoga pants. "Did you see anyone else coming or going? I take it you really hadn't seen Nick fly fishing?"

"No, but I did see him leave with his fishing gear."

"Okay. What about anybody else?"

"Spotted Cami coming and going from the outhouse and then heading in the direction of the creek."

"What about Sandi?"

"Aaron said she was reading in their tent. Never laid eyes on her until we returned." Her face lit up. "But if it helps, we heard Clint snoring logs in his yurt."

"That does help." Lane tucked the note back into her pad. "Were you aware Nancy had brought a gun to camp?"

"Uh... Sure. We all were, I guess." Maddie gave a weak smile. "She wore it on her hip during our ride."

Lane decided to apply some pressure and see if Maddie would flinch.

"What would you say if I told you someone saw you going into the Reyerson's tent?"

"I'd say they're lying." Maddie didn't balk. "Or you are."

"Well, I think out of everyone in camp besides Witt, you had the most motive to wish Nancy dead. She was hanging a disastrous secret over your head—"

"And I gave in to her demand, Sheriff. That is not the actions of a woman willing to kill another."

Lane decided to move on, her bluff unsuccessful.

"Sandi had said she thought everyone had gotten sick from the hamburgers Tanya made on the last night. She stated they were raw in the middle?"

Maddie blinked. "Mine wasn't." She put a hand to her heart. "In fact, Witt didn't even have a hamburger. I'd brought him one, but he never ate it."

"Are you sure about that?"

"Yes, because I hate wasting food and made Nick eat it. He scarfed it right down and has been feeling fine." She blushed again. "We both have."

"Well then, what do you think it was that everyone ate that might have—" Lane stopped, Maddie's eyes growing wide as she slowly stood, her gaze set beyond Lane, the two being approached by a woman dressed in scrubs and a white coat. "Sheriff Lane?

I'm Doctor Andrea Kinser. Mind if we step over here for a moment?" Dr. Kinser gave Maddie a polite smile before turning on her heels and walking Lane to the T-juncture. "I have some bad news," she said once they had paused, her head held close to Lane's. "Mr. Reyerson has passed."

"And Mrs. Carson?"

"It won't be long now." Dr. Kinser tucked a clipboard under her arm. "If we'd seen them twenty, even ten hours sooner, we would have been able to start treatment with charcoals and fluid therapy. Though, with the amount of toxins in their systems, it may have been a moot point in the end."

"I'm sorry... toxins?"

"Yes. Their tests came back with a high amount of amatoxin."

Lane shook her head, unfamiliar with the name.

"Amatoxins are found in poisonous mushrooms. For example, death caps are a common one, mistaken for regular button mushrooms. Which is what I believe to be the culprit in this case. Most likely, our patients ate the equivalent of two or more each. It only takes half a mushroom cap to destroy your liver and shut down all functions."

Lane's mouth dropped open. "Did either say when they ate the mushrooms?"

"By the time we figured it out, both were beyond speech."

"Well, then, what about a timeline?"

"That I can help with. Now, this, of course, depends on the amount consumed, but going off the levels we found, I would estimate they ate the mushrooms sometime Saturday afternoon, feeling ill shortly after." The doctor put up a pausing hand. "Then, after a bout of nausea, cramping, and diarrhea, roughly eight to ten hours later, they probably started feeling better, almost back to normal. Unfortunately, the toxins in their system had already started to attack their liver and kidneys, which led to jaundice, organ failure, coma, and ultimately, death." She gave Lane a mirthless smile. "This comes with the disclaimer that the timing of symptoms varies, depending on the patient and their overall health, along with the amount digested, and how quickly they sought medical help."

"So, no guarantees it was Saturday afternoon."

"None, but from what their admitting physician reported, it's the best I can give you."

"I understand, and Mrs. Carson's husband. He wasn't able to tell you how they—" Lane's cell phone dinged, recognizing the alert as her brother's text tone. "Pardon me, Dr. Kinser." She quickly glanced down at the message, her mouth quirking at Kent's text:

"My kid's Flintstone vitamins are stronger than this junk. Call me when you can."

Lane put her cell phone away. "Sorry about that. Mr. Carson wasn't able to shed light on when or how his wife consumed the mushrooms?"

"He's mentioned there was pizza and a home-made salad eaten for lunch on the day in question. However, he didn't recall mushrooms on either one."

"Might have been diced or thinly cut?"

"And he simply failed to notice? True. However, if that were the case, I'd think we'd have more than two people in our ICU."

"Agreed. And... Mr. Carson..." Lane frowned down at her cell phone, quickly sending a text to Caleb. "He also complained of not feeling well. Is he in danger of—"

Dr. Kinser shook her head. "No, we took a blood sample, and he's fine."

"Then, his stomach ache?"

"He mentioned suffering from an ulcer. Probably a badly timed flare-up." She put a hand on Lane's arm. "I'm sorry to cut this short, but I still have rounds to finish. I'd be happy to send over the final report, and—"

"Dr. Kisner?" A nurse in blue scrubs stood slightly outside of the ICU unit door, her head swiveling up and down the hallway, searching for passing visitors, her voice low, "I'm sorry to interrupt, but I need you to call time of death in room four."

"On my way," Dr. Kisner answered, then turned

to Lane. "I'm sorry, Sheriff. It seems Mrs. Carson has just passed."

CHAPTER 28

"I'm here! Got back as fast as I could," Lane's voice rang out as she burst through the station's door, shrugging out of her coat and barking questions, "Any news from the WSP lab? Is Caleb back, or is he still out picking up Sandi Coletta? Have we heard yet from forensic accounting on Cami's bookkeeping? Why don't you call—"

Martha held out an arm as if stopping traffic and brought Lane to a complete halt. Standing at her desk, she held her phone to her ear and said into the handset, "I'm sorry, Alicia. Can you repeat that?"

"Alicia with ballistics?" Lane half-whispered and crossed the room, receiving a vehement nod from her dispatcher. "She calling with the results?"

Martha shot her a wide-eyed and pointed stare, along with an exaggerated nod, before saying into the phone, "Yes, I'll let her know... hmm, hmm... okay, we appreciate the rush…Email is fine. Thanks so much. Have a good day." Martha hung up and sat down with a huff, "THAT, indeed, was Alicia from ballistics. She wanted me to tell you that all favors have been cashed in, and just as you suspected, they were able to confirm that the victim was shot from the gun Caleb found in the woods. The extracted bullet from the victim and the test shot were a match. She's emailing you the report now."

"I figured they would be. Where's Caleb?"

"Getting Sandi settled in room one." Martha picked up a pink message pad, her voice turning snooty, "MISTER Allister says he's on his way over and not to speak to his client until he gets here." She flopped the pad down onto her desk. "Aaron obviously called him."

"I'm not surprised."

"Oh, and nothing from the forensic accounting team, but…" Martha straightened the white skull on her desk, then plucked a sheet from the printer. "We did get the lab results on the vitamin sample pack you sent over for testing." She handed over the printed email. "Came back with mixed results."

"A little birdie told me the same." Lane quickly scanned the sheet, an eyebrow arching. "Seems as if two of the morning pills are legit. Though, they don't appear to be much more than a basic multivitamin. The mid-day to evening capsules, as suspected, are mostly filler."

"Just enough for a boost in the morning to start your day," Martha tsked. "The rest, vitamin placebo."

"And fraud. Sadly, this is gonna have to wait." Lane tossed the email onto Martha's desk, it wafering like a feather to the surface. "Were you able to track down where the pizza and salad came from?"

"Yes, and just so you know, Sandi has been completely cooperative. Says the Carsons brought two unbaked pizzas to her luncheon, unfrozen, and thinks both had mushrooms."

"Unfrozen... Doesn't sound like it was some cheap pizza they picked up from Hattie's."

"She also admitted to making the salad herself but swears no mushrooms."

"Well, if she's to be believed, then…then it had to have been the pizza. Maybe only one of the pies was contaminated with the bad mushrooms?" Panic suddenly filled Lane's voice, "The only place that does pizza around here is Gelato Deli. Have we spoken to Stephano? He may not realize—"

"That was my first stop on my way back to the office," Caleb's voice carried down the hall, coming from the direction of the interrogation rooms. "He swears up and down that the chopped mushrooms he put on there were standard button mushrooms delivered by his regular produce supplier. Nothing was forested." He put a hand on Lane's shoulder. "And I bagged what mushrooms he had to be tested, just to be on the safe side. They looked normal enough." He dropped his good arm and moved to his desk. "They're in the fridge and labeled. Got a courier on their way over now."

"Good work, Deputy." Lane looked physically relieved. "Any other food poisoning ailments within the community?" This was directed at Martha.

"No, thank goodness. Except, I did hear Amy Holmes has been complaining of feeling periodically ill..." Martha leaned in, her voice dropping into a gossipy whisper, *"Especially in the mornings... if you know what I mean."*

"And what about Sandi?" Lane swept past Martha's juicy piece of gossip. "How is her composure?" She looked at Caleb. "Nervous? Pleased? Sad? Indifferent?"

"Panicked, I'd say, and I can't blame her." He frowned. "Why? You stumble onto something at the hospital?"

"Maybe. An idea hit me coming back over the ferry." Lane started to pace the small lobby. "Aaron is cheating with Maddie Mason. Could be Sandi found out and decided to do something about it."

"Like poison her husband and his lover, except she nailed the wrong set of people?" Caleb sounded doubtful. "I don't know how you'd go about poisoning the right set, let alone the wrong. Are we sure this isn't some weird accident?"

Martha held up a hand, signaling she'd like to interject, "Stephano has been in business for over twenty years, and his father started that deli. They've not once, that I can recall, ever had an issue with food poisoning, let alone death cap mushrooms." Her voice dropped, and she leaned in, her gossipy nature kicking in, "You overwater your lawn, and they'll pop up in your backyard. *Anybody could have picked them!*"

Caleb suddenly jolted in his seat as if slapped. "Picking mushrooms!" He turned to Lane, wide-eyed. "When searching the woods Saturday, I ran into Jay Jamison. Walked up on him unexpected-ly. He was circling the trees like he was looking for something. When I asked what he was searching for, he said he was hunting mushrooms!"

Lane stopped pacing. "You know, I saw him later that afternoon. He was in a hurry, coming from the direction of the bank and stuffing a big wad of cash in his wallet."

"Bank isn't open on Saturday," Martha chimed in. "Probably was visiting the ATM."

"Possibly." Lane sounded doubtful. "He also might have met with someone to exchange poison-ous mushrooms for cash." She hurried on, Martha shaking her head, remembering her earlier statement, "With someone who doesn't have an overwatered yard... like an out-of-towner!"

"So, not Sandi?" Caleb was good and confused.

"I'm just thinking out loud." Lane started to pace again. "It couldn't have been Cami or Nick... they were with me when I saw Jay and his wad of cash."

"Well, I don't see how it could have been a mainlander. How would they even know Jay to arrange such a transaction?" Martha crossed her arms and huffed, "It seems unlikely."

Lane thought she had a good point.

"Martha..." Lane turned on her heels, a slow smile gracing her lips. "Is Jay a big Broncos fan?"

"Oh, well, I don't know," Martha fussed, trying to recall. "I know he enjoys football. Played in high school. Was rumored to be scouted by WSU, but..." Her voice dipped, *"He failed the drug screen for the wacky tobaccky."*

Caleb rolled his eyes. "Sheriff, what do football teams have to do with—"

"Where is that Denver Broncos hat?" Lane could still envision Jay Jamison striding down the sidewalk in the blue and orange baseball cap. "The one we found in the Coletta's suitcase? I wanna look at it."

"I, uh... I didn't bag it."

"Why the hell not?"

"Well, because Sandi came up to me later. Told me she thought the hat might belong to her oldest boy. Said he was always bringing home stuff from school and that it probably got thrown in the laundry," Caleb confessed, his tone somewhat defensive. "She thought she'd swiped it up on accident since she was in a big hurry to pack." He shook his head, clearly confounded as to why Lane looked so upset. "I didn't think it was a big deal."

"It might not be...," Lane admitted, her eyes roaming to the floor in thought. She suddenly jerked her head up, announcing, "I need to talk to Jay." She turned to Martha. "Get Philip on the phone. Tell him I'll pick him up at the ranger's station and that we're heading up to the Jamison place."

"Hey, now!" Caleb jetted from his chair. "If you're going to question Jay, I think I should be the one to go. I was the one who—"

"Normally, Deputy, I wouldn't disagree," Lane cut him off, shooing Martha to make the call as she pulled out her cell phone and quickly snapped a photo of the WSP lab report.

"Good, I'll get my coat."

"Caleb...," Lane started, sending a quick text before tucking the phone into her pocket.

"I'll even let you drive," he said stubbornly, catching the edge in Lane's voice, hoping to win her over.

"I'm sorry, Caleb. But I need you to stay behind." She gave him a leveled look, her eyes pained and tired. "Both the Jamisons are known for carrying firearms, and Jay, especially, is a very large and capable man."

"Your point?" Caleb's face turned red.

"That if things go south, I'll need backup." She moved to the coat rack and yanked her jacket down. "Someone with the use of both of their arms."

"I get that," Caleb snapped, frustrated. "But I don't see why I can't tag along. I'm not completely helpless."

"Allister should be showing up to advise Sandi." Lane shrugged into her coat, then patted the pockets for her keys. "I'd like you present, in case she decides to talk."

"With Allister as her lawyer? Fat chance of that."

"I'm also expecting the forensic financial report on Vita Mineralium. As soon as that comes over, I'll need you to give me the long and short of it."

"But Martha can do that!"

"Deputy Pickens! This is not up for debate!" Lane didn't wait for his response as she made for the door. "Now, stay put, and call me when you get that report!"

CHAPTER 29

"You know..." Martha placed a fresh cup of coffee on the edge of Caleb's desk, her tone chiding, "It's not like you to pout."

"I'm not pouting." Caleb pushed the mug away with a side-eyed frown.

"Yes, you are. You haven't said word one since Allister got here, and that was twenty minutes ago." She crossed her arms and bumped his chair with her hip. "You've done nothing but pout and stare at that screen."

"It's called research, Martha," Caleb mumbled, changing his mind and sliding the coffee closer. "And I'm learning all sorts of things."

"Oh?" She peeked over his shoulder, the screen filled with numerous search engine results varying from specific to vague questions regarding poisonous fungi. "Like what?"

"Like you don't need much to kill somebody, and that it doesn't matter if they're raw or cooked. Their potency doesn't change."

"Well, now." Martha picked up her own coffee and sat at her desk, peering over the rim with a raised eyebrow. "That means those mushrooms could have been served up any which way. Cooked on the pizza or raw in the salad." She looked back towards the interrogation room. *"Maybe Sandi isn't so innocent?"*

"Maybe," Caleb agreed, not sounding convinced. "Then again, maybe not... says here that the first symptoms might not show up until the next day." He flopped back in his chair and put a knuckle to his tired eye, giving it a good rub. "That changes things a bit."

"How so?"

"Well, Sheriff Lane thinks the mushrooms were digested Saturday afternoon, right? But what if it was actually Friday night? When everyone was still up at camp?"

"Wouldn't it depend on how much they ate?"

"Sure. In fact..." Caleb inched closer, his excitement building. "That's my point! What if the timing is off?"

Martha gave a befuddled shake of her head.

"What I'm saying is, what if only a small amount

was consumed? The sheriff didn't mention how much was found in their system. I mean, however much they ate was obviously still deadly in the end, but what if the effects didn't hit until, coincidentally, Saturday evening after lunch?"

"Well, then..." Martha sat back in her chair, relieved. "It was an accidental poisoning after all!"

"No! The complete opposite." Caleb edged closer, desperate for her to understand. "It was totally on purpose!"

"On purpose?" Martha frowned, contemplating. "Are you saying Witt was always a target, like Nancy? That one of his people—"

"No, see, I don't think he was a target! At least, not by one of his employees."

"Sorry, but I'm not following, Caleb."

"The way I figure it, Vita Mineralium needs Witt to survive. To keep things running and the money being paid out. None of them can afford to lose Nancy AND Witt. Which reasons, the poisoner would need to be someone not associated directly with Vita Mineralium! Someone who wouldn't be affected by the company going belly up!" He jetted out of his chair. "Martha! I think I've been right all along!"

"You have?" She stood with him, his excitement contagious. "About what?"

"About Tanya! She poisoned Witt!" Caleb circled

his chair. "Think about it! She was the camp's cook! How easy would it have been for her to pick the damn shrooms herself and then add them to Witt's meal?"

"Not Tanya!" Martha slowly sat down, her enthusiasm instantly draining. "She's an angel!"

"Yes, Tanya!" Caleb turned and began ruffling one handed through his desk papers. "Here!" He yanked a crinkled sheet from the pile and thrusted the paper towards Martha. "Read these text messages and then tell me how angelic she is."

With a doubting frown, Martha slipped on her readers and took the handed sheet, scanning the length of the page.

"Oh, my." She quickly flipped to the other side. "I see what you mean... but..." Martha pulled the readers from her nose and perched them on the top of her head. "I'm confused. Weren't you saying before that you thought Tanya was his accomplice? That she was the one who hid the gun or possibly shot the gun? Maybe both?"

"I did. I still do!" Caleb took a deep breath, almost annoyed. "I believe Witt, be it with pillow talk or good ol' greed, was able to convince Tanya to help kill his wife."

"Caleb, just because the young girl was taken in by a suave Casanova..." Martha handed the sheet back, shaking her head. "Doesn't mean she was foolish enough to actually kill for him."

"She's young, impressible, and alone in this world."

"Not so! She has Angie!"

"Who needs money!" Caleb countered. "She's got motive for helping Witt coming out of her ears if you're willing to see it!"

"If you say so," Martha still sounded unconvinced. "But if Tanya did aid Witt with getting rid of his wife, I highly doubt she'd murder the man a few hours later by poisoning. You can't have it both ways, Caleb." Martha shook her head. "Besides, you're forgetting it wasn't only Witt who was poisoned." She put a pausing hand, Caleb's mouth dropping open to protest. "Now, that's not to say you're completely wrong. For Sandi's sake, I hope you're right."

"You do?"

"Well, in that Tanya accidentally served poisonous mushrooms. I refuse to imagine she did it on purpose." She gave him a slow shake of her head. "I'm sorry, Caleb. Unless you can find a motive as to why Tanya would have taken Mrs. Carson out as well, I can't believe it."

"Hold on! Mrs. Carson... as in MARRIED, Mrs. Carson!" Caleb suddenly leaned over his desk and began using his good arm to sort through the bags of evidence still piled on top. "Martha, help me find the credit card receipts that were stashed in the Carson's glovebox. I want to check something."

"Exactly, what are you looking for?" Martha held up the evidence bag in question.

"Proof." Caleb grabbed Witt's phone log from his desk. "Now, if I remember correctly, among the ATM withdrawals, there were a few receipts where he'd stayed in the hotel attached to the casino."

"Uh, here's one!"

"Give me the date and time."

"Okay." Martha tipped her head up and peered through her readers. "This one says September twentieth. Card was run at two-thirty in the afternoon."

Caleb quickly scanned the call log, a satisfied smile spreading across his face.

"And here's a couple more, but in August. Same time... dates vary... it looks to have been a weekly event. The seventh, fourteenth, the twenty-first. Oh, two times that week. Twenty-fourth..."

"HA! I knew it!" Caleb suddenly flapped the log into the air, snapping it with force. "On each of those days, Witt, shortly after checking into the suite, calls his mistress's cell phone."

"The throwaway one you were telling me about?"

"Yes, but here... right here, and on this date as well, he accidentally dialed Cami's cell phone directly."

"Accidentally?"

"Yeah. I think Mrs. Cami Carson is Witt's long-time mistress." Caleb suddenly handed Martha the call log and lurched to his feet, grabbing his coat from the back of his chair. "I also think, after helping Witt kill Nancy, Tanya figured out she wasn't his only squeeze. Maybe she pieced it together, or maybe he spelled it out for her, either way, she'd been made a fool."

"And she took revenge." Martha slowly dropped into her chair. "I can't believe it."

"Believe it." Caleb gave her a cocky smile. "Show Sheriff Lane the receipts and call log when she gets back in."

"Why?" She sprung back up, her chair rocketing behind her. "Where are you going?"

CHAPTER 30

"Evening, Mr. Jamison. Up for a visit?" Ol'man Jamison, in the midst of securing the corral gate, squinted at the two figures heading his way, his smile reserved, held until his old eyes could make out who was speaking.

"That you, Phil?" His wrinkled face suddenly cleared, and a wide grin replaced the uncertain scowl. He gave a quick hush to Jasper, the grey-muzzled lab following on the visitor's heels, barking a noisy welcome. "See, you brought your girlfriend with you."

"Mr. Jamison," Philip started, grimacing as he felt Lane go rigid at the comment, the two coming to a stop at the corral gate. "I'd like you to meet Sheriff Lane." He then turned and extended a hand towards the old man. "Sheriff, this is Mark Jamison. He and his son Jay own this place and a good five acres bordering the park to the south." Philip turned back to the old man, his face questioning, "Speaking of Jay, he around?"

"Yup, in the house." Mr. Jamison dusted off his hands and offered one to Lane, shushing Jasper at the same time. "Pleasure to meet you, Sheriff. Afraid the boy and I don't go into town all that often." He let go of her hand and leaned an elbow against the metal gate. "So, what brings you two out here?"

"We were just driving around." Philip placed a big-meaty arm around Lane's petite shoulders and gave them a tight squeeze, the openly affectionate action rendering Lane momentarily speechless. "And it dawned on me, you'd not met yet." He hurried on, Lane still crushed against his side, "By the way, we saw Angie's truck and trailer pulling out of your drive, heading back to town." He nodded at the two penned horses, both grazing on a pile of loose hay on the far side of the fence. "These two just get dropped off?"

"They did." Ol'man Jamison turned towards the corral and gave a curt nod of his head, his eyes lingering on the two, a speckled grey and a big appaloosa. "Angie called me up about an hour ago and asked if I wouldn't mind boarding the two for a bit."

With the old man's eyes set on the other side of the corral, Lane weaseled from under Philip's grip, his approach to questioning much different than her own. She preferred the direct method.

"Could we chat with Jay?" She stepped forward and positioned herself directly in front of the old man, her smile sunny but lacking warmth.

"Well, sure." He jerked on the gate, making sure it was secure. "Why don't we head for the house? I can put some coffee on and—"

"I'd prefer it if he came outside."

At her request, the old man's smile dropped, morphing into caution, but he gave an obliging nod and then bellowed into the air, "Jay! Come on out. We got company."

Philip, feeling the sudden tension, pointed a finger towards the end of the corral and asked, "What's the name of the appaloosa again?"

"Tamarack," Both Lane and Mr. Jamison answered at the same time, the old man's eyebrows shooting up in surprise at her knowledge. She gave him a hapless shrug with a smile, the tension of before softening.

"Angie tried to give me riding lessons a couple of summers back." She nodded towards the smaller of the two. "The little one, that's Grailee, isn't it?"

"It is." He smiled down at her. "She loves them two horses as much as she loves to breathe, but I think that one is her favorite. Was a gift from her daddy." His eyes suddenly looked past Lane, and the sound of the front porch door swinging shut met their ears. "Sheriff, this here is my boy, though he's all grown."

Philip and Lane turned to see Jay bounding down the steps in a flannel shirt and dirty jeans, wearing a well-worn cap, the color of hunter's orange.

"Hi, there!" Jay greeted, Jasper running to his side and careening circles around him as he approached. "Sorry, didn't hear you pull up. Was inside cleaning up after unloading the horses."

"Son, though they're being polite, I have a funny feeling the Sheriff and Ranger here want to have a word with you."

"Really?" Jay's smile stayed in place as his head swiveled to Philip and then Lane. "What about?"

"As much as I wish this was just a social call," Lane started, her eyes running the length of both the Jamisons. "I'm afraid I have a few questions for you, Jay. My deputy mentioned he saw you up by Crescent Meadow Saturday morning. Do you remember talking to him?"

Jay's relaxed stance stiffened, and he gave a slow nod of his head. "Yeah, sure."

"He said you'd told him you were picking mushrooms. Can I ask what you did with those?"

"Oh." Jay's shoulders relaxed. "I didn't find any."

"None?" Lane's eyebrow shot up, her voice dripping with disbelief.

"Not a one," Jay's answer was clipped, though his eyes did not waiver from Lane's. "Came back empty-handed. Was hoping to find some morels for our dinner stew."

"I bet."

Lane could feel Philip fidgeting beside her.

"Jay, Witt Reyerson died earlier today," Lane suddenly announced, aiming for shock value with the statement, her attention quickly swiveling between father and son. "From poisoning. Specifically, death cap mushrooms."

The old man, still leaning up against the fence, seemed to slouch at the news, his face registering shock, while Jay's face blanched, his broad shoulders tightening as he stood to attention.

"Sheriff—"

"Hush, now! What are you implying?" Ol' man Jamison pointed a finger at his son. "My boy knows the difference between morels and death caps." His hand flew to his shirt pocket, shakily pulling out a pack of cigarettes with the lighter sitting inside. "They don't even look remotely the same!"

"I also saw you Saturday afternoon, in town, walking down the street, stuffing a wad of cash in your pocket." Lane tilted her head, catching Jay's eye, his attention having switched to his father, who was lighting a trembling cigarette. "You also had on a much nicer baseball cap." She suddenly took a step closer, Philip tensing behind her. "You meet up with Sandi Coletta?"

"The bank manager's wife?" Jay asked, surprise lilting his voice. He looked to his father, then to Philip. "I don't know why you'd think I met up with Mrs. Coletta, but I'll be honest with you..." He gave his father a hard look. "I did go up looking for mushrooms, and no, they weren't morels I was searching for. I lied about that. But my hand to heaven, I didn't find any death caps." He slowly shook his head, his eyes still on his father. "Because they were already picked."

"It's my fault." Ol'man Jamison dropped his elbow from the gate and looked up with brimming eyes, his hand reaching out and grasping Jay's arm for balance. "I should have let it be and kept my trap shut."

"Dad...," Jay warned, his eyes darting to Philip and Lane. "It's not your fault. You're not responsible—"

"The hell I'm not!" He suddenly barked, bringing his cigarette to his mouth and inhaling deeply. His hand shook as he let the breath out, his eyes meeting Lane's. "We'd bumped into Angie and her campers about mid-day on Friday. I'd spotted her, upfront and center, proud as a peach. Sitting there full of airs." Mr. Jamison nodded at Philip. "It was Nancy. Her hair was a different color, but that condescending smile was the same."

Jay stepped closer to his father.

"Angie had been telling us about this gal, a lady named Nancy, who had been helping her out with the camp," Jay cut in, adjusting the baseball cap atop his head. "So, it was a bit of shock when Dad put two and two together that the woman Angie had been talking about was his best friend's widow."

"Took the wind right out of sails, if I'm to be honest." Mr. Jamison dropped the cigarette to the ground, his boot grinding it into the dirt. "When we got back home, well, I couldn't stop thinking about her. How my best pal was rotting in the ground, and she was parading around like she was somebody! How Angie didn't have her daddy, and she'd gone on to have littles of her own. All that money she'd swindled right under Buck's nose!" His hand slammed against the gate in anger. "Wasn't fair, and I decided I was going to do something about it." His face suddenly fell, the anger dissipating. "I'm not a young man anymore, but later on that night, I hiked myself over to Angie's camp. Wasn't hard to find, even as dark as it was, with all of their hootin' and hollering. They seemed to be having a grand time... all but her." A ghost of a smile lifted his lips. "Saw her there, sitting by the fire all by herself, looking... well, miserable is the only word that describes it. Pathetically miserable."

"You felt sorry for her?" Lane ventured, almost afraid to interrupt.

"Not a lick, and it wasn't any less than she deserved." He spat to the side, shaking his head. "But it did keep me from pulling the trigger. No, ma'am. She wouldn't get a reprieve from her rotten life from me."

"But you didn't have the same resolve the next morning?" Lane took a step closer, her hand reaching behind her belt. "You'd hidden yourself within the pines, and when she'd come into view—"

"No!" Jay suddenly lumbered in front of his father, his hands held outward, warding Lane back. "It wasn't him." He reached up and snatched his hat from his head, the hunter's orange bright against his dark plaid flannel. "I think, maybe, we might want to talk to a lawyer."

"That's your right..." Lane tilted her head, her expression calculating. "But I don't think you'll need one."

"They won't?" Philip suddenly blurted, his eyes snapping to Lane, his finger jetting in Jay's direction. "Isn't he who Angie saw in the woods? The person wearing hunter's orange?"

"Yes, he was." Lane put her hand upon Philip's accusatory arm and gently pushed it down to his side. "But he's not the one who shot Nancy, are you, Jay?"

"All the same, it's probably best to wait and talk

to an attorney," Jay answered, his full focus set on his father, the older Jamison now gazing across the pasture. "You have to understand, Buck was the best friend my dad ever had. Those girls are like family."

"I do understand, Jay." Lane joined Mr. Jamison, the pair staring out at the two horses. "Completely."

"Well, I sure don't! Why are you—," Philip was cut off by Lane's cell phone.

"One second." Lane held up a finger and pulled the phone from her pocket, glancing down at the caller ID as she wandered out of earshot, answering the call, "Hey, Martha. Everything go well with Allister and Sandi?"

"Oh, yes, but not really. Just as we predicted, Sandi clammed up. But that's not why I'm calling. The forensic accounting report came through, and you're gonna wanna look at this. Huge amounts of money have been moved, all hopscotched to various accounts along the way, the final destination being an offshore Swiss bank account."

"And I take it this was found all under Witt's name?"

"Um, that part is a bit confusing."

"Martha, that's why I asked Caleb to call me when it came in. Why didn't you hand this over to him? In fact, why isn't he the one —"

"Oh, well, you see, I would have, but I couldn't," Martha hedged, her voice suddenly sounding small.

"He's not back yet."

"Back from where?"

"Angie's farm. He went to talk to Tanya. He figured out... well, he thinks he figured out, that the mushrooms were actually eaten Friday night at the last meal up at camp. And since Tanya was the cook, and Witt was sleeping with Cami... Oh, wait. I probably should have started there. Now, Sheriff, this might get a little muddled." She cleared her throat, excited. "Caleb wanted to look at those casino receipts, the ones found in the Carson's glovebox. So we did, and Caleb found matching dates between Cami and Witt's call logs. Which must mean they were having an affair, and that sweet girl found out, and in retaliation, poor Tanya poisoned—"

"Ranger!" Lane's tone sounded panicked as the cell phone dropped from her ear. "We gotta go now!"

CHAPTER 31

With the evergreens growing sparse and giving way to fenced pasture, Caleb made a left-hand turn at the bent and lopsided mailbox, the rusted name of BENNETT boasted on top, and pulled onto the lonely and rutted dirt lane of Angie's farm. A two-story house, white with blue trim, sat at the very end of the road with two large maples in the yard, giving shade to the chickens pecking at the empty gravel drive. Not far from the main residence stood a steel, modern building that Caleb knew to be the stables, and behind that, an old rustic barn surrounded by a steady fence line and sectioned corrals.

Stepping from his patrol car, Caleb paused, half expecting a farm dog to come tearing around the corner announcing his arrival. Instead, he was greeted by the uproar of clucks and squawks from the chickens. They scattered from his path, drawing just as much attention as a yipping dog as he made his way to Angie's front porch, the steps in dire need of a coat of paint, the screen door propped open, held in place with a rock.

With just a glance around, one could easily see the house and acreage were far too much for Angie to manage on her own. With the exception of the fancy steel building, looking very much out of place to the rest of the rustic charm of the farm, the homestead appeared to be in need of some tender loving care. Caleb didn't doubt that the place had Angie's heart. He figured if she could, she would spruce it up, make it as grand, if not grander, than when her father was alive. But, with her whole summer spent in the park, waiting on people hand and foot, all her free time and energy was spent... and it showed.

Though the driveway was empty, devoid of Angie's pick-up and bumper horse trailer, Caleb gave the door a solid knock, not expecting an answer, the porch boards squeaking under his weight. The assumption was correct, his knock having gone unanswered.

No one at home, Caleb took the steps, two at a time, chickens flying once again from his path, and headed for the stables. Just because there wasn't a car in the drive or an answer at the door didn't mean someone wasn't home. At least, that is what he'd tell Sheriff Lane as his excuse for poking around. Though normally a stickler for the rules, Caleb's curiosity had gotten the best of him, and he'd do everything by the book... after he'd had a good look.

The stables, a large rectangle steel building, appeared to be empty of man and beast, though it was clear someone had been in the middle of mucking out the stalls. A pitchfork and shovel were leaned against the door beside a huge pile of soiled hay and whatnot left in the middle of the alley.

He gave a call of hello, it also unanswered, and skirted around the stinking mound, admiring the place, saddened to see the pens further down the line pristine as if never used. It was clear to see there had been grand plans, which had not come to fruition.

Stepping through the back doors of the building, Caleb's eyes roamed to the right, landing on the original barn, as wide as it was tall, the wood darkened and weather-stained. The back section seemed to list to the side, almost appearing to be propped up by the stacked and tarped hay bales stored in its shadow, though it may have been an illusion, the haystack seeming to be a tumbling waterfall itself of fallen green bales, their edges tawny blonde and dry.

The building looked deserted. Caleb paused, hands on hips, debating if he should venture over, when he heard the bang of a door. Turning to his left, back towards Angie's place, he was surprised to find, parked a few yards behind the main house, an equine RV, and by the worn path leading from the main cabin to the farmhouse, it was clear someone was living inside, mostly likely Tanya.

Caleb, his sense of eagerness taking over, quickly started his way across the low-cut grass, slowing his pace as he grew closer, noting behind the trailer, out of sight from the gravel drive, a stack of hay bales with a large swath of paper attached, one end broke free and flopped over, the printed contents of the sign hidden.

Taking a quick glance towards Tanya's abode, it also appearing deserted, Caleb quickly bent over and pinned the corner of the sign back with his index finger, revealing a large target used for shooting practice. The weather-worn sheet was imprinted with the blackened shadow of a man's outline, bullet holes riddling the center and the far reaches of its sun-bleached edges.

"I frickin' knew it!" Caleb muttered, letting the corner edge drop as he pulled out his cell phone, his fingers trembling, the adrenaline of excitement coursing through his veins. He unsteadily punched the camera icon as he balanced on one foot, using his suspended leg, the toe pointed, to hold the flopped corner back and in place, once again revealing the target so he could take a shaky snapshot.

Successful, though out of focus and not at the best angle, he quickly sent the picture to Martha with the word 'PROOF' before bringing the phone to his ear, having punched Lane's number on speed dial, the call going straight to voicemail.

"She must still be at the Jamison's," he thought, preening to know how proud Lane would be. He'd had suspicions, backed them up with cause and motive, and now, he'd found the actual evidence. They'd have to have forensics come out and go over the place. But Caleb was confident the team would find a few spent bullets still lodged in the stacked hay bales, the deputy envisioning Witt and Tanya target practicing with Nancy's gun. Pleased with himself, Caleb made his way to the front of the trailer and gave the door a one-handed pounding. It slightly bowed under his fist, and he followed up the hardened knock with a friendly holler of, "Anybody home?" which was answered by a stilling silence.

"Guess not," Caleb said with a sigh as he turned, dialing Martha and returning the phone to his ear. His hopes of cornering Tanya, and eliciting a heartfelt confession defeated, he'd have to settle for Martha radioing Sheriff Lane so she could see the target bales for herself.

As the line rang, Caleb's attention swung to the main house, and his hand dropped to his side, his thumb disconnecting the call, his eyes falling on the kitchen window and the swaying drapes, a darkened figure looking out, their attention upon him.

Giving a friendly wave, Caleb followed the worn path from Tanya's trailer up through the back lawn, cornering the house, to the front. Expecting to see Angie's rig, the driveway remained empty for the exception of his patrol car. Had, whoever was at the window, been here all along? Was it between the stables and his wandering the place, that they'd missed each other?

He stepped up onto the porch as the front door preemptively swung open, and Angie stepped out, beaming a courteous yet curious smile.

"Well, Hey, Caleb. You looking for me?"

"Hi, Angie." He returned her grin, his eyes darting past her slim silhouette and into the darkened hallway, finding it empty. "Not exactly. I was hoping Tanya was home?"

"She's not, but she should be back..." She glanced down at her wristwatch, a large and rusted wrench in her hand. "Oh, in I'd say, twenty minutes or so? She's dropping off a couple of horses for me at Mark Jamison's place. Do you..." She tilted her head towards the door. "You wanna wait for her? Or should I have her give you a call?" Her smile turned coy. "I can't tell if this is an official visit or...?" She let the question hang in the air, and Caleb gave a shake of his head, holding up his good arm, warding off the suggestion.

"Purely professional. Just wanted to ask her a couple of questions."

"About?" Angie's brow creased, her smile still friendly.

"The last night up at camp. Just tying up some loose ends is all," Caleb lied smoothly, not wanting to alarm Angie, fearful she'd call her cousin and warn her off.

"Oh, is that all?" Angie waved the rusty wrench, beckoning Caleb into the house. "Might as well wait for her inside. Maybe you can even give me a hand?" She turned with a wink. "No pun intended."

Caleb gave a polite chuckle and followed her down a darkly lit hallway as she angled to the right, passing into the kitchen.

"What are you trying to fix exactly? Got a leak?" He paused at the kitchen table, his eyes falling on the sink, the cabinets below open, cleaning supplies stacked high on the counter with a towel on the floor next to a tipped over bucket. "Or is something clogged?"

"The garbage disposal." She used the wrench to point at the sink. "There's a bolt that won't give, no matter how hard I yank. I've been banging on the thing for a good hour."

"Well, that might explain why you didn't answer when I knocked."

"Yeah, I didn't hear a knock. Did hear a car. Thought it was the mailman or UPS dropping something off." She once again pointed to the window. "Wasn't until I looked outside that I spotted you."

She pulled out a chair and indicated for Caleb to take a seat, dropping the wrench with a clunk by the sink.

"I'll be honest. I was surprised to see you." She leaned against the counter with her arms crossed. "You said something about loose ends and the last night of camp? Are you sure it isn't something I can help you with?"

"Might be. I was curious about the radios," Caleb grunted, being careful of his arm as he took the offered chair.

"The two-ways?" Angie asked. "Those cheap things?"

"Yeah, I was wondering... Sorry, but you wouldn't happen to have any aspirin lying around, would you?" He nodded towards his slung arm. "It's my first day off pain pills."

"Should. Let me check the medicine cabinet." Angie pushed off the counter with a smile, and as she passed, asked, "The two-ways... Like, are you needing to know where I bought them?"

"No." Caleb chuckled, his head swiveling to follow Angie as she strode pass, presumably heading to the bathroom for the aspirin. "I was curious why the radio worked for me, up at Crescent Meadow when I had my accident. But not for you when Nancy was shot."

"Oh, well, that's because they don't always keep a good charge!" Angie's voice carried from the other room. "Those things eat batteries..." There was the sound of a cabinet door opening and then a drawer. "Tanya put fresh batteries in that morning, but when the time came that I needed mine, it was plum dead." Her voice grew closer. "You're lucky they worked for you."

"Guess I am." Caleb slightly turned, Angie coming back into the room and heading for the sink to fill a glass of water. "Did you see Tanya put in the new batteries?"

"No, but if she said she did, I believe her." She handed Caleb the bottled aspirin and glass. "Here."

"Thanks for this." Caleb tilted the bottle in her direction, the pills clinking against the side, worried he'd put Angie on the defensive. "You want me to try my hand at that bolt? I might be able to do it even in this sling."

"Don't think it would hurt to have you try." Angie perked up, giving her shoulders a shrug as she walked to the counter and picked up the wrench. "Good luck," she added, handing the grimy tool to Caleb, who followed her over, taking it from her hand.

"Well, I'd say it probably just needs a little extra elbow grease, but my guess…" He grunted as he bent down to one knee, his head angled, peering up at the pipes. "You've already loosened it for me." He looked back at her, shooting her a flirtatious wink. "I see those horse girl muscles."

Angie flashed him a brilliant smile, pleased by his comment, and inched closer, pointing inside the cabinet space. "That's the bugger."

"I see it." Caleb twisted, angling the wrench, doing his best to squeeze his good shoulder into the small space, without bumping or pressing against his injured one. Situated with Angie still bent over him, watching his every move, he ventured, "So, uh, I… I noticed someone was target practicing. Who's the sharp shooter?" Caleb paused, the wrench biting into the bolt and turning effortlessly. "There! That was easier than I thought. Told you, you probably loos—"

Caleb felt a sharp prick at the back of his neck, a pointed tip digging into his skin as the hairs on his scalp stood on end, Angie's breath hot against his goose-pimpled skin.

"Don't move, Caleb… You don't want me to push the plunger all the way down or heaven forbid, break the needle." Angie's lips brushed against his ear, her hands holding him in place, Caleb frozen, scared to move. "You're going to start feeling a little woozy in a few minutes, so I suggest staying right where you are." She pulled back, grunting as she wrestled the wrench from his hand. "You don't need this," she panted, sending the rusted tool clattering across the kitchen as she stood and placed her foot on his bad shoulder, keeping him pinned.

"Angie..." Caleb strained to see her, twisting his neck as far as he could, still halfway under the sink. "What did you stick..." He blinked, unable to finish the sentence, his mind growing fuzzy. She was right, he was beginning to feel woozy.

"Horse tranquilizer," she answered, deciphering his thick tongued question, and putting her cell phone to her ear, her boot still on his arm. "You starting to feel the effects?"

Caleb blinked, then tried to nod, wanting to do nothing more than sleep.

"I'll take that as a yes." She removed her foot, and took a few steps back, speaking into her phone, her voice hitching, nervous. "I need you to come back right now... I know you just left, but something's happened..." Caleb, his cheek pressed against the laminate, felt her trailing footfall and desperately squirmed, his arm weakly scratching at his pocket, his own cell phone just out of reach.

Angie's voice grew closer, her steps vibrating through the cold floor. "I panicked, okay?... You have to come back!" She stopped, her voice climbing to a shout. "I can't move him on my own! He'll be nothing but dead weight!... Well, you're going to have to figure something out!" She suddenly stomped over, bending down and shoving Caleb's arm away from his pocket, her tone angry, "Don't forget this whole mess was your idea..."

CHAPTER 32

Without argument or question, Philip jumped into Lane's patrol truck, the Jaimsons disappearing through the rear-view mirror in a cloud of dust, Lane's tires rumbling over the cattle guard at the end of the dirt drive, burning rubber as the rig skated onto pavement, tires squealing.

"What is the quickest way to Angie's?" Lane half-shouted, jostled by the transition. "Any back-roads or shortcuts?"

"Not unless you want to take out a few fence posts on your way," Philip answered, struggling to clip his seatbelt and keep his eyes on the road.

"I might!" Lane risked a quick glance, giving him a brazen smile before glaring back at the wind-shield and increasing speed. "I want to get there as quick as we can. I'm worried trouble is brewing at Angie's place."

"Trouble? Lane, I'm still completely baffled as to why you let the Jamisons off the hook!" Philip hitched a thumb back the way they came. "Jay was obviously covering for his old man and—"

"No, not for his dad," Lane cut in, her teeth gritting as she gripped the steering wheel tighter. "For someone else." She took a steadying breath, her knuckles white, feeling Philip's befuddled stare. "Phil... Angie loves those two horses, they're her favorites above all else, right?" She didn't wait for his answer. "They're also the same two horses that, on the morning of the shooting, one had lost a shoe and the other supposedly developed a stone bruise, making both unrideable. Yet, you rode that little grey the same day, who still had all four shoes, and Jerry checked Tamarack, who was perfectly healthy... Why?"

"What do you mean why? Why what?"

"Why come up with lies to keep those two horses from going on that morning ride?" Lane cornered hard, forcing Philip to grab the dash as she shouted the answer, the truck easing out of the curve. "Because she wanted to keep them out of harm's way!"

"Are you saying Angie knew they would be shot at?" Philip's voice was incredulous. "How would she know beforehand... unless?" He shook his head, his mind racing to catch up with Lane, jumping to a terrible conclusion. "Angie knew... because she and Witt were in it together?"

"Yes." Lane took another hard turn, a Y in the road coming into view. "And no."

She veered to the left and smashed her foot down onto the gas as Philip twisted towards her, his voice gruff, "I don't understand..."

"Yes... Angie knew they would be shot at because she was the one doing the shooting. And no, she wasn't working with Witt. I'm still piecing it together, but neither of the Reyersons were ever meant to return from Crescent Meadow." She peeked over, catching Philip's eye, his face pained. "I believe her plan was to make it look like a murder-suicide, but when the time came to shoot Witt, she couldn't pull the trigger."

"Ah, geesh." Philip's head rocked back, his mind racing to the conversation he'd had with Angie. "It was because she couldn't take away those little girl's daddy." Philip, his voice tight, twisted in his seat. "She had started to tell me how guilty she felt, and I... I." He shook his head, his brow furrowing. "But... the gloves and the gun that Caleb found? How did she—"

"As best as I can figure, as planned, she'd guided them up to the meadow, where possibly, everything went as she claimed. The couple was fighting, and Witt rode on, leaving Angie and Nancy alone. With Nancy's back to her, she pulled out the murder weapon—"

"Easily stolen from the Reyerson's tent."

"And called Nancy's name... when Nancy turned in her saddle, Angie shot her in the chest. She then hopped off her horse and ripped off the gloves. Likely hid them in her saddle bag..."

"Wait... Angie was wearing gloves all that morning, Lane! Nice, thin leather riding gloves! Maybe—"

"Phil! The gloves found with the murder weapon would have fit over her riding gloves." Lane gave him a sad smile, understanding his disbelief. "She wore two pairs."

"So, then what? Witt rides back, and she's supposed to shoot him, but she has second thoughts?"

"Angie, by nature, is not a cold-hearted killer, Phil. She... in her head, was righting a wrong. I suppose when the reality of what she'd done had come to bear, she couldn't take another life, and maybe, as you suggested, she was unable to deprive those little girls of both parents."

"She'd know how they'd feel." Philip sighed, his shoulders slumping with the thought. He suddenly sat up, realization dawning. "Hold on, then! So, there never was anyone shooting from within the pines?"

"No, not a shooter. I think Angie was trying to

use that as an excuse to keep Witt distracted from her so she could shoot him unawares, and then surprise, surprise, she does spot someone in the woods. Someone wearing hunter's orange."

"Jay Jamison!"

"And she starts to panic. She's worried someone has seen what she'd done. Someone knows... but she's not sure. Maybe she's seeing things? Witt can't verify what she saw." Lane put herself in Angie's shoes. "She's upset, frantic, needing to get rid of the murder weapon, and like any good guide would, go get help. So, she takes to her horse and flies back to camp."

"Because her radio is conveniently dead." Philip shook his head, disgusted. "And on the ride back, she chucks the murder weapon and the extra gloves into the woods!"

"And then calls us in, pointing to the mystery person in the pines, who she's not sure exists but ends up being the perfect cover. Leading us in several directions. A hunting accident, murder for hire, possibly a crime of opportunity, or better yet, Witt as the gunman himself."

"Angie always denied he was the shooter, though."

"That was her guilt, but her partner, that was what they wanted us to believe. That Witt was guilty."

"Partner?" Philip shifted in his seat, Lane hitting Angie's dirt road. "What partner?"

CHAPTER 33

Wings flapping, speckled and dotted chickens scattered, scampering out of the way as Lane's tires bit into the gravel of Angie's empty driveway, coming to a halt beside the porch steps, the screen door closed, hanging half off its hinges.

"I don't see Caleb's rig." Lane unclicked her seatbelt and wrenched her door open, too distracted to answer Philip's question.

"Or Angie's truck and bumper." Philip scrunched down, peering out the window, his seat belt flying back to the side of the door. "Tanya must not be back."

"And we didn't pass her." Lane pulled out her cell phone to dial Martha, the call picking up after one ring. "Is Caleb back at the office?... What text?...

Proof?... All right, I'll see if I can make sense of it when I get back. Okay, well. I'm at Angie's now. Call if he shows up." She punched the phone and tucked it into her back pocket, her eyes roaming to the house. "No word from Caleb."

"And it doesn't look like anyone is home." Philip stumbled down the stairs, the porch door slamming behind him. "Think Caleb went into town looking for 'em? He came to talk to Tanya, right?" Lane nodded, turning and looking over towards the stable and barn, noting the remaining horses in the far pasture, the grass short and bare. "Could be someone is working in the stables."

"Or out back. Tanya lives in a small RV trailer behind the main house, according to Mr. Jamison."

"All right, why don't we split up? I'll head to the stables, and you see if Tanya is home." Lane turned, giving him a leveled look as she lowered her voice to a whisper, "And play dumb. I don't want anyone clueing into what we know." She started for the stables, tossing over her shoulder, "And holler if you find somebody."

Jogging to the large, metal, rectangular building, Lane cast her gaze towards the pastured horses. As eager as she was to get back to town and track Angie down, along with her deputy, she couldn't shake the feeling that something was off. Why would Angie have Tanya drop the two horses at Mark Jamison's place? And why place the ones left behind as far away from the barn as possible?

Having pieced together the 'how' of Nancy's murder, Lane was now mentally working on the 'why'... wanting the full picture. Angie had spared Witt, but her partner had not been willing... and like Hattie had said, they'd been impatient, rushing to put an end to Witt. She wondered how big of a factor time had played in their decision. Was it simply impatience... or was a clock ticking?

Reaching the stables, Lane yanked on the metal sliding door, finding it locked.

"Angie? Tanya?" She tugged again, bumping into a propped shovel and pitchfork, both tumbling to the ground as she gave another tug, the door holding fast. "Anybody around?"

Her calls unanswered, Lane wondered if there was a side entrance and cornered the building, a fenced corral bordering the side. She walked the length of the stables, her ears perking at what sounded like movement from within, and picked up her pace.

Crawling through the corral bars and steering clear of the electric fence, she passed through and exited out the other side, coming around the end of the building, surprised to find Caleb's patrol car parked against the metal siding, the smell of gasoline stinging her nose.

Approaching with caution, Lane flung the car

door open and found the vehicle empty, two toppled and drained gas cans left in the backseat. She gently shut the door and stepped back, circling the sedan as she reached for her phone, another smell hitting her senses.

Smoke.

Turning on her heels, Lane looked up, spotting plumes of dark smoke seeping from a grated window just below the roof, a weather vane in the shape of a bronze horse perched above it. Dropping her gaze down to the back doors, her heart skipped as she realized they were chained together, held by a silver lock. No doubt, to keep someone in.

"Caleb!"

Lane rushed to the doors, placing a tentative hand against the siding, the metal warm to her touch. "Is anybody in there?" she hollered, placing her ear to the door as she yanked her cell phone from her pocket, stepping back and dialing the station. "Martha! Get the fire department and EMT to Angie's place. The horse stables are on fire." She hung up, her fingers trembling as she hit Philip's phone number, at the same time throwing a hard kick against the stable door, the chain holding it in place.

"Damnit, Ranger!" Sent to voicemail, Lane hastily slipped the phone back into her pocket one-handed and snatched her service weapon from the holster, yelling toward the stable doors, "Caleb? If you're in there, back away from the door!"

She took aim, hoping the gunshot would bring Philip running, and pulled the trigger, jerking the broken lock from the chain and tugging the silver links through the handle, tossing it to the ground.

Grabbing hold of the doors, the metal screeching in protest as she heaved them to the side, a billow of smoke flooded into the open air and Lane blinked against the heat, holstering her gun. Keeping low, she entered the metal barn, her hand trailing against the stable walls, palm flat as she skated against the individual enclosures, her head leaning over each gate, searching through the smoke for a figure. The sound of crackling wood and groaning metal filled her ears as she strained to hear any response to her calls, the decorative timber of the ceiling dropping hot ash, the falling embers cascading down upon her back and shoulders, her lungs burning with each breath.

The intensity of the heat increased as Lane ventured closer to the center of the building, the air scorching hot, becoming unbearable. Realizing she could go no further, she was forced to head back to the opening, dodging across the alley.

Reaching the opposite stalls, her eyes watered, trying to blink away the soot falling from the ceiling as she stumbled, croaking out another call of, "Caleb!"

Lurching forward, her breath winded, she landed

hard against the next stall, groping at the handle as she fell back, the wooden gate unlatched, swinging wide, and revealing two bodies on the floor. Caleb and Angie.

Scrambling across the cement, Lane gripped a hold of Caleb's pant leg, and pulled, her deputy loosely jerking at her tug, but unresponsive, his free arm falling from his chest to the floor, boneless. "Deputy!" Lane barked, not much more than a hoarse croak, and clambered over his leg as she scooted up to his head, Caleb still not rousing, his body jostling loosely with her movements.

"Please, Lord, please," Lane prayed, pushing Caleb's hair from his forehead, and bending down, her other hand landing on his chest, an audible cry of relief escaping as she felt the rise and fall of his shallow breaths. "Oh, thank God," Lane whispered, her hand running along his breast plate and up to his neck, searching for an actual pulse, her hand brushing against a small object, a syringe, it laying on Caleb like discarded garbage. "Oh, no... okay, okay." Realization hit Lane, and she tucked the syringe into Caleb's sling, her eyes moving to Angie, heartbroken to find the girl staring blankly, her unfocused eyes seeing through Lane as if she were glass. "Angie?" Lane nudged her shoulder, already knowing, her fingers fumbling at the girl's neck for a pulse, Angie's head lulling to the side revealing a bloody hole, a bullet darkening her temple.

"Damn it." Lane pulled back and Angie's head rolled to the side, revealing the butt end of a revolver, the girl's own pistol, loosely clutched in her left hand.

With the sound of cracking beams overhead and metal warping a few stalls away, Lane grabbed Caleb's fallen arm, his other limb still slinged and pressed against his body, and flung it across his chest before standing to a crouch, working her way back to the stall door.

Reaching the opening, she grasped Caleb's ankles and pulled, straining at his dead weight, his head skidding and bumping across the concrete floor as she stood half-slouched, her head engulfed in smoke as she dragged him, hot embers and soot raining down. She'd made it a few feet, before she was forced to stop, sweat pouring down her face, her hands aching as her chest constricted. She bent back down, her lungs on fire, and tightened her grip, once again dragging Caleb towards open air.

With a thudding ache, her shoulder hit the metal door and Lane gave a final yank, lurching backwards and out of the stables, Caleb pulled to safety. She gulped in huge breaths of air between coughing fits and managed to stand up, her head held to the sky, giving out a throat wrenching scream, "FIRE!"

She waited for a response, her ears perking at the

sound of running feet as she bent back down, exhaustedly pulling Caleb further out of the building and dragging him away from the gasoline-soaked patrol car.

Caleb safe, she stood and placed her hands on her hips, panting, expecting to hear Philip corner the building. Her breath suddenly hitched as five sharp points pressed into the middle of her back, biting her skin, a voice coming from behind her, the hostility of the words equaling the force of the pitchfork prongs pressed into her back.

"You're making a lot of work for yourself, Sheriff. Now your going to have to drag him back inside."

CHAPTER 34

"Unless you want me to run you through..." Clint Carson inched down the wooden handle of the pitchfork, making sure to keep pressure against Lane's back, blood already soaking through her uniform in fine pointed spots. "I'd advise you stay very still." He wrenched Lane's gun from its holster and dropped the pitch fork, launching it to the side, way out of reach as he pressed the barrel hard against her back. "Okay, now that you've had a breather. Grab his ankles."

Lane didn't move, her gaze set on Caleb, his chest still rising and falling. She closed her eyes and with a prayer on her lips, she slightly turned her head, slowing rotating towards Clint, the pressure of the muzzle easing as she faced him, a pleased smirk etched into his soot-coated skin.

"This is where it started, wasn't it? At Angie's farm?" Lane cautiously nodded towards the stables, smoke billowing into the darkened October sky. "Planting the seeds of revenge." Clint's smirk morphed into a pleased smile, encouraging Lane to continue, "Easy to strike up a friendship. You being the stay-at-home dad-taxi service, dropping off the kids for their riding lessons." Lane shook her head, envisioning their conversations, the girl longing for an understanding shoulder. "I imagine you listened with a sympathetic ear to Angie's past resentments towards Nancy and used her bitterness to reinforce the belief that the Reyerson's wealth was besotted from her father's embezzled funds."

"Why, yes, I did," Clint admitted, his grin dropping, his tone instructive, "Grab. His. Ankles."

"And you fed her belief that Witt and Nancy were responsible for her father's death... Is that how you approached her? A life for a life?"

"You've got this all figured out, huh?" Clint suddenly laughed, cocking his head to the side and shrugging. "Truth is, it didn't take much convincing, what with that old man spouting about revenge and how Nancy and Witt should burn in hell... and Angie being flat broke."

Lane bobbed her head, comprehending Angie's desperation to keep the farm and her horses.

"You promised to return her father's money. With

the Reyersons gone, you'd take over Vita Mineralium and give her what she was owed." Lane's chin dropped to her chest, her eyes scanning the ground, voicing her thoughts. "You purposely got the camp drunk the night before the ride, knowing full well that Nancy would insist Witt go, for appearance's sake alone." She looked up at the sound of Clint moving closer, the gun still pointed at her chest.

"And secured myself a nice alibi."

"Along with making sure there were no witnesses. No one to join the ride and interfere with Angie's mission."

"It would have been perfect, if she's followed my plan," Clint scoffed. "But she grew soft, and in the end, she couldn't take Witt out."

"Which left you to do it." Lane shifted, her eyes on the gun, Clint suddenly thinking twice and taking a tentative step back out of her reach. "Your morning jog on Saturday and your stuffed fanny pack. You had the death cap mushrooms on you at the deli, didn't you?"

"Oh, well, you are impressive, Sheriff." He tightened his grip, his chest puffing out. "Did you know you were also there when I ordered the pizzas? I found that very thrilling." He slightly leaned in, pleased. "Wasn't hard to add death caps to the unbaked pies, and since Witt and my wife loved being waited on hand and foot, I was able to serve them the perfect slices. Of course, if anyone else grew sick, it would simply reinforce the idea of an accidental poisoning." He shook his head. "I was greatly disappointed to find out Maddie was faking. It would have been helpful to have her fall ill as well."

"It was the receipts..." Lane's mouth quirked, realizing. "That's why you killed your wife... and Witt. The casino receipts Witt gave you to give to Cami? You examined them and figured out he was literally handing you proof of your wife's infidelity... with him."

"Yeah, that pretty much sealed their fates. That, and the secret accounts I found. Witt was a brilliant business strategist but a terrible embezzler. He was draining the business dry, and Nancy, though savvy with people, wasn't as brilliant when it came to numbers. The more pressure he applied for investing, the more money he moved around, and with Cami keeping a second set of books, well, it wasn't hard for me to figure out."

"That's rather judgmental, being you were blackmailing the Reyersons." Lane guessed, it hitting the mark. "Over their fake vitamins?"

"How the hell did you figure that out?" Clint's voice was earnestly surprised. "Must not have believed my little story? It was true enough that I found international distributors. However, I did fib about not buying their cheap products. Not only did

I make the purchase, I smuggled the goods into the country. After the deed was done, I had the leverage to put the screws to Nancy, and I didn't need to tell her what fresh hell would break loose if I spilled the beans to the DEA or, worse yet, the media. She rightly opted to pay me to keep my mouth shut, foolishly thinking I was as legally culpable as she and Witt." He waved the gun. "And before you start feeling bad for those two, trust me, their little monthly blackmail payments didn't do much more than cut into Witt's casino play money. They were still racking in the dough. Now..." Clint paused, Lane's eyes darting over his shoulder, searching for help, hoping against her gut that Philip would arrive on the scene. "We need to hurry this up. After I call 9-1-1 and report this tragic event, I still have to make my way home. Pack up my kids, clean out a hefty bank account, and then hit the airport. I think a lovely vacation destination with no extradition laws sounds lovely this time of year... don't you, Sheriff?"

Distant sirens reached their ears, the pulsing wail barely audible over the cracking and groaning of the crumbling stable.

"Well, I'm afraid we're going to have to wrap this up. Seems help is on the way."

"And Angie?" Lane stalled, holding out a pleading hand, her voice hoarse. "You were worried she would talk? To protect Tanya from suspicion?"

"Pick up his ankles, Sheriff." Clint ignored her, his tone forceful as he shifted to the left, heat radiating off the building. "Drag him back inside, and I'll make your end quick."

"And Tanya... is she—" Lane faltered, glancing past Clint's shoulder, white smoke rising from the RV trailer, her heart sinking, realizing why Philip hadn't answered her call.

"What are you looking at?" Clint risked a glance over his shoulder and followed Lane's tearful stare towards the burning trailer. "Oh,..yeah, that." He gave her a humored smile. "I'm afraid your park ranger friend and I had a little run-in."

Lane felt her knees weaken, threatening to buckle from underneath her, her hands falling to her thighs as she bent over, her stomach twisting, sorrow gripping her insides.

"Let's go, Sheriff." Clint suddenly stalked toward her, his finger on the trigger, nudging Lane's shoulder, causing her to stumble backward. She tripped over Caleb's sprawled legs and crashed to the ground, falling on top of her deputy, his eyes fluttering, still unconscious.

Crawling to her knees, Lane held up a pleading hand, catching a quick glimpse of someone ducking back from the corner edge of the building. Stalling for time, she pushed off of Caleb, using his chest as leverage to prop herself up to standing, the syringe hidden in her fist, her thumb positioned on the plunger, unsure if it held anything inside.

"Sirens are getting closer, and I'm losing my patience!" Clint barked as Philip suddenly emerged, blood coating half his face as he stealthily crept from the side of the building, scooping up the chain from the grassed ground, the broken lock still threaded through the last link.

Crouched down, he signaled to Lane his intent, her heart lurching with joy as she lunged to the side, Philip looping the chain over Clint's head and pulling tight against his neck.

Caught in a metal choke hold, Clint's arm flailed wide, and the gun went off, his trigger finger sending shots through the air, tings of ricochet hitting the metal siding as Lane rolled to a stop. He threw a hard elbow into Philip's ribs, before launching his head backward, and connecting with the ranger's bloodied forehead, the chain falling loose from Philip's grip as he crumpled to the ground.

Free from the constrictive links, Clint scrambled to turn around, pointing the gun at Philip and pulling the trigger, dust flying as he missed.

"No!" Lane threw herself at his back, her arm crashing down as the needle bit into his skin, her thumb pressing hard against the plunger before letting go. She lurched away, her palms splayed against his back as she held him at bay, Clint's fist clamping around the syringe, jerking it from his neck.

"Oh, you're gonna pay for that!" He swung towards Lane, eyes wild as she deftly dodged his lurching steps and kicked out his knee, sending Clint crashing to the ground, the gun jetting from his hand.

"It's over, Mr. Carson!" Lane dug her knee into his spine, it cracking under the pressure. "You're done hurting people," she grunted, yanking his arm toward her and snatching the cuffs from her duty belt. "And you better pray my deputy is okay..." She slapped the cuffs in place, clinking them tight while gripping his opposite arm and doing the same. "Otherwise... I promise you..."

The firetruck's blaring siren blotted out the last of her words, though Lane's intent was felt by the cutting pressure of the cuffs and the rough shove to his head as she clambered to her feet.

Torn between rushing to Philip and checking on Caleb, Lane stumbled past them both, escaping the shadow of the stables and running into the open yard, her arms waving above her head, striving to be heard over the blaring wail of the firetruck's sirens and engine's rumbling purr. Strobe lights lit Lane's small frame, dusk having started to fall, and her arms dropped as Ethan Richardson began shouting and pointing in her direction before hopping into the ambulance and taking a wide berth around the burning stables, coming to their rescue.

Exhausted, Lane made her way to the ambulance, Ethan throwing the cube-shaped truck into park and racing to the back. Flinging the doors open, he barked questions as Calvin Morton grabbed the stretcher, the wheels bumping across the grass as Lane pointed to Caleb, her first priority, shouting that they needed Jerry Holmes, his veterinarian medical knowledge a necessity.

Ethan radioed the main fire truck, Jerry, one of the volunteer firemen. Seconds later, the vet was on the scene, able to tell the EMTs the medicine and potency Angie had access to, Jerry asking Lane questions regarding the length of time since injection and given amounts. She was only able to estimate a rough time for Caleb and had no idea of the quantity he received. As for Clint Carson, she couldn't say with any certainty how much tranquilizer she had injected, if any, nor at the moment, did she care.

Shouts of low blood pressure and a slow heart rate were reported as they wheeled Caleb to the ambulance, a bag of saline held high and tracing down to his arm as they loaded and shut the doors behind them, Jerry still working on Clint Carson.

Sirens coming back to life, the ambulance tore across the yard and onto the dirt road, heading for the Heli-pad by the school. Lane was confident a second chopper had already been requested, though, by Jerry's stoic expression, she wondered if it would be a moot point in the end.

With her deputy in good hands and her prayers answered, Lane took to searching the ground, tracking down her gun and quickly holstering the weapon. She then made her way to Philip, finding him laid out flat on his back, his right arm draped over his chest, yet to be treated, having been assessed as less critical than the other medical emergencies.

Stiffly lowering herself to the ground, Lane placed a tender palm against Philip's cheek, her hand sliding up to his hairline, her fingers gently prodding his scalp, locating a large cut in need of stitches.

"You still with me, Ranger?" she whispered, bending down and kissing the large goose egg forming in the middle of his forehead, guessing he'd be walking around with two black eyes once the swelling went down. "Open your eyes for me, Phil."

A groan of protest met her ears, and Lane's concerned face split into a relieved smile as Philip slowly opening his eyes and focused on her face, a pained grimace of a grin crossing his lips. "Hey, Toots."

"You know I hate it when you call me that," Lane huffed, moving back so Philip could prop himself up, leaning on his elbows. "We gotta get you to Dr. Hadley's office. Pretty sure you've got a concussion, and you need stitches."

"I'm right behind you," Philip mumbled, not

moving an inch.

"Come on. I got you," Lane coaxed, wrapping her arm around his and helping Philip heft up to a full sitting position. "We need to get you all fixed up and spit-polished for Sunday."

"What's Sunday?" Philip frowned, his thoughts muddled, as he leaned on Lane, his head pounding.

"Dinner at my brother's," Lane grunted, standing herself and dragging Philip with her. "And I want us to move in together. But I like my cottage better than your place, and with Stinker—"

"No... Sorry, Lane... but no."

"No?" Lane, slowly working them back to Angie's house and her patrol truck, stopped, wondering how hard of a hit he took to the head. "No, to what exactly? Dinner at my brothers? Moving in together, or living at my place?"

"Yes, to dinner, and no to living together." Philip swung his head, looking down at her with a playful smirk. "I've decided I won't live with you either, at least not until we're married."

"And when will that be?" Lane asked, a curious brow arched as a pleased smile lit her lips.

Philip shrugged, instantly regretting the movement, his right hand going to his forehead as he gingerly wrapped an arm around Lane's shoulder, his tone hopeful, "Whenever you decide to say yes."

"Is that a proposal, Ranger?"

CHAPTER 35

"Now, don't be nervous." Lane punched the doorbell, the nerves clearly all hers. "And don't take anything Kent says to heart. He's a big kidder. Oh, and make sure to compliment Mindy on her cooking, even if it tastes like sawdust." She turned and gave Philip a quick smile, anticipating at any moment for the front door to open, and added in a hushed whisper, "Not that her cooking is terrible, it's just... hit and miss sometimes."

After the five-alarm fire at Angie's, the old rustic, lopsided barn being the only structure to survive the two blazes, Sunday dinner had been postponed, Lane far too busy tying up loose ends and dealing with public backlash, Mike Allister leading the charge.

The pompous old lawyer had criticized her handling of the Reyerson's case, his vote of no confidence echoed by the Coletta's, Sandi still bitter at being brought in and questioned regarding the death cap mushrooms.

The small town was divided between those who stood in support of Lane, believing the Sheriff's department had done their job, even putting themselves in harm's way, and those who felt Allister's claims of incompetence were well-founded. These opinions were based on Allister's boast that he'd warned their bungling sheriff, who, in her prideful arrogance, had ignored his theory that Witt was in danger of being a victim himself.

Lane, unable to disagree with his claim, suffered in silence, frustrated that if Mike Allister had kept his client housebound, as she had requested, Witt might never have been exposed to Clint Carson's successful attempt at poisoning in the first place. Allister's lack of respect for her position within the community had put him equally at fault, and she was willing to share the blame.

Pointing fingers aside, Lane was eager for Caleb's return, her deputy still re-cooperating from his injuries. It had been with great relief, a good six hours after arriving at the hospital, that Caleb had awoken from his tranquilized coma, suffering only minor injuries from smoke inhalation. Once Lane got in to see him, he was quick to apologize. Admitting his rogue actions and dire need to be proven correct, his theory ultimately proven wrong, had placed undue pressure upon Angie, his pointed questions and veiled accusations forcing her to take action.

However, despite Caleb's feelings, it wasn't all his fault. The Fire Marshall's report had confirmed the stable fire was set intentionally. Though this was no secret, after questioning Caleb, it was revealed that Angie had built the prye of hay in the middle of the stable herself. Intent on burning the building down, sending her two beloved horses to the Jamison's, and corralling the remaining in the far field to avoid suspicion.

Lane drew the conclusion that Angie was expecting a windfall of money, believing that Clint Carson would stay true to his word and pay her what she felt to be her family's lost wealth. Needing a reason to explain her good fortune and being able to pay back her overdue taxes, she decided to burn down her own stables, planning to claim the influx of cash as a payout from the insurance company. It might have worked if Caleb hadn't found Angie's target practice bales and come pounding on her door, asking questions.

Speaking of questions, there was one that had bothered Lane. The mystery of the orange Broncos cap. With Sandi Colette refusing to speak to the sheriff again without Allister present, Lane had chosen to drag Philip, the ranger sporting two black-eyes as predicted, out to the Jamison's homestead.

When her question was presented, it was met with a hearty laugh.

"No, ma'am. I'm not a Bronco fan." Jay gave Philip a good-natured elbow to the ribs, smiling over at Lane, the small family seated at the kitchen table. "I'm a Seahawk fan, like everyone else on this island!" He'd pointed to his father, Ol'man Jamison seated next to Tanya, the girl smiling along. "Dad bought me that hat for Christmas because it had a horse on the front, and what with his eyesight, he didn't notice the team's logo on the side." Jay tapped the lip of his grimy baseball cap, the rim dirty from wear. "This is my everyday hat. I only wear the horsey hat when I go into town."

It had been good to visit with the Jamisons, though they were clearly mourning the loss of Angie, Tanya, now homeless and jobless, staying with the father and son. If Jay's plans were to come to fruition, he hoped, at the IRS auction, to pick up the Bennett's farm for a song, offering to build Tanya her own little place if she was willing to stay and work the property.

Kody was thrilled at the prospect of his romantic interest remaining on the island. It had been discovered afterward that Tanya, after dropping off the horses, had gone straight to the Ranger Station, completely naïve of Angie's plans, intent on using

Kody's shoulder to cry over Witt's death, having found Mark and Jay Jamison unsympathetic.

Upon leaving the Jamison's, Philip had insisted on visiting Miss Hattie, wanting to show off Lane's diamond ring. Greeted with a denatured smile, the little old lady had gripped both of their hands, her joy apparent as she exclaimed, "Bout time!"

Philip had wanted to ask Hattie if she'd been surprised by the case's outcome, Angie being the shooter and Clint Carson the driving force, but Lane had forbade it, not wanting to taint the happy moment. Besides, by Hattie's own words, the old woman had pieced most of it together long before Lane even had suspicions. The only real unanswered question now was, had Nancy and Witt been responsible for Buck Bennett's death? Hattie seemed to think so, and with her track record, Lane was apt to agree, though opening an investigation would be a moot point.

As for the fate of Vita Mineralium, the DEA opened an official investigation, and Kent was placed at the helm. It was a short-lived case, what with the primary owners both deceased and the guilty party of arranging the illegal purchase, distribution, and smuggling of the illicit vitamins already in police custody, Clint Carson, having survived. And now that things had finally settled down, Lane was bringing Philip to Kent's home for Thanksgiving dinner.

"Here." She quickly straightened Philip's tie, smiling up at him before taking back the cranberry Jello salad from his arms. "You look very handsome."

"I don't know why you're so nervous." Philip chuckled, re-straightening his tie despite Lane having just done so. "I'm sure we'll all get along fine."

The front door suddenly swung open, and Lane's big brother filled the doorway, three more men, all suspiciously resembling in looks, stood behind him, arms crossed, faces scowled.

"Well, looky there, fellas!" Kent greeted, yelling back into the house, his head turned to his siblings standing in force behind him. "He's not half as ugly as Kiddo said." He then offered his hand. "You must be, Phil. Welcome to the family."

THE END

Thank You!

Thank you for reading the fourth book of the Rockfish Island Mysteries series, Within The Pines, A Rockfish Island Mystery:IV. Book Five of the Rockfish Island Mystery series is scheduled and currently being plotted. Make sure to follow J.C. Fuller on her media sites/newsletter for updates on the series.

If you enjoyed Within The Pines, would you be so kind as to put a review on Amazon, Goodreads, and Bookbub? Thank you for your support!

Follow J.C. Fuller on Social Media...

Tiktok: @j.c.fullerauthor

Instagram/Threads: @j.c.fuller

Facebook: @j.c.fuller-Rockfish Island Mysteries Series

GoodReads: J.C.Fuller

ALSO BY J.C. FULLER

A ROCKFISH ISLAND MYSTERY SERIES

Black Bear Alibi

The Push

False Findings

Within the Pines